A DEAD SOMETHING

Hazel Rickerby-Carrick's face, idiotically bloated, looked up: not at Troy, not at anything. Her mouth, drawn into an outlandish rictus, grinned through discoloured froth. She bobbed and bumped against the starboard side. And what terrible disaster had corrupted her river-weed hair and distended her blown cheeks?

The taffrail shot upwards and the trees with it. The voice of the weir exploded with a crack on Troy's head and nothing whatever followed it.

Nothing . . .

CLUTCH OF CONSTABLES

NGAIO MARSH

A JOVE BOOK

This Jove book contains the complete
text of the original hardcover edition.

CLUTCH OF CONSTABLES

A Jove Book / published by arrangement with
Little, Brown and Company

PRINTING HISTORY
Little, Brown and Company edition 1969

Two previous paperback printings
Jove edition / June 1981
Second printing / May 1983

ISBN: 0-515-07105-6

Jove books are published by Jove Publications,
Inc., 200 Madison Avenue, New York, N.Y. 10016.
The words ''A JOVE BOOK'' and the ''J'' with sunburst
are trademarks belonging to Jove Publications, Inc.

PRINTED IN THE UNITED STATES OF AMERICA

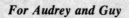
For Audrey and Guy

CONTENTS

CAST OF CHARACTERS

Passenger List, M. V. Zodiac
MRS. RODERICK ALLEYN
MISS HAZEL RICKERBY-CARRICK
MR. CALEY BARD
MR. STANLEY POLLOCK
DR. FRANCIS NATOUCHE, M.D.
MR. EARL J. HEWSON
MISS SALLY-LOU HEWSON
THE REV. J. DE B. LAZENBY

Ship's Company, M.V. Zodiac
JAMES TRETHEWAY—SKIPPER
MRS. TRETHEWAY—COOK AND STEWARDESS
TOM TRETHEWAY—BOY

Persons in or about Tollardwark
JNO. BAGG—LICENSED DEALER
MRS. BAGG—HIS MOTHER
MR. AND MRS. SMITH—A TON-UP COMBO

Police
SUPERINTENDENT ALBERT TILLOTTSON
            —TOLLARDWARK CONSTABULARY
P.C. CAPE—TOLLARDWARK CONSTABULARY
SUPERINTENDENT R. BONNEY
            —LONGMINSTER CONSTABULARY
SUNDRY CONSTABLES—COUNTY POLICE FORCES
SUPERINTENDENT RODERICK ALLEYN
                    —C.I.D. LONDON
INSPECTOR EDWARD FOX—C.I.D. LONDON
DETECTIVE-SERGEANT BAILEY—C.I.D. LONDON
DETECTIVE-SERGEANT THOMPSON
                    —C.I.D. LONDON

I

APPLY WITHIN

"There was nothing fancy about the Jampot," Alleyn said. "The word 'jobs' is entirely appropriate to his activities. He planned carefully, left as little as possible to chance, took a satisfaction in his work and accepted, without dwelling upon them, the occupational hazards which it involved. Retention or abolishment of capital punishment made no difference at all to his professional behaviour: I daresay he looks upon the murders that he did in fact perform, as tiresome and regrettable necessities.

"His talents were appropriate to his employment. They included manual dexterity, a passion for accuracy, a really exceptional intelligence of mathematical precision and a useful imagination offset by a complete blank where nervous anxiety might be expected. Above all he was a superb mimic. Mimics are born not made. From his childhood the Jampot showed an uncanny talent in not only reflecting the mannerisms, speech habits and social behaviour of an extraordinary diversity of persons but in knowing, apparently by instinct, how they would react to given circumstances. Small wonder," Alleyn said, "that he led us up the garden path for so long. He was a masterpiece."

He looked round his audience. Six rows of sharp-cropped heads. Were the dumb-looking ones as dumb as their wrinkled foreheads, lacklustre eyes and slackish mouths seemed to suggest? Was the forward-leaning one in the second row, who had come up from the uniformed branch with an outstanding report, as good as his promise? Protectors of the people, Alleyn thought. If only the people would recognize them as such. He went on.

"I've chosen the Jampot for your consideration," he said, "because he's a kind of bonus in crime. He combines in himself the ingredients that you find singly or in other homicides and hands you the lot in a mixed grill. His real name, believe it or not, is Foljambe."

The forward-leaning, sandy-coloured recruit gave a laugh which he stifled. Several of his companions grinned doubtfully and wiped their mouths. Two looked startled and the rest uneasy.

"At all events," Alleyn said, "that's what he says it is, and as he hasn't got any other name, Foljambe let the Jampot be.

"He was born in Johannesburg, received a good education and is said to have read medicine for two years, but would appear to have been from birth what used to be known as a 'wrong 'un.' His nickname was given him by his South African associates in crime and has been adopted by the police on both sides of the Atlantic. In Paris, I understand he is known as Le Folichon or 'the frisky bloke.'

"I'd like to pick up his story at the time of his highly ingenious escape from gaol which took place on the 7th May the year before last in Bolivia...."

One or two of his hearers wrote this down. He was giving an address by invitation to a ten-week course at the Police College.

"By an outlandish coincidence," Alleyn said, and his deep voice took on the note of continuous narrative, "I was personally involved in this affair: by personally, I mean as a private individual as well as a policeman. It so happened that my wife..."

1

"...above all it must be said of this most distinguished exhibition, that while in scope it is retrospective it is by no means definitive. The painter, one feels, above all her contemporaries, will continue to explore and penetrate: for her own and our sustained enjoyment."

The painter in question muttered: "Oh Lord, Oh Lord," and laid aside the morning paper as stealthily as if she had stolen it. She left the dining-room, paid her bill, arranged to pick up her luggage in time to catch the London train and went for a stroll.

Her hotel was not far from the river. Summer sunshine defined alike ranks of unbudgingly Victorian mercantile buildings broken at irregular intervals by vast upended waffle-irons. Gothic spires and a ham-fisted Town Hall poked up through the early mist. She turned her back on them and made downhill for the river.

As she drew near to it the character of the streets changed. They grew narrower and were cobbled. She passed a ropewalk and a shop called "Rutherfords, Riverview Chandlers," a bakery smelling of new bread, a pawnbroker's and a second-hand machine-parts shop. The River itself now glinted through gaps in the buildings and at the ends of passages. When she finally came within full view of it she thought it beautiful. Not picturesque or grandiloquent but alive and positive, curving in and out of the city with historical authority. It was, she thought, a thing in its own right and the streets and wharves that attended upon it belonged to it and to themselves. "Wharf Lane" she read, and took her way down it to the front. Rivercraft of all kinds were moored along the foreshore.

Half-way down the lane she came upon the offices of the Pleasure Craft and Riverage Company. In their window were posted faded notices of sailing dates and various kinds of cruises. While she was reading these a man in shirtsleeves, looking larger than life in the confined space, edged his way towards the window and attached to its surface with sticky paper a freshly written card.

He caught sight of her, gave her a tentative smile and backed out of the window.

She read the card:

M.V. Zodiac. Last-minute cancellation.
A single-berth cabin is available for
this day's sailing. Apply within.

Placed about the window were photographs of M.V. *Zodiac* in transit and of the places she visited. In the background hung a map of the river and the canals that articulated with it: Ramsdyke. Bullsdyke. Crossdyke. A five-day cruise from Norminster to Longminster and back was offered. Passengers slept and ate on board. The countryside, said a pamphlet that lay on the floor, was rich in historical associations. Someone with a taste for fanciful phrases had added: "For Five Days You Step Out of Time."

She had had a gruelling summer working for her one-man show, and was due in a few weeks to see it launched in Paris and afterwards New York. Her husband was in America and her son was taking a course at Grenoble. She thought of the long train journey south, the gritty arrival, the summer stifle of London and the empty stuffy house. It seemed to her, afterwards, that she behaved like a child in a fairytale. She opened the door, and as she did so she heard something say within her head: "For five days I step out of time."

2

"There is," wrote Miss Rickerby-Carrick, "no bottom, none, to my unquenchable infamy."

She glanced absently at the tip of her propelling pencil and, in falsetto, cleared her throat.

"For instance," she wrote, "let us examine my philanthropy. Or rather, since I have no distaste for colloquialism, my dogoodery. No!" she exclaimed aloud. "That won't wash. That is a vile phrase, dogoodery is a vile phrase." She paused again, greatly put out by the suspicion that these observations were not entirely original. She stared about her and caught the eye of a thin lady in dark blue linen who, like herself, sat on her own suitcase.

"'Dogoodery,'" Miss Rickerby-Carrick repeated. "Is that a facetious word? Do you find it so?"

"Well—it depends, I suppose, on the context."

"You look startled."

"Do I?" said Troy Alleyn, looking startled indeed. "Sorry. I was a thousand miles away."

"I wish *I* were. Or no," amended Miss Rickerby-Carrick. "Wrong again. Correction. I wish I were a thousand miles away from *me*. From myself. No kidding," she added. "To try out another colloquialism."

She wrote again in her book.

Her companion looked attentively at her and might have been said, after her own fashion, also to make notes. She saw a figure, not exactly of fun, but of confusion. There was no coordination. The claret-coloured suit, the disheartened jumper, above all the knitted jockey-cap, all looked to have been thrown at their wearer and fortuitously to have stuck. She had a strange trick with her mouth, letting it fly apart over her teeth and turn up at the corners so that she seemed to grin when in fact she did nothing of the sort. The hand that clutched her propelling pencil was arthritic.

Overhead, clouds bowled slowly across a midsummer sky. A light wind fiddled with the river and one or two small boats bumped at their moorings. The pleasure craft *Zodiac* had not appeared but was due at noon.

"My name," said Miss Rickerby-Carrick, "is Rickerby-Carrick. Hazel. 'Spinster of this parish.' What's yours?"

"Alleyn."

"Mrs.?"

"Yes." After a moment's hesitation. Troy, since it was obviously expected of her, uncomfortably added her first name. "Agatha," she mumbled.

"Agatharallen," said Miss Rickerby-Carrick sharply. "That's funny. I thought you must be K. G. Z. Andropoulos, Cabin 7."

"The cabin *was* taken by somebody called Andropoulos, I believe, but the booking was cancelled at the last moment. This morning, in fact. I happened to be here on—on business, and I saw it advertised in the company's window, so I took it," said Troy, "on impulse."

"Just like that. Fancy." A longish pause followed. "So we're ship-mates? 'Water wanderers'?" Miss Rickerby-Carrick concluded, quoting the brochure.

"In the *Zodiac*? Yes," Troy agreed and hoped she sounded friendly enough. Miss Rickerby-Carrick crinkled her eyes and stripped her teeth. "Jolly good show," she said. She gazed at Troy for some time and then returned to her writing. An affluent-looking car drove half-way down the cobbled passage. Its uniformed driver got out, walked to the quay, looked superciliously at nothing in particular, returned, spoke through the rear window to an indistinguishable occupant and resumed his place at the wheel.

"When I examine in depth the motives by which I am activated," wrote Miss Rickerby-Carrick in her book, "I am appalled. For instance. I have a reputation, within my circle (admittedly a limited one), for niceness, for kindness, for charity. I adore my reputation. People come to me in their trouble. They cast themselves upon my bosom and weep. I love it. I'm awfully good at being good. I think to myself that they must all tell each other how good I am. 'Hay Rickerby-Carrick,' I know they say, 'she's so *good*.' And so I am. I *am*. I put myself out in order to keep up my reputation. I make sacrifices. I am unselfish in buses, upstanding in tubes, and I relinquish my places in queues. I visit the aged, I comfort the bereaved, and if they don't like it they can lump it. I am filled with amazement when I think about my niceness. O misery, misery, misery me," she wrote with enormous relish.

Two drops fell upon her notebook. She gave a loud, succulent and complacent sniff.

Troy thought: "Will she go on like this for five days? Is she dotty? Oh God, has she got a cold!"

"Sorry," said Miss Rickerby-Carrick. "I've got a bid of cold. Dur," she added, making a catarrhal clicking sound and allowing her mouth to fall slightly open. Troy began to wonder if there was a good train to London before evening.

"You wonder," said Miss Rickerby-Carrick in a thick voice, "why I sit on my suitcase and write. I have lately taken to a diary. My self-propelling confessional, *I* call it."

"Do you?" Troy said helplessly.

Down the cobbled lane walked a pleasant-looking man in an ancient knickerbocker suit of Donegal tweed and a cloth cap. He carried, besides a rucksack, a square box on a shoulder-strap and a canvas-covered object that might, Troy thought, almost be a grossly misshapen tennis racquet. He took off his cap when he saw the ladies and kept it off. He was of a sandy complexion with a not unattractive cast in one of his blue eyes, a freckled countenance and a tentative smile.

"Good morning," he said. "We must be fellow-travellers."

Troy agreed. Miss Rickerby-Carrick, blurred about the eyes and nose, nodded, smiled and sniffed. She was an industrious nodder.

"No signs of the *Zodiac* as yet," said the newcomer. "Dear me," he added, "that's a pitfall of a joke, isn't it? We shall all be making it as punctually as the tides, I daresay." Miss Rickerby-Carrick, after a moment's thought, was consumed with laughter. He looked briefly at her and attentively at Troy. "My name's Caley Bard," he said.

"I'm Troy Alleyn and this is Miss Rickerby-Carrick."

"You said you were Agatha," Miss Rickerby-Carrick pointed out. "You said Agatharallen," and Troy felt herself blushing.

"So I am," she muttered, "the other's just a sort of a joke— my husband—" her voice died away. She was now extremely conscious of Mr. Bard's scrutiny and particularly aware of its dwelling speculatively on the veteran paintbox at her feet. All he said, however, was, "Dear me," in a donnish tone. When she looked her apprehension he tipped her a wink. This was disconcerting.

She was relieved by the arrival on an apocalyptic motor-bicycle of a young man and his girl. The noonday sun pricked at their metal studs and turned the surface of their leather suits and calf-high boots into toffee. From under crash helmets hair veiled in oil and dust fell unevenly to their shoulders. Their machine belched past the stationary chauffeur-driven car and came to a halt. They put their booted feet to the ground and lounged, chewing, against their bicycle. "There is nothing," Troy thought, "as insolent as a gum-chewing face," and at the same time she itched to make a sharp, black drawing of the riders.

"Do you suppose—?" she ventured in a low voice.

"I hardly think water-wandering would present a very alluring prospect," Mr. Bard rejoined.

"In any case, they have no luggage."

"They may not need any. They may bed down as they are."

"Oh, do you think so? All those steel knobs."

"There is that, of course," Mr. Bard agreed.

The young people lit cigarettes, inhaled deeply, stared at nothing and exhaled vapour. They had not spoken.

Miss Rickerby-Carrick gazed raptly at them and then wrote in her book.

"—two of our Young Independents," she noted. "Is it to gladiators that one should compare them? Would they like it if one did? Would I be able to get on with them? Would they like me? Would they find me *simpática* or is it *simpático*? Alas, there I go again. Incorrigible, hopeless old Me!"

She stabbed down an ejaculation mark, clicked off her pencil with an air of quizzical finality, and said to Troy: "How did you get here? I came by bus: from good old Brummers."

"I drove," Mr. Bard said. "From London and put up at a pub. Got here last night."

"I did too," said Troy. "But I came by train."

"There's a London train that connects this morning," Miss Rickerby-Carrick observed. "Arrives 11:45."

"I know. But I—there was—I had an engagement," Troy mumbled.

"Such as going to the pictures?" Mr. Bard airily suggested to nobody in particular. "Something of that sort?" Troy looked at him but he was staring absently at the river. "*I* went to the pictures," he said. "But not last night. This morning. Lovely."

"The *pictures!*" Miss Rickerby-Carrick exclaimed. "This morning! Do you mean the cinema?"

But before Mr. Bard could explain himself if indeed he intended to do so, two taxis, one after the other, came down the cobbled lane and discharged their passengers.

"There! The London train must be in," Miss Rickerby-Carrick observed with an air of triumph.

The first to alight was an undistinguished man of about forty. Under a belted raincoat he wore a pinstriped suit which, revealed, would surely prove abominable. His shirt was mauve and his tie a brightish pink. His hair was cut short, back and sides. He had a knobbly face and pale eyes. As he approached, carrying his fibre suitcase and wearing a jaunty air, Troy noticed that he limped, swinging a built-up boot. "Morning all," he said. "Lovely day, innit?"

Troy and Mr. Bard agreed and Miss Rickerby-Carrick repeated: "Lovely! Lovely!" on an ecstatic note.

"Pollock's the name," said the new arrival, easily. "Stan." They murmured.

Mr. Bard introduced himself and the ladies. Mr. Pollock responded with sideways wags of his head.

"That's the ticket," he said. "No deception practised."

Miss Rickerby-Carrick said: "*Isn't* this going to be *fun*,"

in a wildish tone that modulated into one of astonishment.
Her gaze had shifted to the passenger from the second taxi
who, with his back to the group, was settling his fare. He was
exceedingly tall and very well-dressed at High Establishment
level. Indeed his hat, houndstooth checked overcoat and
impeccable brogues were in such a grand conservative style
that it surprised—it almost shocked—Troy to observe that
he seemed to be wearing black gloves like a Dickensian
undertaker. Some yards distant, his bell-like voice rang out
enormously. "Thank you. Good morning to you. Good
morning."

He lifted his suitcase and turned. His hat tilted a little
forward; the brim shadowed the face but could not be seen to
do so as the face itself was darker than a shadow; the latest
arrival was a coloured man.

Miss Rickerby-Carrick gave out an ejaculation. Mr. Bard
after the briefest glance continued talking to Troy. Mr.
Pollack stared, faintly whistled and then turned aside with a
shuttered face. The motor-cyclists for some private reason
broke into ungentle laughter.

The newcomer advanced, lifted his hat generally and
moved through the group to the wharf's edge where he stood
looking upstream towards the bend in the river: an
incongruous but impressive and elegant figure against a
broken background of rivercraft, sliding water and buildings
advertising themselves in a confusion of signs.

Troy said quickly: "That makes five of us, doesn't it?
Three more to come."

"One of whom occupies that very affluent-looking car, no
doubt," said Mr. Bard. "I tried to peer in as I came past but an
open newspaper defeated me."

"Male or female, did you gather?"

"Oh, the former, the former. A large manicured hand. The
chauffeur is one of the stony kind. Now what is your guess?
We have a choice of two from our passenger list, haven't we?
Which do you think?" He just indicated the figure down by
the river. "Dr. Natouche? Mr. J. de B. Lazenby? Which is
which?"

"I plump for J. de B. L. in the car," Troy said. "It sounds
so magnificent."

"Do you? No; my fancy lies in the contrary field. I put Dr.

Natouche in the car. A specialist in some esoteric upper reaches of the more impenetrable branches of medicine. An astronomical consulting fee. And I fetch our friend on the wharf from Barbados. He owns a string of hotels and is called Jasper de Brabazon Lazenby. Shall we have a bet on it?"

"Well," Troy said, "propose your bet."

"If I win you have a drink with me before luncheon. If you win, I pay for the drinks."

"Now then!" Troy ejaculated.

Mr. Bard gave a little inward laugh.

"We shall see," he said. "I think that I might—" He smiled at Troy and without completing his sentence walked down to the quay.

"Are you," Troy could just hear him say, "joining us? I'm sure you must be."

"In the *Zodiac*?" the great voice replied. "Yes. I am a passenger."

"Shall we introduce ourselves?"

The others all strained to hear the exchange of names.

"Natouche."

"Dr. Natouche?"—

"Quite so."

Mr. Bard sketched the very vaguest and least of bows in Troy's direction.

"I'm Caley Bard," he said.

"Ah. I too have seen the passenger list. Good-morning, sir."

"Do," said Caley Bard, "come and meet the others. We have been getting to know each other."

"Thank you. If you wish."

They turned together. Mr. Bard was a tall man but Dr. Natouche diminished him. Behind them the river, crinkled by a breeze and dappled with discs of sunlight, played tricks with the two approaching figures. It exaggerated their size, rimmed them in a pulsing nimbus and distorted their movement. As they drew nearer, the pale man and the dark, Troy, bemused by this dazzle, thought: "There is no reason in the wide world why I should feel apprehensive. It will be all right unless Mr. Pollock is bloody-minded or the Rickerby-Carrick hideously effusive. It must be all right." She glanced up the lane and there were the cyclists, stock-still except for their jaws: staring, staring.

She held out her hand to Dr. Natouche who was formal and bowed slightly over it. His head, uncovered, showed grey close-cut fuzz above the temples. His skin was not perfectly black but warmly dark with grape-coloured shadows. The bony structure of his face was exquisite.

"Mrs. Alleyn," said Dr. Natouche.

Miss Rickerby-Carrick was, as Troy had feared she would be, excessive. She shook Dr. Natouche's hand up and down and laughed madly: "Oh—ho—ho," she laughed, "how perfectly splendid."

Mr. Pollock kept his hands in his pockets and limped aside thus avoiding an introduction.

Since there seemed to be nothing else to talk about Troy hurriedly asked Dr. Natouche if he had come by the London train. He said he had driven up from Liverpool, added a few generalities, gave her a smile and a slight inclination of his head, returned to the river and walked for some little distance along the wharves.

"Innit marvellous?" Mr. Pollock asked of nobody in particular. "They don't tell you so you can't complain."

"They?" wondered Miss Rickerby-Carrick. "Tell you? I don't understand?"

"When you book in." He jerked his head towards Dr. Natouche. "What to expect."

"Oh, but you *mustn't!*" she whispered. "You *mustn't* feel like that. Truly."

"Meant to be class, this carry-on? Right? That's what they tell you. Right? First class. Luxury accommodation. Not my idea of it. Not with that type of company. If I'd known one of that lot was included I wouldn't have come at it. Straight, I wouldn't."

"How very odd of you," said Mr. Bard lightly.

"That's your opinion," Mr. Pollock angrily rejoined. He turned towards Troy, hoping perhaps for an ally. "I reckon it's an insult to the ladies," he said.

"Oh, go along with you," Troy returned as good-naturedly as she could manage, "it's nothing of the sort. Is it, Miss Rickerby-Carrick?"

"Oh *no*. No. Indeed, no."

"I know what I'm talking about," Mr. Pollock loudly asserted. Troy looked nervously at the distant figure on the riverage. "I own property. Once that sort settles in a district—look—it's a slum. Easy as that."

"Mr. Pollock, this man is a doctor," Troy said.

"You joking? Doctor? Of what?"

"Of medicine," Mr. Bard said. "You should consult your passenger-list, my dear fellow. He's an M.D."

"You can tell people you're anything," Mr. Pollock darkly declared. "Anything. I could tell them I was a bloody earl. Pardon the French, I'm sure." He glared at Troy, who was giggling. The shadow of a grin crept into his expression. "Not that they'd credit it," he added. "But still."

The young man on the motor-cycle sounded a derisive call on his siren. "*Taa* t'-ta ta ta. *Ta-Taa.*" He and his girl-friend were looking towards the bend in the river.

A rivercraft had come into view. She was painted a dazzling white. A scarlet and green houseflag was mounted at her bows and the red ensign at her stern. Sunlight splashed her brasswork, red curtains glowed behind her saloon windows. As she drew towards her moorings her name could be seen, painted in gold letters along her bows.

M.V. *Zodiac.*

The clock in a church tower above the river struck twelve.

"Here she is," Mr. Bard said. "Dead on time."

3

The *Zodiac* berthed and was made fast very smartly by a lad of about fifteen. Her Skipper left the wheelhouse and said goodbye to his passengers who could be heard to thank him, saying they wished the voyage had been longer. They passed through the waiting group. A woman, catching Troy's eyes, said: "You're going to love it." And a man remarked to his wife: "Well, back to earth, worst luck," with what seemed almost excessive regret after a five-day jaunt.

When they had all gone the new passengers moved down to the *Zodiac* and were greeted by the Skipper. He was a pleasant-looking fellow, very neat in his white duck shirt and dark blue trousers and tie. He wore the orthodox peaked cap.

"You'd all like to come aboard," he said. "Tom!" The boy began to collect the luggage and pile it on the deck. The Skipper offered a hand to the ladies. Miss Rickerby-Carrick made rather heavy going of this business. "Dear me!" she said, "Oh. Oh, thank you," and leapt prodigiously.

She had a trick of clutching with her left hand at her dun-coloured jumper: almost, Troy thought, as if she carried her money in a bag around her neck and wanted continuously to assure herself it was still there.

From amidships and hard-by the wheelhouse the passengers descended, by way of a steep little flight of steps and a half-gate of the loosebox kind, into the saloon. From there a further downward flight ended in a passage through the cabin quarters. Left of this companionway a hatch from the saloon offered a bird's-eye view into the cuddy which was at lower deck level. Down there a blonde woman assembled dishes of cold meats and salads. She wore a startched apron over a black cotton dress. Her hair, pale as straw, was drawn back from a central parting into a lustrous knob. As Troy looked down at it the woman turned and tilted back her head. She smiled dazzlingly and said: "Good morning. Lunch in half an hour. The bar will be open in a few minutes." The bar, Troy saw, was on the port side of the saloon, near the entry.

The boy came down with Troy's suitcase and paintbox. He said: "This way, please," and she followed him to the lower deck and to her cabin.

No. 7 was the third on the starboard side, and was exactly twice the size of its bunk. It had a cupboard, a washbasin and a porthole near the ceiling. The counterpane and curtains were cherry-red, and in a glass on the bedside shelf there was a red geranium mixed with a handful of fern and hedgerow flowers. This pleased Troy greatly. The boy put her suitcase on the bunk and her paintbox under it. For some reason she felt diffident about tipping him. She hesitated but he didn't. He gave her a smile that was the very print of the woman's and was gone. "He's her son," thought Troy, "and perhaps they're a family. Perhaps the Skipper's his father."

She unpacked her suitcase and stowed it under her bunk, washed her hands and was about to return to the saloon when, hearing voices outside, she knelt on her bunk and looked through the porthole. It was at dockside level and there, quite close at hand, were the shiny leggings and polished boots of the smart chauffeur, his brown breeches and his gloved hands each holding a suitcase. They moved out of sight, towards the boarding plank, no doubt, and were followed by shoes and clerical grey trousers. These legs paused and formed a truncated triangular frame through which Troy saw, as if in an artfully directed film, the distant black-leathered cyclists, still glinting, chewing and staring in the cobbled lane. She had the oddest notion that they stared at her, though that, as she told herself, was ridiculous. They had just been joined by the boy from the *Zodiac* when all of them were blotted out by a taxi that shot into her field of vision and halted. The framing legs moved away. The door of the taxi began to open but Troy's attention was abstracted by a loud rap on her cabin door. She sat down hurriedly on her bunk and said: "Come in." Miss Rickerby-Carrick's active face appeared round the door.

"I say," she said. "Bliss! A shower and *two* loos! *Aren't* we lucky!"

Before Troy could reply she had withdrawn. There were sounds within the craft of new arrivals.

"Thank you very much . . . Er, here—" the voice was lowered to an indistinguishable murmur. A second voice said: "Thank you, sir." A door was shut. Boots tramped up the companionway and across the deck overhead. "The chauffeur," Troy thought. "And Mr. J. de B. Lazenby." She waited for a moment listening to the movements of the other passengers. There was a further confusion of arrival and a bump of luggage. A woman's voice said: "That's correct, Stooard, we do have quite a bit of photographic equipment. I guess I'll use No. 3 as a regular stateroom and No. 6 can accommodate my brother and the overflow. O.K.? O.K., Earl?"

"Sure. Sure."

The cabin forward of Troy's was No. 6. She heard sounds of the bestowal of property and a number of warnings as to its fragility, all given with evident good humour. The man's voice said repeatedly: "Sure. Sure. Fine. Fine." There was an unsuccessful attempt to tip the boy. "Thanks all the same,"

Troy heard him say. He departed. There followed a silence and an ejaculation from the lady. "Do you look like I feel?" and the man's answer: "Forget it. We couldn't know."

Troy consulted her passenger list. Mr. Earl J. and Miss Sally-Lou Hewson had arrived. She stowed away her baggage and then went up to the saloon.

They were all there except the three latest arrivals. Dr. Natouche sat by himself reading a newspaper with a glass of beer to hand. Miss Rickerby-Carrick, in conversation with Mr. Pollock, occupied a seat that ran around the forward end of the saloon under the windows. Mr. Caley Bard, who evidently had been waiting for Troy, at once reminded her that she was to have a drink with him. "Mrs. Tretheway," he said, "mixes a superb martini."

She was behind the little bar, displayed in the classic manner within a frame of bottles and glasses, many of which were splintered by sunlight. She herself had a kind of local iridescence: she looked superb. Mr. Pollock kept glancing at her with a half-smile on his lips and then turning away again. Miss Rickerby-Carrick gazed at her with a kind of anguished wonder. Mr. Bard expressed his appreciation in what Troy was to learn was a very characteristic manner.

"The bar at the Folies-Bergères may as well shut up shop," he said to Troy. "Manet would have changed his drinking habits. You, by the way, could show him where he gets off." And he gave Troy a little bow and a very knowing smile. "You ought to have a go," he suggested. "Don't," she said hurriedly. "Please." He laughed and leant across the bar to pay for their drinks. Mrs. Tretheway gave Troy a woman-to-woman look that included her fabulous smile.

Even Dr. Natouche lowered his paper and contemplated Mrs. Tretheway with gravity for several seconds.

At the back of the bar hung a framed legend, rather shakily typed.

The Signs of the *Zodiac*
The Hunt of the Heavenly Host begins
With the Ram, the Bull and the Heavenly Twins.
The Crab is followed by the Lion
The Virgin and the Scales,

The Scorpion, Archer and He-Goat
The Man that carries the Watering-Pot
And the Fish with the Glittering Tails.

"Isn't that charming?" Mr. Bard asked Troy. "Don't you think so?"

"The magic of the proper name," Troy agreed. "Especially those names. It always does the trick, doesn't it?"

Mrs. Tretheway said, "A chap that cruised with us gave it to me. He said it was out of some kid's book."

"It's got the right kind of dream-sound for that," Troy said. She thought she would like to make a picture of the signs and put the rhyme in the middle. Perhaps before the cruise was over—

"To make it rhyme," Mrs. Tretheway pointed out, "you have to say 'pote.' 'The Man that carries the Watering-pote.' "

She pushed their drinks across the bar. The back of her hand brushed Mr. Bard's fingers.

"You'll join us, I hope," he said.

"Another time, thanks all the same. I've got to look after your lunch. It's cold—what do they call it—smorgasbord, for today. If everybody would help themselves when they're ready."

She went over to the hatch into the cuddy. Tom, the boy, had gone below and handed up the dishes to his mother who set them out on the tables that had been pushed together and covered with a white cloth.

"Whenever you're ready," Mrs. Tretheway repeated, "please help yourselves," and returned to the bar where she jangled a handbell.

Without consulting Troy, Mr. Bard ordered two more dry martinis. This was not Troy's favorite drink and in any case the first had been extremely strong.

"No, really, thank you," she said. "*Not* for me. I'm for my lunch."

"Well," he said. "P'rhaps you're right. We'll postpone until dinner-time. Let moderation be our cry."

It now occurred to Troy that Mr. Bard was making a dead set at her. Gratifying though this might or might not be, it did not fit in with her plan for a five days' anonymous dawdle along the British Inland Waterways. Mr. Bard, it was

evident, had twigged Troy. He had this morning visited her
one-man show for the opening of which, last evening, she had
come up from London. He had been cunning enough to
realize that she wanted to remain unrecognized. Evidently he
was disposed to torment her about this and to set up a kind of
alliance on the strength of it. Mr. Bard was a tease.

There was a place beside Dr. Natouche at the end of a
circular seat that ran under the forward windows of the
saloon. Troy helped herself to cold meat and salad and sat
beside him. He half-rose and made her a little bow. "I hope
you are pleased with the accommodation," he said. "I find it
perfectly satisfactory."

There was an extraordinary quality in Dr. Natouche,
Troy suddenly decided. It was a quality that made one
intensely aware of him, as if with the awareness induced by
some drug: aware of his thin, charcoal wrist emerging from a
white silk cuff, of the movements of his body under his
clothes, of his quiet breathing, of his smell which was of
wood: cedarwood or even sandalwood.

He had neatly folded his newspaper and laid it beside his
plate. Troy, glancing at it, saw herself having her hand
shaken by the Personage who had opened her show. Was it
possible that Dr. Natouche had not recognized this
photograph. "I really don't know," she thought, "why I fuss
about it. If I were a film star it would be something to take on
about but who cares for painters? The truth of the matter is,"
Troy thought, "I never know what to say when people who
don't paint talk to me about my painting. I get creaky with
shyness and hear myself mumbling and am idiotic."

Dr. Natouche, however, did not talk about painting. He
talked about the weather and the days to come and he
sounded a little like one of the Pleasure Craft and Riverage
Company's pamphlets. "There will be a great deal of historic
interest," he said, calmly.

He had moved away from Troy to give her plenty of room.
She was as conscious of the distance between them as if she
had measured it in inches.

"All the arrangements are charming," concluded Dr.
Natouche.

Mr. and Miss Hewson now appeared. They seemed to be
the dead norm of unpretentious American tourists. Miss

Hewson was fairish, shortish and compact in shape. Her brother was tall, thin and bespectacled and wore a hearing-aid. They both looked hygienic and practical.

"Well, now," Miss Hewson said, "if we aren't just the slowest things to settle. Pardon us, folks."

Mrs. Tretheway from behind the bar introduced them to the assembled company and in a pleasant, sensible fashion they repeated each name as they heard it while the British murmured and smiled. Dr. Natouche reciprocated in this ritual and Troy wondered if he too was an American but could hear no trace of it in his voice. West Indian? African? Pakistani?

"One to come," Miss Rickerby-Carrick presently announced, excitedly tossing salad into her mouth. "You're not the last." She had been talking energetically to the Hewsons who looked dazed and baffled. She indicated a copy of the passenger list that had been put on the table. Troy had already noticed that the name K. G. Z. Andropoulos had been struck out opposite Cabin 7 and that her own had not been substituted. Mr. Bard, with one of his off-beat glances at her, now reached out for the card and made good this omission. "We may as well," he said, "be all shipshape and Bristol fashion." Troy saw that he had spelt her surname correctly but obligingly prefaced it merely by the initials A. T. She couldn't help giving him a look in return and he tipped her another of his squinny winks.

Miss Rickerby-Carrick began playfully to whisper: "What do you think? Shall we guess? What will he be?" She pointed to Mr. J. de B. Lazenby's name on the card and looked archly round the company.

They were spared the necessity of reply by the entrance of Mr. Lazenby himself.

In a way, Troy felt, it was something of an anticlimax. Mr. Lazenby was a clergyman.

It was also a surprise. One did not, somehow, associate the clergy, except in the upper reaches of their hierarchy, with expensive cars and uniformed chauffeurs. Mr. Lazenby gave out no particular air of affluence. He was tall, rather pink and thinly crested, and he wore dark glasses, an immaculate clerical grey suit, a blue pullover and the regulation dog-collar.

Mrs. Tretheway, from behind the bar where, to Troy's fancy, she had become a kind of oracle, pronounced his name and added sensibly that he would no doubt find out in due course who everybody was.

"Surely, surely," said Mr. Lazenby in a slightly antipodean, faintly parsonic voice.

"But," cried Miss Rickerby-Carrick, "it doesn't say in the passenger list. It doesn't say Reverend. Now, why is that?"

"I expcet," said Mr. Lazenby, who was helping himself to luncheon, "it was because I applied for my reservation by letter. From Melbourne. I didn't, I think, declare my cloth." He smiled at her, composed himself, bent his head for a moment, scratched a miniature cross on his jumper and sat down by Mr. Pollock. "This looks delicious," he said.

"Very tasty," said Mr. Pollock woodenly and helped himself to pickles.

Luncheon went forward in little desultory gusts of conversation. Items of information were exchanged. The Hewsons had come up from the Tabard Inn at Stratford-upon-Avon where on Saturday night they had seen a performance of *Macbeth* which they had thought peculiar. Mr. Lazenby had been staying with the Bishop of Norminster. Mr. Pollock had caught the London train in Birmingham where he had lodged uncomfortably at the Osborn Hotel. Dr. Natouche and Miss Rickerby-Carrick had come from their respective homes. Miss Hewson guessed that she and her brother were not the only non-Britishers aboard, addressing her remark to Mr. Lazenby but angling, Troy thought, for a reaction from Dr. Natouche who did not, however, respond. Mr. Lazenby expounded to the Hewsons on Australia and the Commonwealth. He also turned slightly towards Dr. Natouche though it was impossible to see, so dark were his spectacles, whether he really looked at him.

"Well, now," Miss Hewson said, "I just don't get this Commonwealth. It's the British Commonwealth but you're not a Britisher and you got the British Queen but you don't go around saying you're a monarchy. I guess the distinctions are too refined for my crass American appreciation. What do you say, dear?" she asked Mr. Hewson.

"Pardon me, dear?"

Miss Hewson articulated carefully into her brother's

hearing-aid and he began to look honest-to-God and dryly humorous.

Miss Rickerby-Carrick broke into the conversation with confused cries of regret for the loss of Empire and of admiration for the Monarchy. "I know one's not meant to talk like this," she said with conspiratorial glances at Troy, Mr. Pollock and Mr. Bard. "But sometimes one can't help it. I mean I'm *absolutely all* for freedom and civil rights and integ—" she broke off with an air of someone whose conversation has bolted with her, turned very red and madly leant towards Dr. Natouche. "Do forgive me," she gabbled. "I mean, of course, I don't know. I mean, am I right in supposing—?"

Dr. Natouche folded his hands, waited a moment and then said: "Are you wondering if I am a British subject? I am. As you see, I belong to a minority group. I practise in Liverpool." His voice was superbly tranquil and his manner entirely withdrawn.

The silence that followed his little speech was broken by the Skipper who came crabwise down the companionway.

"Well, ladies and gentlemen," he said. "I hope you are comfortably settled. We'll be on our way in a few minutes. You will find a certain amount of information in the brochures supplied. We don't go in for mikes and loudspeakers in the *Zodiac* but I'm very much at your service to answer questions if I can. The weather forecast is good although at this time of year we sometimes get the Creeper, which is a local name for River fog. It usually comes up at night and can be heavy. During the afternoon we follow the upper reaches of the River through low-lying country to Ramsdyke Lock. We wind about and about quite a lot which some people find confusing. You may have noticed, by the way, that in these parts we don't talk about the River by name. To the locals it's always just the River. You may think Shakespeare had a good notion of this river when he described the Trent as being 'smug and silver.' It was over this country that Archbishop Langton chased King John. But long before that the Romans made the Ramsdyke canal as an addition to the River itself. The waterways were busy in Roman times. We take a little while going through the lock at Ramsdyke and you might fancy a stroll up the field and a look at a hollow alongside the Dyke Way. The wapentake courts were held there in Plantagenet times. Forerunners of our judges circuits. You can't miss the wapentake hollow. Matter of five minutes' walk. Thank you."

He gave a crisp little nod and returned to the upper deck. An appreciative murmur broke out among the passengers.

"Come," Mr. Bard exclaimed. "Here's a sensible and heartening start. A handful of nice little facts and a fillip to the imagination. Splendid. Mrs. Alleyn, you have finished your luncheon. Do come on deck and witness the departure."

"I think we should all go up," Troy said.

"Oh ra-*ther!*" cried Miss Rickerby-Carrick. "Come on, chaps!"

She blew her nose vigorously and made a dash for the companionway. There was a printed warning at the top: "Please note deeper step" but she disregarded it, plunged headlong through the half-door at the top and could be heard floundering about with startled cries on the other side. Troy overheard Mr. Hewson say to Miss Hewson: "To me she seems kind of fabulous," and Miss Hewson reply: "Maybe she's one of the Queen's Beasts," and they both looked dryly humorous. Illogically Troy felt irritated with them and exasperated by Miss Rickerby-Carrick, who was clearly going to get on everybody's nerves. Mr. Pollock for instance, after contemplating her precipitate exit, muttered: "Isn't it marvellous!" and Mr. Bard, for Troy's benefit, briefly cast up his eyes and followed the others to the upper deck. Mr. Lazenby, who was still at his luncheon, waved his fork to indicate that he would follow later.

Dr. Natouche rose and looked out of the saloon windows at the wharf. Troy thought: "How *very* tall he is." Taller, she decided, than her husband, who was over six feet. "He's waiting," she thought, "for all of us to go up first," and she found herself standing by him.

"Have you ever done this before Dr. Natouche?" she asked. "Taken a waterways cruise?"

"No." he said. "Never before. It is a new experience."

"For me too. I came on an impulse."

"Indeed? You felt the need of a break perhaps after the strain of your public activities."

"Yes," Troy agreed, unaccountably pleased that he did,

after all, know of her show and had recognized her. Without so much as noticing that she felt none of her usual awkwardness she said: "They *are* a bit of a hurdle, these solemn affairs."

Dr. Natouche said: "Some of your works are very beautiful. It gave me great pleasure in London to see them."

"Did it? I'm glad."

"They are casting off, if that is the right phrase. Would you like to go up?"

Troy went up on deck. Tom, the boy, had loosed the mooring lines and laid them out smartly. The Skipper was at the wheel. The *Zodiac*'s engines throbbed. She moved astern, away from her wharf and out into the main stream.

The motor-cyclists were still in the lane. Troy saw young Tom signal, not very openly, to them and they slightly raised their hands in return. The girl straddled her seat, the boy kicked and their engine broke out in pandemonium. The machine curved, belched and racketed up the lane out of sight.

Dr. Natouche appeared and then Mr. Lazenby. The eight passengers stood along the rails and watched the riverbanks take on a new perspective and become remote. Spires and waffle-irons, glass boxes, mansard roofs and the squat cupola of the Norminster Town Hall were now merely there to be stared at with detachment. They shifted about, very slowly, and looked over one another's shoulders and grew smaller. The *Zodiac*, now in midstream, set her course for Ramsdyke Lock.

II

THE WAPENTAKE

"He had been operating," Alleyn said, "in a very big way in the Middle East. All among the drug barons with one of whom he fell out and who is thought to have grassed on him. From drugs he turned to the Old Master racket and was certainly behind several very big jobs in Paris. Getting certificates for good fakes from galleries and the widows of celebrated painters. He then crossed to New York where he worked off the fruits of this ploy until Interpol began to make interested noises. By the way, it may be noted that at this juncture he had not got beyond a Blue Circular which means of course—"

The boots of the intelligent-looking sandy man in the second row scraped the floor. He made a slight gesture and looked eager. "I see you know," Alleyn said.

"Ay, Sir, I do. A Blue International Circular signifies that Interpol cannot place the identity of the creeminal."

"That's it. However, they were getting warmer and in 1965 the Jampot found it necessary to transfer to Bolivia where for once he went too far and was put in gaol. From there, as I've said, he escaped in May of last year, and sometime later arrived with an efficiently cooked-up passport in a Spanish freighter in England. At that juncture the Yard had no specific charge against him, although he featured heavily in the discussions we were holding in San Francisco. He must have already been in touch with the British group he subsequently directed, and one of them booked him in for a late summer cruise in the *Zodiac*. The object of this manoeuvre will declare itself as we go along.

"At this point I'd like you to take particular note of a

disadvantage under which the Jampot laboured. In doing this I am indulging in hindsight. At the time we are speaking about we had no clear indication of what he looked like and our only photograph was a heavily bearded job supplied by the Bolivian police. The ears are hidden by flowing locks, the mouth by a luxuriant moustache and the jaw and chin by rich and carefully tended whiskers.

"We now know, of course, that there was in his appearance something that set him apart, that made him, physically speaking, an odd man out. Need I," Alleyn asked, "remind you what this was?"

The intelligent-looking Scot in the second row made a slight gesture. "Exactly." Alleyn said and enlarged upon it to the class.

"I'm able," he went on, "to give you a pretty full account of this apparently blameless little cruise because my wife wrote at some length about it. In her first letter she told me—"

1

"And there you are," Troy wrote. "All done on the spur of the moment and I think I'm going to be glad I saw that notice in the Pleasure Craft Company's office window.

"It's always been you that writes in cabins and on trains and in hotel bedrooms and me that sits at the receiving end, and now here we are, both at it. The only thing I mind is not getting your letters for the next five days. I'll post this at Ramsdyke Lock and unless they're very carefree about mail it should reach you in New York when I'm at Longminster on the turning point of my little journey. At that rate it'll travel about two thousand times as fast as I do, so whar's your relativity, noo? I'm writing it on my knee from a deck chair. I can't tell you how oddly time behaves on the River, how fantastically remote we are from the country that lies so close on either hand. There go the cars and lorries, streaking along main arteries and over bridges and there are the sound-breakers belching away overhead, but they belong to another world. Truly.

"Our world is watery: details of eddies and reeds and wet

banks. Beyond it things move in a very rum and baffling kind
of way. You know how hopeless I am about direction. Well,
what goes on over there beyond our banks completely
flummoxes me. There's a group of vast powerhouses that has
spent the greater part of the afternoon slowly moving from
one half of our world to the other. They retire over our
horizon on the port side and just as one thinks that's the last
of *them*, there they are moving in on the starboard.
Sometimes we approach them and sometimes we retreat, and
at one dramatic phase we sailed close by and there were
lilliputians halfway up one of them, being busy. Yes: O.K.
darling, I know rivers wind.

"Apart from the powerhouses the country beyond the
River is about as empty as anywhere in England: flat, flat, flat
and according to the Skipper almost hammered so by the
passage of history. Red roses and white. Cavaliers and
Roundheads. Priests and barons. The Percies of the North.
The Jockeys of Norfolk. The lot: all galumphing over the
landscape through the centuries. Did you know that
Constable stayed here one summer and painted? Church
spires turn up with minimal villages and of course, the locks.
Do you remember the lock in *Our Mutual Friend:* a great
slippery drowning-box? I keep thinking of it although the
weirs are more noisily alarming.

"It seems we are going towards the sea in our devious
fashion and so we sink in locks.

"As for the company: I've tried to introduce them to you.
We're no more oddly assorted, I suppose, than any other
eight people that might take it into their heads to spend five
days out of time on the River. Apart from Miss Rickerby-
Carrick who sends me up the wall (you know how *beastly* I
am about ostentatious colds-in-the-head), and Dr. Natouche
who is black, there's nothing at all remarkable about us.

"I'm not the only one who finds poor Miss R.-C. difficult.
Her sledgehammer tact crashes over Dr. N. like a shower of
brickbats, so anxious is she to be unracial. I saw him flinch
two minutes ago under a frontal assault. Mr. Bard said just
now that a peep into her subconscious would be enough to
send him round more bends than the *Zodiac* negotiates in a
summer season. If only she'd just pipe down every now and
then. But no, she doesn't know how to. She has a bosom

friend in Birmingham called—incredibly I forget what—
Mavis something—upon whom we get incessant bulletins.
What Mavis thinks, what she says, how she reacts, how she
has recovered (with setbacks) from Her Operation (coyly left
unspecified). We all, I am sure, now dread the introduction of
the phrase: My special chum, Mavis. All the same, I don't
think she's a stupid woman. Just an inksey-tinksey bit dotty.
The Americans clearly think her as crazy as a coot but
typically British. This is maddening. She keeps a diary and
keeps is the operative word: she carries it about with her and
jots. I am ashamed to say it arouses my curiosity. *What* can
she be writing in it? How odious I sound.

   "I don't like Mr. Pollock much. He is so very sharp and
pale and he so obviously thinks us fools (I mean Mr. Bard
and me and, of course, poor Miss R.-C.) for not sharing his
dislike of coloured people. Of course one does see that if they
sing calypsos all night in the no doubt ghastly tenements he
exorbitantly lets to them and if they roar insults and
improper suggestions at non-black teenagers, it doesn't send
up the tone. But don't non-black tenants ever send the tone
down, for pity's sake? And what on earth has all this got to do
with Dr. Natouche whose tone is superb? I consider that one
of the worst features of the whole black-white thing is that
nobody can say: 'I don't much like black people' as they
might say: 'I don't like the Southern Scot or the Welsh or
antipodeans or the Midland English or Americans or the
League of British Loyalists or the *Reader's Digest*.' I happen
to be attracted to the dark-skinned (Dr. Natouche is
remarkably attractive), but until people who are or who are
not attracted can say so unself-consciously it'll go on being a
muddle. I find it hard to be civil to Mr. Pollock when he
makes his common little racial gestures.

   "He's not alone in his antipathy. Antipathy? I suppose
that's the right word but I almost wrote 'fear.' It seems to me
that Pollock and the Hewsons and even Mr. Lazenby, for all
his parsonic forbearance, eye Dr. Natouche with something
very like fear.

   "We are about to enter our second lock—the Ramsdyke, I
think. More later.

   "Later (about 30 minutes), Ramsdyke. An incident. We
were all on deck and the lock people and our Tom were doing

their things with paddles and gates and all, and I noticed on the far bank from the lockhouse a nice lane, a pub, some wonderful elms, a ford and a pond. I called out to nobody in particular:

"Oh, look! The place is swarming with Constables. Everywhere you look—a perfect clutch of them."

"Rory, it was as if someone had plopped a dirty great weight overboard into the lock. Everybody went dead still and listened. At least—this is hard to describe—*someone* did in particular but I don't know which because nobody moved. Then Dr. Natouche in mild surprise said: 'The police, Mrs. Alleyn? Where? I don't see them,' and I explained and he, for the first time, gave a wonderful roar of laughter. Pollock gaped at me, Caley Bard said he'd thought for a moment his sins had caught up with him, Mr. Lazenby said what a droll mistake to be sure and the Hewsons looked baffled. Miss Rickerby-C. (her friends call her, for God's sake, Hay) waited for the penny to drop and then laughed like a hyena. I still don't know which of them (or whether it was more than one of them) went so very quiet and still and what's more I got the idiotic notion that my explanation had been for—someone— more disturbing than the original remark. And on top of all this, I cannot get rid of the feeling that I'm involved in some kind of performance. Like one of those dreams actors say they get when they find themselves on an unknown stage where a play they've never heard of is in action.

"Silly? Or not silly? Rum? Or not rum?

"I'll write again at Tollardwark. The show looked all right: well hung and lit. The Gallery bought the black and pink thing, and seven smaller ones sold the first night. Paris on the 31st and New York in November. Darling, if, and only if, you have a moment I *would* be glad if you could bear to call at the Guggenheim just to say..."

2

Troy enjoyed coming into the locks and Ramsdyke, as she observed in her letter, was a charming one: a seemly house, a modest plot, the towpath, a bridge over the River, and the Ramsdyke itself, a neat wet line, Roman-ruled across the fens. On the farther side was the "Constable" view and further downstream a weir. The *Zodiac* moved quietly into the lock but before she sank with its waters Troy jumped ashore, posted her letter and followed the direction indicated by the Skipper's tattooed arm and pointed finger. He called after her, "Twenty minutes," and she waved her understanding, crossed the towpath, and climbed a grassy embankment.

She came into a field bordered by sod and stone walls, and on the left beyond the wall, by what seemed to be a narrow road leading down to the bridge. This was the Dyke Way of the brochures. Troy remembered that it came from the village of Wapentake, which her map showed as lying about a mile and a half from the lock. She walked up the field. It rose gently and showed, above its crest, trees and a distant spire.

The air smelt of earth and grass and, delicately, of woodsmoke. It seemed lovely to Troy. She felt a great uplift of spirit and was so preoccupied with her own happiness that she came upon the wapentake itself, just where the Skipper had said it would be, before she was aware of it.

It was a circular hollow, sometimes called, the brochure said, a pot, and it was lined with grass, mosses and fern. Here the Plantagenet knights-of-the-shire had sat at their fortnightly hundreds, dealing out justice as they saw it in those days and as the growing laws directed them. Troy wondered if, when the list was a heavy one, they stayed on into the evening and night and if the torches were lit.

Below the wapentake hollow and quite close to the lock, another, but a comparatively recent, depression had been cut into the hillside: perhaps to get a load of gravel of which there seemed to be a quantity in the soil, or perhaps by archeological amateurs. An overhanging shelf above this excavation had been roughly shored up by poles with an old door for roof. The wood had weathered and looked to be rotting. "A bit of an eyesore," thought Troy.

She went into the wapentake and sat there, and fancied she felt beneath her some indication of a kind of bench that must have been chopped out of the soil, she supposed, seven centuries ago. "I'm an ignoramus about history," Troy thought, "but I do like to feel it in my bones," and she peopled the wapentake with heads like carven effigies, with robes in the colours of stained glass and with glints of polished steel.

She began to wonder if it would be possible to make a very formalized drawing—dark, and thronged with seated, law-giving shapes. A puff of warm air moved the grass and the hair of her head, and up the sloping field came Dr. Natouche.

He was bareheaded and had changed his tweed jacket for a yellow sweater. When he saw Troy he checked and stood still, formidable because of his height and colour against the mild background of the waterways. Troy waved to him. "Come up," she called. "Here's the wapentake."

"Thank you."

He came up quickly, entered the hollow and looked about him. "I have read the excellent account in our little book," he said. "So here they sat, those cold chaps." The colloquialism came oddly from him.

"You sit here, too," Troy suggested, wanting to see his head and his torso in its yellow sweater, against the moss and fern.

He did so, squaring himself and resting his hands on his knees. His teeth and the whites of his eyes were high accents in the picture he presented for Troy. "You ask for the illustration of an incongruity," he said.

"You would be nice to paint. Do you really feel incongruous? I mean is this sort of thing quite foreign to you?"

"Not altogether. No."

They said nothing for a time and Troy did not think there was any awkwardness in their silence.

A lark sang madly overhead and the sound of quiet voices floated up from the lock. Above the embankment they could see the top of the *Zodiac*'s wheelhouse. Now it began very slowly to sink. They heard Miss Rickerby-Carrick shout and laugh.

A motor-cycle engine crescendoed out of the distance, clattered and exploded down the lane and then reduced its speed and noise and stopped.

"One would think it was those two again," said Troy.

Dr. Natouche rose. "It is," he said, "I can see them. Actually, it is those two. They are raising their hands."

"How extraordinary," she said idly. "Why would they turn up?"

"They may be staying in the district. We haven't come very far, you know."

"I keep forgetting. One's values change on the River."

Troy broke off a fern frond and turned it between her fingers. Dr. Natouche sat down again.

"My father was an Ethiopian," he said presently. "He came to this country with a Mission fifty years ago and married an Englishwoman. I was born and educated in England."

"Have you never been to your own country?"

"Once. But I was alien there. And like my father, I married an Englishwoman. I am a widower. My wife died two months ago."

"Was that why you came on this cruise?"

"We were to have come together."

"I see," Troy said.

"She would have enjoyed it. It was something we could have done," he said.

"Have you found many difficulties about being as you are? Black?"

"Of course. How sensible of you to ask, Mrs. Alleyn. One knows everybody thinks such questions."

"Well," Troy said, "I'm glad it was all right to ask."

"I am perfectly at ease with you," Dr. Natouche stated, rather, Troy felt, as he might have told a patient there was nothing the matter with her and really almost arousing a comparable pleasure. "Perfectly," he repeated after a pause. "I don't think, Mrs. Alleyn, you could ever say anything to me that would change that condition."

Miss Rickerby-Carrick appeared at the top of the embankment. "Hoo-hoo!" she shouted. "What's it like up there?"

"Very pleasant," Troy said.

"Jolly good."

She floundered up the field towards them, blowing her nose as she came. Troy was suddenly very sorry for her. Were there, she asked herself, in Birmingham where Miss Rickerby-Carrick lived, people, apart from Mavis, who actually welcomed her company?

Dr. Natouche fetched a sigh and stood up. "I see a gate over there into the lane," he said. "I think there is time to walk back that way if you would care to do so."

"You go," Troy muttered. "I'd better wait for her."

"Really? Very well."

He stayed for a moment or two, politely greeted Miss Rickerby-Carrick and then strode away.

"*Isn't* he a dear?" Miss Rickerby-Carrick panted. "*Don't* you feel he's somebody awfully special?"

"He seems a nice man," Troy answered and try as she might, she couldn't help flattening her voice.

"I do think we all ought to make a special effort. I get awfully worked-up about it. When people go on like Mr. Pollock, you know. I tackled Mr. Pollock about his attitude. I do that, you know, I do tackle people. I said: 'Just because he's got another pigmentation,' I said, 'why should you think he's different.' They're *not* different. You do agree, don't you?"

"No," Troy said. "I don't. They are different. Profoundly."

"Oh! How *can* you say so."

"Because I think it's true. They are different in depth from Anglo-Saxons. So are Slavs. So are Latins."

"Oh! If you mean like *that*," she said and broke into ungainly laughter. "Oh, I see. Oh, yes. Then you *do* agree that we should make a special effort."

"Look, Miss Rickerby-Carrick—"

"I say, do call me Hay."

"Yes—well—thank you. I was going to say that I don't think Dr. Natouche would enjoy special efforts. Really, I don't."

"*You* seem to get on with him like a house on fire," Miss Rickerby-Carrick pointed out discontentedly.

"Do I? Well I find him an interesting man."

"There you are, you see!" she cried, proclaiming some completely inscrutable triumph, and a longish silence ensued.

They heard the motor-cycle start up and cross the bridge and listened to the diminishment of sound as it made off in the direction of Norminster.

One by one the other passengers struggled up the field. Mr. Pollock behind the rest, swinging his built-up boot. The Hewsons were all set-about with cameras while Caley Bard had a box slung from his shoulder and carried a lepidopterist's net. So *that*, Troy thought, was what it was. When everybody was assembled the Hewsons took photographs of the wapentake by itself and with their fellow-travellers sitting self-consciously round it. Mr. Lazenby compared it without, Troy felt, perceptible validity, to an aboriginal place of assembly in the Australian outback. Mr. Pollock read his brochure and then stared with a faint look of disgust at the original.

Caley Bard joined Troy. "So this is where you lit off to," he murmured. "I got bailed up by that extraordinary lady. She wants to get up a let's-be-sweet-to-Natouche move-ment."

"I know. What did you say?"

"I said that as far as I am concerned, I consider I'm as sweet to Natouche as he can readily stomach. Now, tell me all about the wapentake. I'm allergic to leaflets and I've forgotten what the Skipper said. Speak up, do."

Troy did not bother to react to this piece of cheek. She said: "So you're a lepidopterist?"

"That's right. An amateur. Do you find it a sinister hobby? It has rather a sinister reputation, I fear. There was that terrifying film and then didn't somebody in the *Hound of the Baskervilles* flit about Dartmoor with a deceiving net and killing-bottle?"

"There's Nabokov on the credit side."

"True. But *you* don't fancy it, all the same," he said. "That I can see, very clearly."

"I like them better alive and on the wing. Did you notice those two motor-cyclists? They seem to be hunting us."

"Friends of young Tom, it appears. They come from Tollardwark where we stay tonight. Did you know it's pronounced Toll'ark? It will take us an hour or more to get there by water but by road it's only a short walk from Ramsdyke. There's confusion for you!"

"I wouldn't want to walk: I've settled into the River-time-space-dimension."

"Yes, I suppose it would be rather spoiling to break out of it. Hullo, that'll be for us."

The *Zodiac* had given three short hoots. They returned hurriedly and found her waiting downstream from the lock.

There was a weir at Ramsdyke, standing off on their port side. Below the green slide of the fall, the whole surface of the river was smothered in foam: foam in islands and in pinnacles, iridescent foam that twinkled and glinted in the late afternoon sunlight, that shredded away from its own crests, floated like gossamer and broke into nothing.

"Oh!" cried Miss Rickerby-Carrick in ecstasy. "*Isn't* it lovely! Oh, *do* look! Look, look, *look!*" she insisted, first to one and then to another of her fellow-passengers. "Who would have thought our quiet old river could froth up and behave like a fairytale? Like a dream isn't it? *Isn't* it?"

"More like washing-day I'm afraid, Miss Rickerby-Carrick," said Mrs. Tretheway looking over the half-door. "It's detergent. There's a factory beyond those trees. Tea is ready in the saloon," she added.

"Oh, *no!*" Miss Rickerby-Carrick lamented. A flying wisp of detergent settled on her nose. "Oh, *dear!*" she said crossly and went down to the saloon, followed by the others.

"How true it is," Caley Bard remarked, "that Beauty is in the Eye of the Beholder."

He spoke to Troy, but Dr. Natouche, who was behind her, answered him.

"Surely," Dr. Natouche said, "not so much in the eye as in the mind. I remember that on a walk—through a wood, you know—I looked into a dell and saw, deep down, an astonishing spot of scarlet. I thought: 'Ah! A superb fungus secretly devouring the earth and the air.' You know? One of those savage fungi that one thinks of as devils? I went down to look more closely at it and found it was a discarded fish-tin with a red label. Was it the less beautiful for my discovery?"

He had turned to Troy. "Not to my way of looking," she said. "It was a good colour and it had made its effect."

"We are back aren't we," Caley Bard said, "at that old Florentine person with the bubucular nose. We are to assume that the painter doted on every blackhead, crevasse and bump."

"Yes," Troy said. "You are."

"So that if a dead something—a fish or a cat—popped up through that foam, for instance, and its colour and shape made a pleasing mélange with its surroundings, it would be a paintable subject and therefore beautiful?"

"You take," she said drily, "the very words from my mouth."

Mr. Bard looked at her mouth for a second or two.

"And what satisfaction," he said under his breath, "is there in that?" He turned away and Troy thought, almost at once, that she must have misheard him.

Miss Rickerby-Carrick flapped into the conversation like a wet sheet. "Oh *don't* stop. Go on. Do, do, go on. I don't want to lose a word of this," she cried. "Because it makes a point that I'm most awfully keen on. Beauty is everywhere. In everything," she shouted and swept her arm past Mr. Lazenby's spectacles. "'Beauty is Truth; Truth, Beauty,'" she quoted. "That's all we need to know."

"That's a very, very profound observation, Miss Rickerby-Carrick," Mr. Hewson observed kindly.

"I just don't go along with it," his sister said. "I've seen a whole lot of Truth that wasn't beautiful. A whole heap of it."

Mr. Pollock, who had been utterly silent for a very long time now heaved an enormous sigh and, as if infected by his gloom, the other passengers also fell silent.

Somebody—Mr. Lazenby?—had left the morning's newspaper on the settle, the paper in which her own photograph had appeared. Troy, who did not eat with her tea, picked it up and, seeing nothing to interest her, idly turned over a page.

"Man found strangled.

"The body of a man who had been strangled was found at 8 P.M. last night in a flat in Cyprus Street, Soho. He is believed to have been a picture-dealer and the police who are making inquiries give his name as K. G. Z. Andropoulos."

The passenger list was still on the table. Troy looked at the name Caley Bard had crossed out in favour of her own.

She rose with so abrupt a movement that one or two of her companions glanced up at her. She dropped the newspaper on the seat and went down to her cabin. After some thought, she said to herself: "If nobody has read it there's no reason why I should point it out. It's a horrible bit of news."

And then she thought that if, as seemed probable, the paragraph had in fact not been noticed, it might be as well to get rid of the paper, the more especially since she would like to repress her own photograph before it went into general circulation. She could imagine Miss Rickerby-Carrick's ejaculations: "And there you both are, you and the murdered

man who was to have your berth. Fancy!" She hunted out her
sketchbook and returned to the saloon.

The newspaper was nowhere to be seen.

3

Troy waited for a minute or two in the saloon to collect her
thoughts. Her fellow-passengers were still at tea and
apparently quite undisturbed. She went up on deck. The
Skipper was at the wheel.

"Everything all right, Mrs. Alleyn?" he asked.

"Yes, thank you. Yes. Everything," said Troy and found
herself a chair.

Most of the detergent foam had been left behind by now.
The *Zodiac* sailed towards evening through clear waters, low
fields and occasional groups of trees.

Troy began to draw the signs of the zodiac, placing them
in a ring and giving them a wonderfully strange character.
Mrs. Tretheway's rhyme could go in the middle and later on
there would be washes of colour.

She was vaguely aware of a sudden burst of conversation
in the saloon. After a time a shadow fell across her hand and
there was Caley Bard again. Troy didn't look up. He moved
to the opposite side and stood with his back towards her,
leaning on the taffrail.

"I'm afraid," he said presently, "that they've rumbled you.
Lazenby spotted the photograph in this morning's paper. I
wouldn't have told them."

"I believe you."

"The Rickerby-Carrick is stimulated, I fear."

"Hell."

"And the Hewsons are gratified because they've read an
article about you in *Life* magazine so they know you're O.K.
and famous. They just can't think how they missed
recognizing you."

"Too bad."

"Pollock, surprisingly, seemed to be not aware of your
great distinction. Lazenby himself says you are regarded in
Australia as being the equal of Drysdale and Dobell."

"Nice of him."

"There's this about it: you'll be able to do what you are doing now, without everybody exclaiming and breathing down your neck. Or I hope you will."

"I won't be doing anything that matters," Troy mumbled.

"How extraordinary!" he said lightly.

"What?"

"That you should be so shy about your work. You!"

"Well, I can't help it. Do pipe down like a good chap."

She heard him chuckle and drag a deck chair into position. Presently she smelt his pipe. "Evidently," she thought, "they haven't spotted the Andropoulos bit in the paper." She considered this for a moment and then added: "Or have they?"

The River now described a series of loops so extreme and so close together that the landscape seemed to turn about the *Zodiac* like a diorama. Wapentake church spire advanced and retreated and set to partners with a taller spire in the market town of Tollardwark which they approached with the utmost slyness, now leaving it astern and now coming round a bend and making straight for it. The water darkened with the changing sky. Along its banks and in its backwaters and eddies the creatures that belonged to the River began to come out on their evening business: water-rats, voles, toads and leaping fish as well as the insects: dragon-flies in particular. Once, looking up from her drawing, Troy caught sight of a pair of ears against the sky and thought: "There goes Wat, the hare." A company of ducks in close formation paddled past the *Zodiac*. Where trees stood along the banks the air pulsated with high formless, reiterative bird-chittering.

Troy thought: "Cleopatra on the river Cydnus wasn't given more things to hear and look at."

At intervals she stopped drawing in order to observe, but the signs of the zodiac grew under her hand. She amused herself by mentally allotting one to each of her fellow-passengers. The Hewsons, of course, belonged to the Heavenly Twins, and Mr. Pollock, because his club foot affected his gait, would be the Crab. Miss Rickerby-Carrick might be assigned to Taurus because she ran like a Bull at every Gate, but almost certainly, thought Troy, Virgo was entirely appropriate. So she gave a pair of bovine horns to the

rampaging motor-cyclist. Because of a certain sting in the tail
of many of his observations, she decided upon Scorpio for
Caley Bard. and Mr. Lazenby? Well: he seemed to be
extremely ill-sighted, his dark spectacles gave him a blind
look like Justice, and Justice carried Scales. Libra for him.
As for Dr. Natouche, he must be a splendour in the
firmament: Sagittarius the Archer with open shoulders and
stretched bow. She began to draw the Archer in his image.
Mrs. Tretheway didn't seem to fit anywhere except perhaps,
as they had a sexy connotation, under the Fish with the
Glittering Tails. She observed the Skipper at his wheel, noted
the ripple of muscles under his immaculate shirt and the
close-clipped curly poll beneath his cap. The excessive
masculinity, she decided, belonged to the Ram and Tom-of-
all work could be the Man who carried the Watering-pot.

And having run out of passengers she raised one of the
Lion's eyebrows and thus gave him a look of her husband.
"Which leaves me for the Goat," thought Troy, "and very
suitable too, I daresay."

One by one the passengers, with the exception of Dr.
Natouche, came on deck. In their several fashions and with
varying degrees of success, they displayed tact towards Troy.
The Hewsons smiled at each other and retired, with
brochures and *Reader's Digests,* to their chairs. Mr. Lazenby
turned his dark spectacles towards Troy, nodded three times
and passed majestically by. Mr. Pollock behaved as if she
wasn't there until he was behind her and then, she clearly
sensed, had a good long stare over her shoulder at what she
was doing.

Miss Rickerby-Carrick was wonderful. When she had
floundered, with her customary difficulty, through the half-
door at the top of the companionway, she paused to converse
with the Skipper but as she talked to him she rolled her eyes
round until they could take in Troy. Presently she left him
and archly biting her underlip advanced on tiptoe. She bent
and whispered, close to Troy's ear: "Don't put me in it," and
so passed on gaily to her deck chair.

The general set-up having now become quietly ridiculous,
Troy swung round to find Mr. Pollock close behind her.

His eyes were half-closed and he looked at her drawing,

unmistakably with the air of someone who knew. For a moment they faced each other. He turned away, swinging his heavy foot.

Caley Bard, with a startling note of anger in his voice, said: "Have you been given an invitation to a Private View, Mr. Pollock?"

A silence followed. At last Mr. Pollock said in a stifled voice: "It's very nice. Lovely," and retired to the far end of the deck.

Troy shut her sketchbook and with a view to papering over what seemed to be some kind of crisis, made conversation with everybody about the landscape.

The *Zodiac* reached Tollard Lock at 6:15 and tied up for the night.

III

TOLLARDWARK

"At that time," Alleyn said, "I was on my way to Chicago and from there to San Francisco. We were setting up a joint plan of action with U.S.A. to cope with an international blow-up in the art-forgery world. We were pretty certain, though not positive, that the Jampot was well in the phoney picture trade and that the same group was combining it with a two-way drug racket. My wife's letters to me from her river cruise missed me in New York and were forwarded to Chicago and thence to San Francisco.

"On reading them I put through a call to the Yard."

1

". . . This will probably arrive with the letter I posted this morning at Ramsdyke. I'm writing in my cabin having returned from Tollardwark where we spend our first night and I'm going to try and set out the sequence of events as you would do it—economically but in detail. I'm almost certain that when they are looked at as a whole they will be seen to add up to nothing in particular.

"Indeed, I only tell you about these silly little incidents, my darling, because I know you won't make superior noises, and because in a cock-eyed sort of way I suppose they may be said to tie in with what you're up to at the moment. I know, very well, that they may amount to nothing.

"You remember the silly game people used to play: making up alphabetical rhymes of impending disaster? 'T. is for Tiger decidedly plumper. What's that in his mouth? Oh it's Agatha's jumper!'

"There are moments on this otherwise enchanting jaunt when *your* Agatha almost catches the sound of something champing in the jungle.

"It really began tonight at Tollardwark..."

2

They had berthed on the outskirts of the little market town and after dinner the passengers explored it. Troy sensed frontal attacks from Miss Rickerby-Carrick and possibly Caley Bard, so, having a plan of her own, she slipped away early. There was an office on the wharf with a telephone booth at the disposal of the passengers. As it was open and nobody seemed to be about, she went straight in.

There was one thing about that number, Troy thought, you did get through quickly. In seconds she was saying: "Is Inspector Fox in the office? Could I speak to him? It's Mrs. Roderick Alleyn," and almost immediately. "Br'er Fox? Troy Alleyn. Listen. I expect you all know: but in case you don't: It's about the Soho thing in this morning's paper. The man was to have been a passenger in the..." She got it out as tidily and succinctly as she could, but she had only given the briefest outline when he cut in.

"Now, that's very kind of you, Mrs. Alleyn," the familiar paddy voice said. "That's very interesting. I happen to be working on that job. And you're speaking from Tollardwark? And you've got the vacant cabin? And you're talking from a phone box? From where?...I see...Yes." A pause. "Yes. We heard yesterday from New York and he's having a very pleasant time."

"What?" Troy ejaculated. "Who? You mean Rory?"

"That's right, Mrs. Alleyn. Very nice indeed to have heard from you. We'll let you know, of course, if there's any change of plan. I think it might be as well if you didn't say very much

at your end," Mr. Fox blandly continued. "I expect I'm being
unduly cautious, indeed I'm sure I am, but if you can do so
without drawing attention to it, I wonder if you could drop in
at our place in Tollardwark in about half an hour or so? It
could be, if necessary, to ask if that fur you lost at your
exhibition has been found. Very nice to hear from you. My
godson well? Goodbye, then."

Troy hung up abruptly and turned. Through the
obscured-glass door panel which had a hole in one corner,
she saw a distorted figure move quickly backwards. She came
out and found Mr. Lazenby standing by the outside entrance.

"You've finished your call, Mrs. Alleyn?" he jovially
asked. "Good-oh. I'll just make mine then. Bishopscourt at
Norminster. I spent the week there and this will let me off my
bread-and-butter stint. You don't know the Bishop I
suppose? Of Norminster? No? Wonderfully hospitable old
boy. Gave the dim Aussie parson a memorable time. Car,
chauffeur, the lot. Going to explore?"

Yes, Troy said, she thought she would explore. Mr.
Lazenby replied that he understood from the Bishop that the
parish church was most interesting. And he went into the
telephone booth.

Troy, strangely perturbed, walked up a narrow cobbled
street into the market square of Tollardwark.

She found it enchanting. It had none of the selfconscious-
ness that settles upon too many carefully preserved places in
the Home Counties, although, so the *Zodiac* brochure said, it
had in fact been lovingly rescued from the clumsy blotting of
Victorian meddlers. But no care, added the brochure, could
replace in their niches the delicate heads, hands, leaves and
curlicues knocked off by Cromwell's clean-living wreckers.
But the fourteenth-century inn had been wakened from
neglect, a monstrous weather-cock had been removed from
the crest of the Eleanor Cross, and Lady Godiva's endowed
church of St. Crispin-in-the-Fields was in good heart. As if to
prove this, it being practice-night for the bell-ringers,
cascades of orderly rumpus were shaken out of the belfry as
Troy crossed the square.

There were not many people about. She felt some
hesitation in asking her way to the police station. She walked
round the square and at intervals caught sight of her fellow-

passengers. There, down a very dark alley, were Mr. and
Miss Hewson, peering in at an unlit Tudor window of a
darkened shop. Mr. Pollock was in the act of disappearing
round a corner near the church where, moving backwards
through a lychgate, was Miss Rickerby-Carrick. It struck
Troy that the whole set had an air of commedia dell'arte
about them and that the Market Square might be their
painted backdrop. She was again plagued by the vague
feeling that somewhere, somehow, a masquerade of sorts was
being acted out and that she was involved in it. "The people
of the *Zodiac,*" she thought, "all moving in their courses and I
with them, but for the life of me I don't know where we're
going."

She suspected that Caley Bard had thought it would be
pleasant if they explored Tollardwark together and she was
not surprised to see him across the square, turning with a
disconsolate air into the Northumberland Arms. She would
have enjoyed his company, other things being equal. She had
almost completed her walk round the market-place and was
wondering which of the few passersby she should accost,
when she came to the last of the entrances into the Square
and, looking down it, she saw the familiar blue lamp.

The door swung to behind her, shutting out the voices of
the bells, and she was in another world smelling of linoleum,
disinfectant and uniforms. The sergeant on duty said at once:
"Mrs. Alleyn would it be? I thought so. The Superintendent's
expecting you, Mrs. Alleyn. I'll just: oh, here you are, sir.
Mrs. Alleyn."

He was the predictable large, hard-muscled man just
beginning to run to overweight, with extremely bright eyes
and a sort of occupational joviality about him.

He shook Troy warmly by the hand. "Tillottson," he said.
"Nice to meet you, Mrs. Alleyn," and took her into his office.

"Very pleased," said Superintendent Tillottson, "to meet
Roderick Alleyn's good lady. His textbook's known as the
Scourge of the Service in these parts and I wouldn't mind if
you passed that on to him."

He laughed very heartily at this joke, placed the palms of
his hands on his desk, and said: "Yes. Well now, I've been
talking to Mr. Fox at Head Office, Mrs. Alleyn, and he

suggested it might be quite an idea if we had a little chat. So, if it's not putting you to too much trouble..."

He led Troy, very adroitly, through the past eight hours and she was surprised that he should be so particular as to details. Evidently he was aware of this reaction because when she had finished he said he supposed she would like to know what it was all about and proceeded to give her a neat report.

"This character, this K. G. Z. Andropoulos, was mixed up in quite a bit of trouble: trouble to the Yard, Mrs. Alleyn, before and after the Yard got alongside him. He was, as you may have supposed, of Greek origin and he's been involved in quite a number of lines: a bit of drug-running here, a bit of receiving there, some interest in the antique lay, a picture-dealing business in Cyprus Street, Soho, above which he lived in the flat where his body was found yesterday evening. He wasn't what you'd call a key figure but he became useful to the Yard by turning informer from spite, having fallen out with a much bigger man than himself. A very big man indeed in the international underworld, as people like to call it, a character called Foljambe and known as the Jampot, in whom we are very, very interested."

"I've heard about *him,*" Troy said. "From Rory."

"I'll be bound. Now, it's a guinea to a gooseberry, to our way of thinking, that this leading character—this Jampot—is behind the business in Cyprus Street and therefore the Department is more than ordinarily concerned to get to the bottom of it and anything that connects with Andropoulos, however slightly, has to be followed up."

"Even to Cabin 7 in the rivercraft *Zodiac*?"

"That's right. We'd like to know, d'you see, Mrs. Alleyn, just why this chap Andropoulos took the freakish notion to book himself in and when he did it. And, very particularly, we'd like to know whether any of the other passengers had any kind of link with him. Now Teddy Fox—"

"*Who!*" Troy ejaculated.

"Inspector Fox, Mrs. Alleyn. He and I were in the uniformed branch together. Edward Walter Fox, he is."

"I suppose I knew," Troy mused. "Yes, of course I knew. We always call him Br'er Fox. He's a great friend."

"So I understood. Yes. Well, he's a wee bit concerned

about you going with this lot in the *Zodiac*. He's wondering what the Chief-Super—your good man, Mrs. Alleyn—would make of it. He's on his way to this conference in Chicago and Ted Fox wonders if he shouldn't try and talk to him."

"Oh, *no!*" Troy ejaculated. "Surely not."

"Well now, frankly it seems a bit far-fetched to me but there it is. Ted Fox cut you short, in a manner of speaking, when you rang him from the Waterways office down there and he did so on the general principle that you can't be too careful on the public phone. He's a careful sort of character himself, as you probably know, and, by Gum, he's thorough."

"He is, indeed."

"Yes. That's so. Yes. Now Ted's just been called out of London, following a line on the Andropoulos business. It may take him across the Channel. In the meantime he's asked me to keep an eye on *your* little affair. So what we'd like to do is take a wee look at the passenger list. In the meantime I just wonder about these two incidents you've mentioned. Now, what are they? First of all you get the impression that someone, you're not sure who, got a fright or a shock or a peculiar reaction when you said there were Constables all over the place, and second: you see this bit about Andropoulos in the paper, you drop the paper on the seat and go to your cabin. You get the idea it might be pleasanter for all concerned not to spread the information that an intended passenger had been murdered. You go back for the purpose of confiscating the paper and find it's disappeared. Right? Yes. Now, for the first of these incidents. I just wonder if it wouldn't be natural for any little gathering of passengers waiting in a quiet lock in peaceful surroundings to get a bit of a jolt when somebody suddenly says there are police personnel all over the place. Swarming, I think you said was the expression you used. And clutch. Swarming with a clutch of Constables. *You* meaning the artist. *They* assuming the police."

"Well—yes. But they didn't all ejaculate at once. They didn't all say: 'Where, where, what do you mean, policemen?' or things like that. Miss Rickerby-Carrick did and I think Miss Hewson did a bit and I rather fancy Mr. Caley Bard said something like: 'What *can* you mean?' But I felt terribly strongly that someone had had a shock. I—Oh," Troy said impatiently, "how silly that sounds! Pay no attention to it. Really."

"Shall we take a wee look at the second item, then? The disappearance of the newspaper? Isn't it possible, Mrs. Alleyn, that one of them saw you were put out and when you went to your cabin picked up the paper to see what could have upset you? And found the paragraph? And had the same reaction as you did: don't put it about in case it upsets people? Or maybe, *didn't* notice your reactions but read the paragraph and thought it'd be nice if you didn't know you'd got a cabin that was to have been given to a murder victim? Or they might all have come to that conclusion? Or, the simplest of all, the staff might just have tidied the paper away?"

"I feel remarkably foolish," Troy said. "How right you are. I wish I'd shut up about it and not bothered poor Br'er Fox."

"Oh no," Tillottson said quickly. "Not at all. No. We're very glad to have this bit about the booking of Cabin 7. Very glad indeed. We'd very much like to know why Andropoulos fancied a waterways cruise. Of course we'd have learnt about it before long but it can't be too soon for us and we're much obliged to you."

"Mr. Tillottson, you don't think, do you, that any of them could have had anything to do with that man? Andropoulos? Why should they have?"

Tillottson looked fixedly at the top of his desk. "No," he said after a pause. "No reason at all. You stay at Toll'ark tonight don't you? Yes. Crossdyke tomorrow? And the following day and night at Longminster? Right? And I've got the passenger list from you and just to please Mr. Fox we'll let him have it and also do a wee bit of inquiring at our end. The clerical gentleman's been staying with the Bishop at Norminster, you say? And he's an Australian? Fine. And the lady with the double name comes from Birmingham? Mr. S. H. Caley Bard lives in London, S.W.3, and collects butterflies. And—er—this Mr. Pollock's a Londoner but he came up from Birmingham where he stayed, you said—? Yes, ta. The Osborn. And the Americans were at the Tabard at Stratford. Just a tick, if you don't mind."

He went to the door and said: "Sarge. Rickerby-Carrick. Hazel: Miss. Birmingham. Natouche: Doctor. G. M.

Liverpool. Caley Bard, S.H. S.W.3. London. Pollock, Saturday and Sunday, Osborn Hotel, Birmingham. Hewson. Americans. Two. Tabard. Stratford. Yes. Check, will you?"

"I mustn't keep you," Troy said and stood up.

"If you don't mind waiting, Mrs. Alleyn. Just another tick."

He consulted a directory and dialled a number. "Bishopscourt?" he said. "Yes. Toll'ark Police Station here. Sorry to trouble you, but we've had an Australian Passport handed in at our office. Name of Bollinger. I understand an Australian gentleman—oh. Oh, yes? Lazenby? All last week? I see. Not his, then. Very sorry to trouble you. Thank you."

He hung up, beamed at Troy and asked if she could give him any help as to the place of origin of the remaining passengers. She had heard the Hewsons speak of Apollo, Kansas, and of a Hotel Balmoral in the Cromwell Road, and she rather fancied Caley Bard did tutorial cramming work. Mr. Stanley P. K. Pollock was a cockney and owned property in London; where, she had no idea. The Superintendent made notes and the Sergeant came in to say he'd checked his items and they were all O.K. Dr. Natouche had been in his present practice in Liverpool for about seven years. He had appeared for the police in a road fatality case last week and had been called in at the site of another one last Sunday. Miss Rickerby-Carrick was a well-known member of a voluntary social workers' organizaton. The other passengers had all been where they had said they had been. The Superintendent said there you were, you see, for what it was worth. As Troy shook hands with him he said there was a police station in the village of Crossdyke, a mile from Crossdyke Lock, and if, before tomorrow night, anything at all out of the way occurred he'd be very glad if she'd drop in at the station and give him a call or, if he was free, he might pop over himself in case she did look in.

"Don't," said Mr. Tillottson apparently as an after-thought, "if I may make a suggestion, begin thinking everybody's behaving suspiciously, Mrs. Alleyn. It'd be rather easy to do that and it'd spoil your holiday. Going to take a look round Toll'ark? I'm afraid I've used up some of your time. Good-night, then, and much obliged, I do assure you."

Troy went out into the street. The church bells had stopped ringing and the town was quiet. So quiet that she quite jumped when some distance away a motor-cycle engine started up explosively. It belched and puttered with a now familiar diminuendo into the distance and into silence.

"But I suppose," Troy thought, "all these infernal machines sound exactly alike."

3

Evening was now advanced in Tollardwark. The Market Square had filled with shadow and only the top of St. Crispin's tower caught a fugitive glint of day. Footsteps sounded loud and hollow in the darkling streets and the voices of the few people who were abroad underlined rather than diminished the sense of emptiness. Some of the shop-windows had all-night lamps in them but most were unlit and their contents hard to distinguish.

Troy loved to be in a strange town at nightfall. She would have chosen always to arrive anywhere at dusk. None of the other passengers were in sight and she supposed they had gone back to the *Zodiac*. Except Caley Bard, perhaps, who might still be taking out his sightseeing in the Northumberland Arms which glowed with classic geniality behind its red-curtained windows. The church windows also glowed: with kaleidoscopic richness.

She crossed the square, went through the lychgate up a short path and entered the west porch. There were the usual notices about parish meetings and restoration funds and the usual collection boxes. When she passed into the church itself she saw that it was beautiful: a soaring place with a feeling of certainty and aliveness not always to be found in churches.

They were saying compline by candlelight to a tiny congregation amongst whom Troy spotted the backs of Miss Rickerby-Carrick's and Mr. Lazenby's heads. As she slipped into a pew at the rear of the nave, a disembodied alto voice admonished its handful of listeners.

"Be sober, be vigilant:" said the lonely voice, "because your adversary the devil, as a roaring lion, walketh about seeking whom he may devour."

She waited until almost the end and then slipped away as unobtrusively as she had come. "If it were all true," she thought, "and if the devil really was out and about in the streets of Tollardwark! What a thing *that* would be to be sure!"

She chose to return down a different street from the one she had come up by. It was very narrow, indeed an alleyway rather than a street, and roughly cobbled. She saw a glimmer of the River at the bottom and knew she couldn't lose her way. At first she passed between old adjoining houses, one or two of them being half-timbered with overhanging upper stories. There was an echo here, she thought, of her own steps. After a minute or two she stopped to listen. The other footfall stopped too but was it an echo or was someone else abroad in the alley? She looked behind her but it was now quite dark and she could see nobody. So she went on again, walking a little faster, and the echo, if it had been an echo, did not follow her.

Perhaps this was because the houses had thinned out and there were open places on either side as if buildings had been demolished. The alley seemed unconsciously long. The moon rose. Instead of being one of general darkness the picture was now, Troy thought, set out in ink and luminous paint: it glittered with light and swam with shadows and through it the River ran like quicksilver. The downhill slope was steep and Troy walked still faster. She made out the ramshackle shape of a house or shed at the bottom where the alley ended in another lane that stretched along the riverfront.

The footfalls began again, some way behind her now but coming nearer and certainly not an echo.

Her way might have been uphill rather than down, so senselessly hard-fetched was her heartbeat.

She had reminded herself of Mr. Tillottson's injunction and had resisted an impulse to break into a run when she came to the building at the bottom of the alley. As she did this two persons moved out of the shadow into her path. Troy caught back her breath in a single cry.

"Gee, Mrs. Alleyn, is that you?" Miss Hewson said. "Earl, it's Mrs. Alleyn!"

"Why, so it is," agreed her brother. "So it is. Hello, there, Mrs. Alleyn. Kind of murky down here, isn't it? I guess the progressive elements in Tollardwark haven't caught up with street-lighting. Still in the linkman phase."

"Golly," Troy said, "you made me jump."

They broke into an apology. If they had known it was Troy they would have hailed her as she approached. Miss Hewson herself was nervous in the dark and wouldn't stir without Brother. Miss Hewson, Mr. Hewson said, was a crazy hunter after old-time souvenirs and this place looked like it was some kind of trash shop and yard and nothing would do but they must try and peer in at the windows. And, interjected his sister, they had made out a number of delectable objects: the cutest kind of work-box on legs. Heaps of portfolios. And then—it was the darndest thing— their flashlamp had gone dead on them.

"It's old pictures," Miss Hewson cried, "that I just can't keep my hands off, Mrs. Alleyn. Prints. Illustrations from Victorian publications. Those cute little girls with kittens and nosegays? Military pieces? Know what I mean?"

"Sis makes screens," Mr. Hewson explained tolerantly. "Real pretty, too. I guess, back home, she's gotten to be famous for her screens."

"Listen to you!" his sister exclaimed. "Talking about my screens to Mrs. Alleyn!"

Troy, whose heart had stopped behaving like a water-ram, said she too admired Victorian screens and reminded the Hewsons that they would be able to explore Tollardwark on the return trip. "I guess Sis'll be heading for this antique joint," Mr. Hewson said, "before we're tied up. Come on, now, girls, why don't we go?"

He had taken their arms when the footsteps broke out again, quite near at hand. Mr. Hewson swung his ladies round to face them.

An invisible man strode towards them through the dark: a set of pale garments and shoes without face or hands. Miss Hewson let out a sharp little scream but Troy exclaimed: "Dr. Natouche!"

"I am so sorry," the great voice boomed. "I have alarmed you. I would have called out back there before the moon rose but did not know if you were a stranger or not. I waited for you to get away from me. Then, just now, I heard your voices. I am so very sorry."

"No harm done I guess, Doctor," Mr. Hewson said stiffly.

"Of course not," Troy said. "I was in the same case as you, Dr. Natouche. I wondered about calling out and then thought you might be an affronted local inhabitant or a sinister prowler."

Dr. Natouche had produced a pocket torch no bigger than a giant pencil. "The moon has risen," he said, "but it's dark down here."

The light darted about like a firefly and for a moment a name flashed out: "Jno. Bagg: Licensed Dealer," on a small dilapidated sign above a door.

"Well," Miss Hewson said to her brother. "C'mon. Let's go."

He took her arm again and turned invitingly to Troy. "We can't walk four-abreast," Troy said. "You two lead the way."

They did so and she fell in beside Dr. Natouche.

The bottom lane turned out to be treacherous underfoot. Some kind of slippery lichen or river-weed had crept over the cobblestones. Miss Hewson slithered, clung to her brother and let out a yelp that flushed a company of ducks who raised their own rumpus and left indignantly by water.

The Hewsons exclaimed upon the vagaries of nature and stumbled on. Troy slipped and was stayed up expertly by Dr. Natouche.

"I think perhaps you should take my arm," he said. "My shoes seem to be unaffected. We have chosen a bad way home."

His arm felt professional: steady and very hard. He moved with perfect ease as his forefathers might have moved, Troy thought, barefoot across some unimaginable landscape. When she slipped, as she did once or twice, his hand closed for a moment about her forearm and she saw his long fingers pressed into her white sleeve.

The surface of the land improved but she felt it would be uncivil to withdraw her arm at once. Dr. Natouche spoke placidly of the beauties of Tollardwark. He talked Troy thought indulgently, rather like the ship's brochure. She experienced a great contentment. What on earth, she thought gaily, have I been fussing about; I'm loving my cruise.

Miss Hewson turned to look back at Troy, peered, hesitated, and said: "O.K., Mrs. Alleyn?"

"Grand, thank you."

"There's the *Zodiac*," Mr. Hewson said. "Girls—we're home."

She looked welcoming indeed, with her riding lights and glowing windows. "Lovely!" Troy said lightheartedly. Dr. Natouche's arm contracted very slightly and then relaxed and withdrew, closely observed by the Hewsons. Mr. Hewson handed the ladies aboard and accompanied them down to the saloon, which was deserted.

Miss Hewson, carefully lowering her voice, said cosily: "Now, dear, I hope you were not too much embarrassed; we couldn't do one thing, could we, Earl?" She may have seen a look of astonishment in Troy's face. "Of course," she added, "we don't just know how you Britishers feel—"

"I don't feel anything," Troy said inaccurately. "I don't know what you mean."

"Well!" Mr. Hewson said. "You don't aim to tell us, Mrs. Alleyn, that there's no distinction made in Britain? Now, only last week I was reading—"

"I'm sure you were, Mr. Hewson, but honestly, we don't all behave like that. Or believe like that. Really."

"Is that so?" he said. "Is—that so? You wait awhile, Mrs. Alleyn. You wait until you've a comparable problem. You haven't seen anything yet. Not a thing."

"I guess we'll just leave it, dear," Miss Hewson said. "Am I looking forward to my bed! Boy, oh boy!"

"We'll say good-night then, Mrs. Alleyn," Mr. Hewson said rather stiffly. "It's a privilege to make your acquaintance."

Troy found herself saying good-night with much more effusiveness than she normally displayed and this, she supposed, was because she wanted everything to be pleasant in the *Zodiac*. The Hewsons seemed to cheer up very much at these signs of cordiality and went to bed saying that it took all sorts to make a world.

Troy waited for a moment and then climbed the little companionway and looked over the half-door.

Dr. Natouche stood at the after-end of the deck looking, it

appeared, at the silhouette of Tollardwark against the night
sky. He has a gift, Troy thought, for isolating himself in
space.

"Good-night, Dr. Natouche," she said, quietly.

"Good-night. Good-night, Mrs. Alleyn," he returned,
speaking as low as his enormous voice permitted. It was as if
he played softly on a drum.

Troy wrote a letter to her husband which she would post
before they left Tollard Lock in the morning and it was
almost midnight when she had finished it.

What a long, long day, she thought as she climbed into her
bed.

4

She fell asleep within half a minute and was fathoms deep
when noises lugged her to the surface. On the way up she
dreamed of sawmills, of road-drills and of dentists. As she
awoke her dream persisted: the rhythmic hullabaloo was
close at hand, behind her head, coming in at her porthole—
everywhere. Her cabin was suffused in moonlight reflected
off the River. It looked like a sanctuary for peace itself, but
on the other side of the wall Miss Rickerby-Carrick in Cabin
8 snored with a virtuosity that exceeded anything Troy had
ever heard before. The pandemonium she released no more
resembled normal snoring than the "1812 Overture"
resembles the "Harmonious Blacksmith." It was monstrous.
It was insupportable.

Troy lay in a sort of incredulous panic, half-giggling, half-
appalled as whistles succeeded snorts, and plosives followed
upon whistles. A door on the far side of the passage angrily
banged. She thought it was Caley Bard's. Then Mr. Hewson,
in Cabin 6 forward of Troy's, thudded out of bed, crossed the
passage to his sister's room and knocked.

"Sis! Hey Sis!" Troy heard him wail. "For Pete's sake!
Sis!" Troy reached out and opened her own door a crack.

Evidently Miss Hewson was awake. Brother and sister
consulted piteously together in the passage. Troy heard Miss
Hewson say: "O.K., dear. O.K. Go right ahead. Rouse her
up. But don't bring me into it."

Another door, No. 5, Troy thought, had been opened and the admonitory sound: "Ssh!" was sharply projected into the passage. The same door was then smartly shut. Mr. Lazenby. Finally Mr. Pollock unmistakably erupted into the mêlée.

"Does everybody mind!" Mr. Pollock asked in a fury. "Do me a favour, ladies and gents. I got the funny habit of liking to sleep at night!" A pause, sumptuously filled by Miss Rickerby-Carrick. "Gawd!" Mr. Pollock said. "Has it been offered to the Zoo?"

Troy suddenly thumped the wall.

Miss Rickerby-Carrick trumpeted, said "Wha-a-a?" and fell silent. After perhaps thirty wary, listening seconds her fellow-passengers returned to their beds and as she remained tacit, all, presumably, went to sleep.

Troy again slept deeply for what seemed to her to be a very long time and was sickeningly roused by Miss Rickerby-Carrick herself, standing like the first Mrs. Rochester beside her bed and looking, Troy felt, not dissimilar. Her cold was heavy on her.

"*Dear* Mrs. Alleyn," Miss Rickerby-Carrick whispered. "Do, do, do forgive me. I'm so dreadfully sorry but I simply can*not* get off! Hour after hour and *wide* awake. I—I had a shock. In Tollardwark. I can't tell you—at least—I—might. Tomorrow. But I can't sleep and I can't find my pills. I can—not—lay my hands upon my pills. Have you by any chance an aspirin? I feel so dreadful, waking you, but I get quite frantic when I can't sleep—I—I've had a shock. I've had an awful shock."

Troy said: "It's all right. Yes. I've got some aspirin. Would you turn on the light?"

When she had done this, Miss Rickerby-Carrick came back to the bed and leant over Troy. She wore a dull magenta dressing gown and dark blue pyjamas. Something depended from her not very delicious neck. It swung forward and hit Troy on the nose.

"*Oh,* I'm so sorry. I *am* so sorry."

"It's all right. If you'll just let me up, I'll find the aspirins." While Troy did this Miss Rickerby-Carrick whispered indefatigably. "You'll wonder what it is. That thing. I'll tell you. It's a romantic story, no denying it. Never leaves me. You'll be surprised," the strange whisper gustily confided.

"No kidding. An heirloom. Honestly. My grandfather—surgeon—Czar—Fabergé. I promise you!" Troy had found the aspirin.

"Here they are. I really think you shouldn't tell people about it, you know."

"Oh—but *you*!"

"I wouldn't—really. Why don't you put it in safe-keeping?"

"You're talking like the insurance people."

"I can well believe it."

"I'ts my *Luck,*" said Miss Rickerby-Carrick. "That's how I feel about it. I can't be without my Luck. I did try once, and immediately fell down a flight of concrete steps. There, now!"

"Well, I wouldn't talk about it if I were you."

"That's what Miss Hewson said."

"For Heaven's sake!" Troy ejaculated and gave up.

"Well, she's awfully interested in antiques."

"Have you shown it to her?"

She nodded coyly, wagging her ungainly head up and down and biting her lower lip. "You'll never guess," she said, "what it *is*. The design I mean. Talk about coincidence!" She put her face close to Troy's and whispered. "In diamonds and emeralds and rubies. The signs of the zodiac. Now!"

"Hadn't you better go to bed?" Troy asked wearily.

Miss Rickerby-Carrick stared fixedly at her and then bolted.

When Mrs. Tretheway at eight o'clock brought her a cup of tea, Troy felt as if the incidents of the night had been part of her dream. At breakfast Mr. Pollock and the Hewsons had a muttering session about Miss Rickerby-Carrick. Caley Bard openly asked Troy if she was keen on "Ein Kleine Nacht Musik" and Mr. Lazenby told him not to be naughty. As usual Dr. Natouche took no part in this general, if furtive, conversation. Miss Rickerby-Carrick herself retired at mid-morning to a corner of the deck where, snuffling dreadfully and looking greatly perturbed, she kept up her diary.

The *Zodiac* cruised tranquilly through the morning. After luncheon Mr. Lazenby occasioned some surprise by appearing in a bathing slip, blowing up an inflatable mattress, and sun-bathing on deck. "Once an Aussie, always an Aussie," he observed. Mr. and Miss Hewson were so far encouraged as to change into Hawaiian shorts and floral tops. Dr. Natouche had already appeared in immaculate blue linen and Caley Bard in conservative slacks and cotton shirt. Troy settled at a table in the saloon, finished her drawing and treated it to a lovely blush of aquarelle crayons which she had bought for fun and because they were easy to carry. Each of the signs now bore a crazy resemblance to the person she had assigned to it. Caley Bard's slew-eyed glance looked out of the Scorpion's head. Virgo was a kind of ethereal whiff of what Miss Rickerby-Carrick might have been. The Hewsons *stylisées,* put their heads together for the Twins. Mr. Lazenby, naked, blindfold and in elegant retreat, displayed the Scales. Something about the stalked eyes of the Crab quoted Mr. Pollock's rather prominent stare. Mrs. Tretheway, translated into classic splendour, presented the Fish on a celestial platter. The Ram had a steering wheel between his hoofs, and the boy, Tom Aquarius, carried water in a ship's bucket. Troy's short dark locks tumbled about the brow of the Goat while her husband glanced ironically through the Lion's mask. The Bull, vainglorious, rode his motor-bike. Splendidly alone, the dark Archer drew his bow. Troy was amused with her picture but sighed at the thought of doing the lettering.

The Hewsons, passing through the saloon, devoured by curiosity and swathed in tact, asked if they might have a peep. This led to everybody, except Dr. Natouche, gathering round her.

"Just see what you've done with children's chalks and a drop of ink!" Caley Bard exclaimed. "What magic!" He gave a little crowing sound, burst out laughing and looked round at his fellow-passengers. "Do you see!" he cried. "Do you see what she's done?"

After some reflection they did, each recognizing the others more readily than him—or her—self. It appeared that Troy had been lucky in three of her choices. The Hewsons were, in fact, twins and, by an extraordinarily felicitous chance, had been born under Gemini, while Miss Rickerby-Carrick confessed, with mantling cheeks and conscious looks, as Caley Bard afterwards put it, to Virgo. She still seemed frightened and stared fixedly at Troy.

"Natouche," Caley Bard called up the companionway, "you must come down and see this."

He came down at once. Troy gave him the drawing and for the second time heard his laugh. "It is beautiful and it is comical," he said presently and handed it back to Troy. "I know, of course, that one must not frivolously compare the work of one great artist with another but may I say that Erni is perhaps your only contemporary who would have approached the subject like this."

"Very perceptive of you," said Caley Bard.

"I want to put the rhyme in the middle," Troy said, "but my lettering's hopeless: it takes ages to do and is awful when it's finished. I suppose nobody here would do a nice neo-classic job of lettering?"

"I would," said Mr. Pollock.

He was close behind Troy, staring over her arm at the drawing. "I—" he paused, and most unaccountably, Troy was revisited by yesterday's impression of an impending crisis. "I started in that business," Pollock said and there seemed to be a note of apology in his voice. "Commercial art. You know? Gave it up for real estate. I—if you show me what you'd like—the type of lettering—I'll give satisfaction."

He was looking at the drawing with the oddest expression in his barrow-boy face: sharp, appreciative and somehow—what?—shameface? Or—could Mr. Pollock possibly be frightened?

Troy said, cordially, "Will you really? Thank you so much. It just wants to be a sort of Garamond face. A bit fantasticated if you like."

Dr. Natouche had a book in his hand with the dust-jacket titled in Garamond. "That sort of thing," Troy said pointing to it.

Mr. Pollock looked reluctantly but sharply at it and then bent over the drawing. "I could do that," he said. "I don't know anything about fantasticate," and added under his breath something that sounded like: "I can copy anything."

Mr. Lazenby said loudly: "You're very sure of yourself, Mr. Pollock, aren't you?" and Caley Bard ejaculated: "Honestly, Pollock. How you dare!"

There followed a brief silence. Pollock mumbled: "Only a

suggestion, isn't it? No need to take it up, is there?"

"I'd be very glad to take it up," Troy said. "There you are; it's all yours."

She moved away from the table and after a moment's hesitation he sat down at it.

Troy went up on deck where she was soon joined by Caley Bard.

"You didn't half snub that little man," she said.

"He irritates me. And he's a damn sight too cool about your work."

"Oh come!"

"Yes, he is. Breathing down your neck. My God, you're *you*. You're 'Troy.' How he dares!"

"Do come off it."

"Have you noticed how rude he is to Natouche?"

"Well, that—yes. But you know I really think direct antagonism must be more supportable than the 'don't let's be beastly' line."

"The Rickerby-Carrick line, in fact?"

"If you like. Yes."

"You know," he said, "if you weren't a passenger in the good ship *Zodiac* I think I'd rat."

"Nonsense."

"It's not. Where did you get to last night?"

"I had a telephone call to make."

"It couldn't have taken you all the evening."

Remembering Fox's suggestion, Troy, who was a poor liar, lied. "It was about a fur I left at the gallery. I had to go to the police station."

"And then?"

"I went to the church."

"You'd much better have come on a one-pub crawl with me," he grumbled. "Will you dine tomorrow night in Longminster?"

Before Troy could reply, Miss Rickerby-Carrick, looking scared, came up from below, attired in her magenta wrapper. Her legs were bare and her arthritic toes emerged like roots from her sandals. She wore dark glasses and a panama hat and she carried her lie-low and her diary. She paused by the wheelhouse for her usual chat with the Skipper, continued on her way and to Troy's extreme mortification avoided her and

Bard with the kind of tact that breaks the sound-barrier, bestowing on them as she passed an understanding smile. She disappeared behind a stack of chairs covered by a tarpaulin, at the far end of the deck.

Troy said: "Not true, is she? Just a myth?"

"What's she writing?"

"A journal. She calls it her self-propelling confessional."

"Would you like to read it?"

"Isn't it awful—but, yes, I can't say I wouldn't fancy a little peep."

"How about tomorrow night? Dinner ashore, boys, and hey for the rollicking bun."

"Could we decide a bit later?"

"In case something more interesting turns up, you cautious beast."

"Not altogether that."

"Well—what?"

"We don't know what everybody will be doing," Troy said feebly and then: "I know. Why don't we ask Dr. Natouche to come?"

"We shall do nothing of the sort and I must say I think that's a pretty cool suggestion. I invite you to dine, tête-à-tête, and—"

Miss Rickerby-Carrick screamed.

It was a positive, abrupt and piercing scream and it brought everybody on deck.

She was leaning over the after-taffrail, her wrapper in wild disarray. She gesticulated and exclaimed and made strange grimaces.

"My diary! Oh stop! Oh please! My diary!" cried Miss Rickerby-Carrick.

Somehow or another she had dropped it overboard. She made confused statements to the effect that she had been observing the depths, had leant over too far, had lost her grip. She lamented with catarrhal extravagance, she pointed aft where indeed the diary was to be seen, open and fairly rapidly submerging. Her nose and eyes ran copiously.

The Tretheways behaved with the greatest address. The Skipper put the *Zodiac* into slow-astern, Tom produced a kind of long-handled curved hook used for clearing river-weed, and Mrs. Tretheway, placidity itself, emerged from below and attempted to calm Miss Rickerby-Carrick.

The engine was switched off and the craft, on her own momentum, came alongside Miss Rickerby-Carrick's diary. Tom climbed over the taffrail, held to it with his left hand and with his right, prepared to angle.

"But no!" screamed Miss Rickerby-Carrick. "Not with that thing! You'll destroy it! Don't, don't, don't! Oh, please. Oh please."

"Stone the crows!" Mr. Lazenby astonishingly ejaculated. With an air of hardy resignation he rose from his lie-low, turned his back on the company, removed his spectacles and placed them on the deck. He then climbed over the taffrail and neatly dived into the River.

Miss Rickerby-Carrick screamed again, the other passengers ejaculated and, with the precision of naval ratings, lined the port side to gaze at Mr. Lazenby. He was submerged but quickly reappeared with his long hair plastered over his eyes and the diary in his hand.

The Skipper instructed him to go ashore and walk a couple of chain downstream where it was deep enough for the *Zodiac* to come alongside. He did so, holding the diary clear of the water. He climbed the bank and squatted there, shaking the book gently and separating and turning over the leaves. His hair hung to one side like a caricature of a Carnaby Street fringe, completely obscuring the left eye.

Miss Rickerby-Carrick began to give out plaintive little cries interspersed with gusts of apologetic laughter and incoherent remarks upon the waterproof nature of her self-propelling pen. She could not wait for Mr. Lazenby to come aboard but leant out at a dangerous angle to receive the book from him. The little lump of leather, Troy saw, still dangled from her neck.

"Oh ho, ho!" she laughed, "my poor old confidante. Alas, alas!"

She thanked Mr. Lazenby with incoherent effusion and begged him not to catch cold. He reassured her, accepted his dark glasses from Troy who had rescued them, and turned aside to put them on. When he faced them all again it really seemed as if in some off-beat fashion and without benefit of dog-collar, he had resumed his canonicals. He even made a little parsonic noise: "N'yer I'll just get out of my wet bathers," he said. "There's not the same heat in the English sun: not like Bondi." And retired below.

"Well!" said Caley Bard. "Who says the church is effete?"

There was a general appreciative murmur in which Troy did not join.

Had she or had she not seen for a fractional moment, in Mr. Lazenby's left hand, a piece of wet paper with the marks of a propelling pencil across it?

While Troy still mused over this, Miss Rickerby-Carrick, who squatted on the deck examining with plaintive cries the ruin of her journal, suddenly exclaimed with much greater emphasis.

The others broke off and looked at her with that particular kind of patient endurance that she so pathetically inspired.

This time, however, there was something in her face that none of them had seen before: a look, not of anxiety or excitement but for a second or two, Troy could have sworn, of sheer panic. The dun skin had bleached under its freckles and round the jawline. The busy mouth was flaccid. She stared at her open diary. Her hands trembled. She shut the drenched book and steadied them by clutching it.

Miss Hewson said: "Miss Rickerby-Carrick, are you O.K.?"

She nodded once or twice, scrambled to her feet and incontinently bolted across the deck and down the companionway to the cabins.

"And *now,*" Troy said to herself. "What about *that* one? Am I still imagining?"

Again she had sensed a kind of stillness, of immense constraint and again she was unable to tell from whom it emanated.

"Like it or lump it," Troy thought, "Superintendent Tillottson's going to hear about that lot and we'll see what he makes of it. In the meantime—"

In the meantime, she went to her cabin and wrote another letter to her husband.

Half an hour later the *Zodiac* tied up for the afternoon and night at Crossdyke.

IV

CROSSDYKE

"As I told you," Alleyn said. "I rang up the Yard from San Francisco. Inspector Fox, who was handling the Andropoulos Case, was away but after inquiries I got through to Superintendent Tillottson at Tollardwark. He gave me details of his talks with my wife. One detail worried me a good deal more than it did him."

Alleyn caught the inevitable glint of appreciation from the man in the second row.

"Exactly," he said. "As a result I talked to the Yard again and was told there was no doubt that Foljambe had got himself to England and that he was lying doggo. Information received suggested that Andropoulos had tried a spot of blackmail and had been fool enough to imply that he'd grass on the Jampot if the latter didn't come across with something handsome. Andropoulos had in fact talked to one of our chaps in the way they do when they can't make up their minds to tell us something really useful. It was pretty obvious he was hinting at the Jampot.

"So he was murdered for his pains.

"The method used had been that of sudden and violent pressure on the carotids from behind and that method carries the Jampot's signature. It is sometimes preceded by a karate chop which would probably do the trick anyway, but it's his little fancy to make assurance double-sure."

The man in the second row gave a smirk to indicate his recognition of the quotation. "If I'm not careful," Alleyn thought, "I'll be playing up to that chap."

"There had," he said, "been two other homicides, one in Ismailia and one in Paris, where undoubtedly Foljambe had been the expert. But not a hope of cracking down on him. The latest line suggested that he had lit off for France. An envelope of the sort used by a well-known travel agency had been dropped on the floor near Andropoulos's body and it had a note of the price of tickets and times of departure from London scribbled on the back. It had, as was afterwards realized, been planted by the Jampot and had successfully decoyed Mr. Fox across the Channel. A typical stroke. I've already talked about his talent—it amounts to genius—for type-casting himself. I don't think I mentioned that when he likes to turn it on he has a strong attraction for many, but not all, women. His ear for dialects of every description is phenomenal, of course, but he not only speaks whatever it may be—Oxbridge, superior grammar, Australasian, barrow-boy, or Bronx, but he really seems to think along the appropriate wave-lengths. Rather as an actor gets behind the thought-pattern of the character he plays. He can act stupid, by the way, like nobody's business. He is no doubt a great loss to the stage. He is gregarious, which you'd think would be risky, and he has a number of unexpected, offbeat skills that occasionally come in very handy indeed.

"Well, you'll appreciate the situation. Take a look at it. Andropoulos has been murdered, almost certainly by the Jampot, and the Jampot's at large. Andropoulos, scarcely a candidate, one would have thought, for the blameless delights of British inland waterways, was to have been a passenger in the *Zodiac.* My wife now has his cabin. There's no logical reason in the wide world why his murderer should be her fellow-passenger; indeed the idea at first sight is ludicrous, and yet and yet—my wife tells me that her innocent remark about 'Constables' seemed to cast an extraordinary gloom upon someone or other in the party, that the newspaper report of Andropoulos's murder has been suppressed by someone in the *Zodiac,* that she's pretty sure an Australian padre who wears dark glasses and conceals his left eye has purloined a page of a farcical spinster's diary, that she half-suspects him of listening in to her telephone conversation with Mr. Fox and that she herself can't escape a feeling of impending disaster. And there's one other feature of this unlikely set-up that, however idiotically, strikes me as being more disturbing than all the rest put together. I wonder if any of you—"

But the man in the second row already had his hand up.

"Exactly," Alleyn said when the phenomenon had delivered himself of the correct answer in a strong Scots accent. "Quite so. And you might remember that I am five thousand-odd miles away in San Francisco on an extremely important conference.

"What the hell do I do?"

After a moment's thought the hand went up again.

"All right, all right," Alleyn said. "*You* tell *me*."

1

Hazel Rickerby-Carrick sat in her cabin turning over with difficulty the disastrous pages of her diary.

They were not actually pulp; they were stuck together, buckled, blistered and disfigured. They had half parted company with the spine and the red covers had leaked into them. The writing, however, had not been irrevocably lost. She used one side only of the page.

She separated the entries for the previous day and for that afternoon.

"I'm at it again," she read dismally. "Trying too hard, as usual. It goes down all right with Mavis, of course, but not with these people: not with Troy Alleyn. If only I'd realized who she was from the first! Or if only I'd heard she was going to be next door in Cabin 7; I could have gone to the Exhibition. I could have talked about her pictures. Of course, I don't pretend to know anything about—" Here she had had second thoughts and had abstained from completing the aphorism. She separated the sopping page from its successor, using a nailfile as a sort of slice. She began to read the final entry. It was for that afternoon, before the diary went overboard.

"—I'm going to write it down. I've got my diary with me: here, now. I'm lying on my lie-low on deck (at the 'blunt end'!!!) behind a pile of chairs covered with a tarpaulin. I'm having a sun-tan. I suppose I'm a goose to be so shy. In this day and age! What one *sees!* And of course it's much healthier and anyway the body is beautiful: *beautiful*. Only mine isn't so very. What I'm going to write now, happened last night. In Tollardwark. It was so frightful and so strange and I don't know what I ought to do about it. I think what I'll do is I'll tell Troy Alleyn. She can't say it's not extraordinary because it is.

"I'd come out of church and I was going back to the *Zodiac*. I was wearing what the Hewsons call 'sneakers.' Rubber soles. And that dark maroon jersey thing, so I suppose I was unnoticed because it was awfully dark. Absolutely pitchers. Well, I'd got a pebble or something in my left 'sneaker' and it hurt so I went into a dark shop-entry where I could lean against a door and take it off. And it was while I was there that those others came down the street. I would have hailed them: I was just going to do it when they stopped. I didn't recognize the voices at once because they spoke very low. In fact the one of them who whispered, I *never* recognized. But the others! Could they have said what I'm sure they did? The *first words* froze me. But literally. *Froze* me. I was *riveted*. Horror-stricken. I can hear them now. It—"

She had reached the bottom of the page. She picked at it gingerly, slid the nailfile under it, crumpled it and turned it.

The following pages containing her last entry were gone.

The inner margins where they were bound together had to some extent escaped a complete soaking. She could see by the fragments that remained that they had been pulled away. "But after all, that's nothing to go by," she thought, "because when he dived, Mr. Lazenby may have grabbed. The book was open. It was open and lying on its face when it sank. That's it. That's got to be it."

Miss Rickerby-Carrick remained perfectly still for some minutes. Once or twice she passed her arthritic fingers across her eyes and brow almost as if she tried to exorcise some devil of muddlement within.

"He's a clergyman," she thought, "a clergyman! He's been staying with a bishop. I could ask him. Why not? What could he say? Or do? But I'll ask Troy Alleyn. She'll jolly well have to listen. It'll interest her. Her *husband!*" she suddenly remembered. "Her husband's a famous detective. I *ought* to tell Troy Alleyn: and then she may like me to call her Troy. We may get quite chummy," thought poor Hazel Rickerby-Carrick without very much conviction.

She put the saturated diary open on her bedside shelf where a ray of afternoon sunlight reached it through the porthole.

A nervous weakness had come upon her. She suffered a terrible sense of constraint as if not only her head was iron-bound but as if the tiny cabin contracted about her. "I shan't sleep in here," she thought. "I shan't get a wink or if I do there'll be beastly dreams and I'll make noises and they'll hate me." And as she fossicked in an already chaotic dresser for Troy's aspirin she was visited by her great idea. She would sleep on deck. She would wait until the others had settled down and then she would take her lie-low from its jolly old hidy-hole behind the tarpaulin and blow it up and sleep, as she phrased it to herself, 'under the wide and starry sky.' And perhaps—perhaps.

"I've always been one to go straight at a thing and tackle it," she thought, and finding Troy's aspirins with the top off inside her sponge bag, she took a couple, lay on her bunk and made several disastrous plans.

2

For Troy, the evening at Crossdyke began farcically. The passengers were given an early dinner to enable them to explore the village and the nearby ruin of a hunting lodge where King John had stayed during his misguided antics in the north.

Troy, who had the beginning of a squeamish headache, hoped to get a still earlier start than she had achieved at Tollardwark and to make her call at the police station before any of her fellow-passengers appeared on the scene. Her story of the lost fur was now currency in the ship and would explain the visit if explanation was needed but she hoped to avoid making one.

Throughout dinner Miss Rickerby-Carrick gazed intently at Troy, who found herself greatly put out by this attention: the more so because what her husband once described as her

King-Size Bowels of Compassion had been aroused by Miss
Rickerby-Carrick. The more exasperating she became, the
more infuriatingly succulent her cold, the more embarrass-
ingly fixed her regard, the sorrier Troy felt for her and the less
she desired her company. Either, she thought, the wretched
woman was doing a sort of dismal lion-hunt or, hideous
notion, had developed a *schwarm* for Troy herself. Or was it
possible, she suddenly wondered, that this extraordinary
lady had something of moment to communicate.

Miss Rickerby-Carrick commanded rather less tact than a
bulldozer, and it must be clear, Troy thought, to everybody
in the saloon that a happening was on the brew.

Determined to look anywhere but at her tormentor, Troy
caught the ironical, skew-eyed glance of Caley Bard. He
winked and she lowered her gaze. Mr. Pollock stared with
distaste at Miss Rickerby-Carrick and the Hewsons caught
each other's glances and assumed a mask-like air of
detachment. Mr. Lazenby and Dr. Natouche swapped bits of
mediaeval information about the ruins.

Troy went straight on deck when she had finished her
dinner and was about to go ashore when up came Miss
Rickerby-Carrick from below, hailing her in a curious kind
of soft-pedalled shout.

"Mrs. Alleyn! I say! Mrs. Alleyn!"

Troy paused.

"Look!" said Miss Rickerby-Carrick coming close to her
and whispering. "I—are you going up to the village? Can I
come with you? I've got something—" she looked over her
shoulder and up and down the deck though she must have
known as well as Troy that the others were all below. "I want
to ask your advice. It's awfully important. Really. I promise,"
she whispered.

"Well—yes. All right, if you really think—"

"*Please.* I'll just get my cardi. I won't be a tick. Only as far
as the village. Before the others start—it's awfully important.
Honest injun. *Please.*"

She advanced her crazy-looking face so close that Troy
took an involuntary step backward.

"Be kind!" Miss Rickerby-Carrick whispered. "Let me tell
you. Let me!"

She stood before Troy: a grotesque, a dreadfully

vulnerable person. And the worst of it was, Troy thought, she herself was now so far caught up in a web of intangible misgivings that she could not know, could not trust herself to judge, whether the panic she thought she saw in those watery eyes was a mere reflection of the ill-defined anxiety which was building itself up around her own very real delight in the little cruise of the *Zodiac*. Or whether Miss Rickerby-Carrick's unmistakable *schwarm* was about to break out in a big way.

"Oh please!" she repeated. "For God's sake! Please."

"Well, of course," Troy said, helplessly. "Of course."

"Oh, you *are* a darling," exclaimed Miss Rickerby-Carrick and bolted for the companionway.

She collided with Mr. Pollock and there was much confusion and incoherent apology before she retired below and he emerged on deck.

He had brought back to Troy the signs of the zodiac with the lettering completed. It was beautifully done, right in scale and manner and execution, and Troy told him so warmly. He said in his flat voice with its swallowed consonants and plummy vowels that she need think nothing of it, the obligation was all his, and he hung about in his odd way offering a few scraps of disjointed information to the effect that he'd gone from the signwriting into the printing trade but there hadn't been any money in that. He made remarks that faded out after one or two words and gave curious little sounds that were either self-conscious laughs or coughs.

"Do you paint?" Troy asked. "As well as this? Or draw?"

He hastened to assure her that he did not. "Me? A flippin' awtist? Do you mind!"

"I thought from the way you looked at this thing—"

"Then you thought wrong," he said with an unexpected slap of rudeness.

Troy stared at him and he reddened. "Pardon my French," he said. "I'm naturally crude. I do not paint. I just take a fancy to look."

"Fair enough," Troy said pacifically.

He gave her a shamefaced grin and said Oh well he supposed he'd better do something about the nightlife of Crossdyke. As he was evidently first going below Troy asked him to keep the drawing for the time being.

He paused at the companionway for Miss Rickerby-Carrick. She erupted with monotonous precipitancy through the half-door, saw Mr. Pollock, who had the zodiac drawing open in his hands, looked at it as if it was a bomb and hurried on to Troy.

"Do let's go," she said. "Do come on."

They took their long strides from the gunwale to the bank, a simple exercise inevitably made complex by Miss Rickerby-Carrick, who, when she had recovered herself, seized Troy's arm and began to gabble.

"At once. I'll tell you at once before anyone can stop me. It's about—about—" She drove her free hand through her dishevelled hair and began distractedly to whisper and stammer quite incomprehensibly.

"—about last evening—and—and—Oh God!—And—"

"About *what?*"

"And—wait—and—"

But it was not to be. She had taken a deep breath, screwed up her eyes and opened her mouth, almost as if she were about to sneeze, when they were hailed from the rear.

"Hi! Wait a bit! What are you two up to?"

It was Mr. Lazenby. He leapt nimbly ashore and came alongside Troy. "We can't have these exclusive ladies' excursions," he said roguishly. "You'll have to put up with a mere man as far as the village."

Troy looked up at him and he shook a playful finger at her. "He's rescued me," she thought and with what she herself felt to be a perverse change of mood suddenly wanted to hear Miss Rickerby-Carrick's confidences. "Perhaps," Troy thought, "she'll tell us both."

But she didn't. By means of sundry hard-fingered squeezes and tweaks she conveyed her chagrin. At the same time Mr. Lazenby went through much the same routine with Troy's left arm and she began to feel like Alice between the Queens.

She produced, once more, her story of the lost fur and said she was going to inquire at the local police station.

"I suppose," Miss Rickerby-Carrick observed, "they make great efforts for you. Because—I mean—your husband—and everything."

"Ah!" Mr. Lazenby archly mocked. "How right you are!

Police protection every inch of the way. Big drama. You heard her say yesterday, Miss Rickerby-Carrick. The landscape's swarming with Constables."

The hand within Troy's right arm began to tremble. "She meant the painter," whispered Miss Rickerby-Carrick.

"That's only her cunning. She's sly as you make 'em, you may depend upon it. We're none of us safe."

The fingers on Troy's right arm became more agitated while those on her left gave it a brief conspiratorial squeeze. "Arms," Troy thought. "Last night Dr. Natouche and tonight these two, and I'm not the sort to link arms." But she was aware that while these contacts were merely irksome, last night's had both disturbed and reassured her.

She freed herself as casually as she could and talking disjointedly they walked into the village where they were over-taken by Caley Bard, complete with butterfly net and collector's box. All desire for the Rickerby-Carrick disclosures had left Troy. She scarcely listened to madly divergent spurts of information: "... my friend, Mavis ... you would love her ... such a brilliant brain ... art ... science ... butterflies even, Mr. Bard ... though not for me— Lamborine ... my friend, Mavis ... Highlands ... *how* I wish she was here ... Mavis ..."

The undisciplined voice gushed and dwindled, gabbled and halted. Troy had an almost overwhelming urge to be alone with her headache.

They came up with the cottage police station. A small car and a motor-cycle stood outside.

"Shall we wait for you?" Bard asked. "Or not?"

"Not, please, I may be quite a time. They'll probably want to telephone about it. As a matter of fact," Troy said, "I believe when I've finished here I'll just go back to the *Zodiac*. For some reason I've got a bit of a headache."

It was an understatement. Her headache was ripening. She was subject to occasional abrupt onsets of migraine and even now a thing like a starburst pulsed in one corner of her field of vision and her temple had begun to throb.

"You *poor* darling," cried Miss Rickerby-Carrick. "Shall I come back with you? Would you like a sleep-pill? Miss Hewson's got some. She's given me two for tonight. Shall I wait for you? Yes?"

"But *of course* we'll wait," Mr. Lazenby fluted.

Caley Bard said that he was sure Troy would rather be left to herself and proposed that he and Mr. Lazenby and Miss Rickerby-Carrick should explore the village together and then he would teach them how to lepidopterize. Troy felt this was a truly noble action.

"Don't let those bobbies worry you," he said. "Take care of yourself, do. Hope you recover your morsel of mink."

"Thank you," Troy said and tried to convey her sense of obligation without alerting Miss Rickerby-Carrick whose mouth was stretched in an anxious grin. She parted with them and went into the police station where at once time slipped a cog and she was back in last evening, for there was Superintendent Tillottson blandly remarking that he had just popped over from Toll'ark in case there had been any developments. She told him (speaking against the beat of her headache and with the sick dazzle in her vision making nonsense of his face) about Mr. Lazenby and the page from the diary and about the odd behavior of Mr. Pollock and Miss Rickerby-Carrick. And again, on describing them, these items shrank into insignificance.

Mr. Tillottson with his hands in his pockets, sitting easily on the corner of the local sergeant's desk said with great geniality that there didn't seem to be much in any of *that* lot did there and she agreed, longing to be rid of the whole thing and in bed.

"Yerse," Mr. Tillottson said. "So that's the story." And he added with the air of making conversation: "And this chap Lazenby had his hair all over his right eye like a hippie? Funny idea in a clergyman. But it was wet, of course."

"Over his left eye," Troy corrected as a sharp stab of pain shot through her own.

"His *left* eye, was it," said Mr. Tillottson casually. "Yes. Fancy. And you never got a look at it. The eye I mean."

"Well, no. He turned his back when he put on his dark spectacles."

"P'rhaps he's got some kind of disfigurement," Mr. Tillottson airily speculated. "You never know, do you? Jim Tretheway's a very pleasant kind of chap, isn't he? And his wife's smashing, don't you think, Mrs. Alleyn? Very nice couple the Tretheways."

"Very," Troy agreed and stood up to a lurching spasm of migraine.

They shook hands again and Mr. Tillottson produced, apparently as an afterthought, the suggestion that she should drop in at "their place in Longminster" where she would find Superintendent Bonney a most sympathetic person: "a lovely chap" was how Mr. Tillottson described him.

"I honestly don't think I need trouble him," Troy said. She was beginning to feel sick.

"Just to keep in touch, Mrs. Alleyn," he said and made a little sketch plan of Longminster, marking the police station with a cross. "Go to the point marked X," he said facetiously. "We may have a bit of news for you," he playfully added. "There's been a slight change in your good man's itinerary. We'll be pleased to let you know."

"Rory!" Troy ejaculated. "Is he coming back earlier?"

"I understand it's not quite settled yet, Mrs. Alleyn."

"Because if he is—"

"Oh, it wouldn't be anything you might call immediate. If you'd just look in on our chaps at Longminster we'd be much obliged. Very kind of you."

By this time Troy could have hurled the local sergeant's ink-pot at Mr. Tillottson but she took her leave with circumspection and made her way through nauseating sunbursts back to the River. Before she reached it her migraine attained its climax. She retired behind a briar bush and emerged, shaken but on the mend.

Her doctor had advanced the theory that these occasional onsets were associated with nervous tension and for the first time she began to think he might be right.

She would quite have liked to look at the ruins, which were visible from her porthole, doing their stuff against the beginning of a spectacular sunset, but the attack had left her tired and sleepy and she settled for an early night.

There seemed to be no other passengers aboard the *Zodiac*. Troy took a shower and afterwards knelt in her dressing gown on the bed and watched the darkling landscape across which, presently, her companions began to appear. There on the rim of a hillside rising to the ruins was Caley Bard in silhouette with his butterfly net. He gave a ridiculous balletic leap as he made a sweep with it. He was followed by Miss Rickerby-Carrick in full cry. Troy saw them put their heads together over the net and thought: "She's driving him crackers." At that moment Dr. Natouche came down the lane and Miss Rickerby-Carrick evidently spied him. She seemed to take a hasty farewell of Bard and, in her precipitancy, became almost air-borne as she plunged downhill in pursuit of the Doctor. Troy heard her hail him.

"Doctor! Doctor Na-tooo-sh."

He paused, turned and waited. He was incapable, Troy thought, of looking anything but dignified. Miss Rickerby-Carrick closed in. She displayed her usual vehemence. He listened with that doctor's air which is always described as being grave and attentive.

"Can she be consulting him?" Troy wondered. "Or is she perhaps confiding in him instead of me."

Now she was showing him something in the palm of her hand. Could it be a butterfly, Troy wondered. He bent his head to look at it. Troy saw him give a little nod. They walked slowly towards the *Zodiac* and as they approached, the great booming voice became audible.

"—your own medical man...something to help you... quite possibly...indeed."

"She *is* consulting him," thought Troy.

They moved out of her field of vision and now there emerged from the ruins the rest of the travellers: the Hewsons, Mr. Lazenby and Mr. Pollock. They waved to Caley Bard and descended the hill in single file, like cut-out figures in black paper against a fading screen sky. Commedia dell'arte again, Troy thought.

The evening was very warm. She lay down on her bunk. There was little light in the cabin and she left it so, fearing that Miss Rickerby-Carrick would call to inquire. She even locked her door and, obscurely, felt rather mean for doing so. The need for sleep that always followed her migraines must now be satisfied and Troy began to dream of voices and of a mouselike scratching at somebody's door. It persisted, it established itself over her dream and nagged her back into wakefulness. She struggled with herself, suffered an angry spasm of conscience and finally, in a sort of bemused fury, got out of bed and opened the door.

On nobody.

The passage was empty. She thought afterwards that as she opened her own door another one had quietly closed.

She waited but there was no stirring or sound anywhere, and wondering if after all she had dreamt the scratching at her door, she went back to bed and at once fell fathoms deep into oblivion that at some unidentifiable level was disturbed by the sound of an engine.

3

She half-awoke to broad daylight and the consciousness of a subdued fuss: knocking and voices, footsteps in the passage and movements next door in Cabin 8. While she lay half detached and half resentful of these disturbances, there was a tap on her own door and a rattle of the handle.

Troy, now fully awake, called out: "Sorry. Just a ~~moment~~," and unlocked her door.

Mrs. Tretheway came in with tea.

"Is anything wrong?" Troy asked.

Mrs. Tretheway's smile broke out in glory all over her face. "Well," she said, "not to say wrong. It's how you look at it, I suppose, Mrs. Alleyn. The fact is Miss Rickerby-Carrick seems to have left us."

"*Left* us? *Gone?*"

"That's right."

"Do you mean—"

"It must have been very early. Before any of us were about and our Tom was up at six."

"But—"

"She's packed her suitcase and gone."

"No message?"

"Well now—yes—scribbled on a bit of newspaper. 'Called away. So sorry. Urgent. Will write.'"

"How very extraordinary."

"My husband reckons somebody must have come in the night. Some friend with a car or else she might have rung Toll'ark or Longminster for a taxi. The telephone booth at the lockhouse is open all night."

"*Well,*" Troy muttered, "she is a rum one and *no* mistake."

Mrs. Tretheway beamed. "It may be all for the best," she remarked. "It's a lovely day, anyhow," and took her departure.

When Troy arrived in the saloon she found her fellow-passengers less intrigued than might have been expected and she supposed that they had already exhausted the topic of Miss Rickerby-Carrick's flight.

Her own entrance evidently revived it a little and there was a short barrage of rather flaccid questions: had Miss Rickerby-Carrick "said anything" to Troy? She hadn't "said anything" to anyone else.

"Shall we rather put it," Caley Bard remarked sourly, "that she hadn't said anything of *interest*. Full stop. Which God knows, by and large, is only too true of all her conversation."

"Now, Mr. Bard, isn't that just a little hard on the poor girl?" Miss Hewson objected.

"I don't know why we must call her 'poor,'" he rejoined.

"Of course you do," Troy said. "One can't help thinking of her as 'poor Miss Rickerby-Carrick' and that makes her all the more pitiful."

"What a darling you are," he said judicially.

Troy paid no attention to this. Dr. Natouche, who had not taken part in the conversation, looked directly at her and gave her a smile of such clear understanding that she wondered if she had blushed or turned pale.

Mr. Lazenby offered one or two professional aphorisms to the effect that Miss Rickerby-Carrick was a dear soul and kindness itself. Mr. Hewson looked dry and said she was just a mite excitable. Mr. Pollock agreed with this. "Talk!" he said. "Oh, dear!"

"They are all delighted," Troy thought.

On that note she left them and went up on deck. The *Zodiac* was still at Crossdyke, moored below the lock, but Tom and his father were making their customary preparations for departure.

They had cast off and the engine had started when Troy heard the telephone ringing in the lock-keeper's office. A moment later his wife came out and ran along the tow-path towards them.

"Skipper! Hold on! Message for you."

"O.K. Thanks."

The engine fussed and stopped and the *Zodiac* moved back a little towards the wharf. The lock-keeper came out and arched his hands round his mouth.

"Car Hire and Taxi Service, Longminster," he called "Message for you, Skipper. Miss something-or-another Carrick asked them to ring. She's been called away to a sick friend. Hopes you'll understand. O.K.?"

"O.K."

"Ta-ta, then."

"So long, then, Jim. Thanks."

The Skipper returned to his wheelhouse doing "thumbs up" to Troy on the way. The *Zodiac* moved out into midstream, bound for Longminster.

Dr. Natouche had come on deck during this exchange. He said: "Mrs. Alleyn, may I have one word with you?"

"Yes, of course," Troy said. "Where? Is it private?"

"It is, rather. Perhaps if we moved aft."

They moved aft. Round the tarpaulin-covered heap of extra chairs. There, lying on the deck, was an inflated, orange-coloured lie-low mattress.

Dr. Natouche stooped, looked down at it and up at Troy. "Miss Rickerby-Carrick slept here last night. I think," he said.

"She did?"

"Yes. That, at least, was her intention."

Troy waited.

"Mrs. Alleyn, you will excuse me, I hope, for asking this question. You will, of course, not answer it if you do not wish. Did Miss Rickerby-Carrick speak to you after she returned to the ship last evening?"

"No. I went very early to my cabin. I'd had a go of migraine."

"I thought you seemed to be not very well."

"It was soon over. I think she may have—sort of scratched—at my door. I fancy she did but I was asleep and by the time I opened my door there was nobody."

"I see. She intimated to me that she had something to tell you."

"I know. Oh, dear!" Troy said. "*Should* I have gone to her cabin, do you think?"

"Ah, no! No. It's only that Miss Rickerby-Carrick has a very high opinion of you and I thought perhaps she intended—" He hesitated and then said firmly. "I think I must explain that this lady spoke to me last evening. About her insomnia. She had been given some tablets—American proprietary product—by Miss Hewson and she asked me what I thought of these tablets."

"She offered me one."

"Yes? I said that they were unknown to me and suggested that she should consult her own doctor if her insomnia was persistent. In view of her snoring performance on the previous night I felt it might, at least in part, be an imaginary condition. My reason for troubling you with the incident is this. I formed the opinion that Miss Rickerby-Carrick was overwrought, that she was experiencing some sort of emotional and nervous crisis. It was very noticeable—very marked. I felt some concern. You understand that she did not consult me on the score of this condition; if she had, it would be improper for me to speak to you about it. I think she may have been on the point of doing so when she suddenly broke off, said something incoherent and left me."

"Do you think she's actually—well—mentally unbalanced?"

"That is a convenient phrase without real definition. I think she is disturbed—which is another such phrase. It is because I think so that I am a little worried about this departure in the middle of the night. Unnecessarily so, I dare say."

"You heard the telephone message, just now?"

"Yes. A friend's illness."

"Can it," Troy ejaculated, "be Mavis!"

She and Dr. Natouche stared speculatively at each other. She saw the wraith of a smile on his mouth.

"No. Wait a bit," Troy went on. "She walked up to the village with Mr. Lazenby and me. My head was swinging with migraine and I scarcely listened. He might remember. Of course she talked incessantly about Mavis. I think she said Mavis is in the Highlands. I'm sure she did. Do you suppose Miss Rickerby-Carrick has shot off by taxi to the Highlands in the dead of night?"

"Perhaps only to Longminster and thence by train?"

"Who can tell! Did nobody hear anything?" Troy wondered. "I mean, somebody must have come on board with this news and roused her up. It would be a disturbance."

"Here? At the stern? It's far removed from our cabins."

"Yes," Troy said, "but how would they *know* she was back here?"

"She told me she would take her tablet and sleep on deck."

Troy stooped down and after a moment, picked up a blotched, red scrap of cloth.

"What's that?" she asked.

The long fingers that looked as if they had been imperfectly treated with black cork, turned it over and laid it in the pinkish palm. "Isn't it from the cover of her diary?" Troy said.

"I believe you're right."

He was about to drop it overboard, but she said: "No—don't."

"No?"

"Well—only because—." Troy gave an apologetic laugh. "I'm a policeman's wife," she said. "Put it down to that."

He took out a pocket-book and slipped the scrap of cloth into it.

"I expect we're making a song about nothing," Troy said.

Suddenly she felt an almost overwhelming impulse to tell Dr. Natouche about her misgivings and the incidents that had prompted them. She had a vivid premonition of how he would look as she confided her perplexity. His head would be courteously inclined and his expression placid and a little withdrawn—a consulting-room manner of the most reassuring kind. It really would be a great relief to confide in Dr. Natouche. An opening phrase had already shaped itself in her mind when she remembered another attentive listener.

"And by-the-way, Mrs. Alleyn," Superintendent Tillottson had said in his infuriatingly bland manner, "we won't mention this little matter to anybody, shall we? Just a routine precaution."

So she held her tongue.

V

LONGMINSTER

"I suppose one of his greatest assets," Alleyn said, "is his ability to instill confidence in the most unlikely people. An infuriated Bolivian policeman is supposed to have admitted that before he could stop himself he found he was telling the Jampot about his own trouble with a duodenal ulcer. This may not be a true story. If not, it was invented to illustrate the more winning facets in the Foljambe façade. The moral is: that it takes all sorts to make a thoroughly bad lot and it sometimes takes a conscientious police officer quite a long time to realize this simple fact of unsavoury life. You can't type criminals. It's just as misleading to talk about them as if they never behave out of character as it is to suppose the underworld is riddled with charmers who only cheat or kill by some kind of accident.

"Foljambe has been known to behave with perfect good-nature and also with ferocity. He is attracted by beauty at a high artistic level. His apartment in Paris is said to have been got up in the most impeccable taste. He likes money better than anything else in life and he enjoys making it by criminal practices. If he was left a million pounds it's odds on he'd continue to operate the rackets. If people got in his way he would continue to remove them.

"I've told you that my wife's letters missed me in New York and were forwarded to San Francisco. By the time they reached me her cruise in the *Zodiac* had only two nights to go. As you know I rang the Department and learnt that Mr. Fox was in France, following what was hoped to be a hot line on Foljambe. I got through to Tillottson who in view of this development was inclined to discount the *Zodiac* altogether. I was not so inclined.

"Those of you who are married," Alleyn said, "will understand my position. In the Force our wives are not called upon to serve in female James-Bondage and I imagine most of you would agree that any notion of their involvement in our work would be outlandish, ludicrous and extremely unpalatable. My wife's letters, though they made very little of her misgivings, were disturbing enough for me to wish her out of the *Zodiac*. I thought of asking Tillottson to get her to ring me up but I had missed her at Crossdyke and if I waited until she reached Longminster I myself would miss my connection from San Francisco. And if, by any fantastic and most improbable chance, one of her fellow-passengers in some way tied in with the Andropoulos-Jampot show, the last thing we would want to do was to alert him by sending police messages to lock-keepers asking her to leave the cruise. My wife is a celebrated painter who is known, poor thing, to be married to a policeman."

The Scot in the second row smirked.

"Well," Alleyn said, "in the upshot I told Tillottson I thought my present job might finish earlier than expected and I would get back as soon as I could. I would remind you that at this stage I had no knowledge of the disappearance of Miss Rickerby-Carrick. If I had heard that bit I would have taken a very much stronger line.

"As it was I told Tillottson..."

1

There was no denying it, the cruise was much more enjoyable without Miss Rickerby-Carrick.

From Crossdyke to Longminster the sun shown upon fields, spinnies, villages and locks. It was the prettiest of journeys. Everybody seemed to expand. The Hewsons' cameras clicked busily. Mr. Lazenby and Mr. Pollock discovered a common interest in stamps and showed each other the contents of sad-looking envelopes. Caley Bard told Troy a great deal about butterflies but she refused, nevertheless, to look at the Death's Head he had caught last evening on Crossdyke Hill. "Well," he said gaily, "don't look at it if it's going to set you against me. Why can't you be more like Hay? She said she belonged to the R.S.P.C.A. but lepidoptera didn't count."

"Do you call her Hay?"

"No. Do you?"

"No, but she asked me to."

"Standoffish old you, as usual," he said, and for no reason at all Troy burst out laughing. Her own apprehensions and Dr. Natouche's anxiety had receded in the pleasant atmosphere of the third day's cruise.

Even Dr. Natouche turned out to have a hobby. He liked to make maps. If anyone as tranquil and grave as Dr. Natouche could be said to exhibit coyness, he did so when questioned by Troy and Bard about his cartography. He was, he confessed, attempting a chart of their cruise; it could not be called a true chart because it was not being scientifically constructed but he hoped to make something of it when he had consulted ordnance maps. Troy wondered if persons of Dr. Natouche's complexion ever blushed, and was sure, when he was persuaded to show them his little drawing, that he felt inclined to do so.

It was executed in very hard lead-pencil and was in the style of the sixteenth-century English cartographers, with tiny drawings of churches and trees in their appropriate places and with extremely minute lettering.

Troy exclaimed with pleasure and said: "That we should have two calligraphers on board! Mr. Pollock, do come and look at this."

Pollock, who had been talking to the Hewsons, hesitated, and then limped over and looked at the map but not at Dr. Natouche.

"Very nice," he said and returned to the Hewsons.

Troy had made a boldish move. Pollock, since the beginning of the cruise, had only just kept on the hither side of insulting Dr. Natouche. He had been prevented, not by any tactics that she and Caley Bard employed, but rather by the behaviour of Dr. Natouche himself, who skillfully avoided giving Pollock any chance to exhibit ill-will. Somehow it came about that at meal-times Dr. Natouche was as far removed as possible from Mr. Pollock. On deck,

Dr. Natouche had conveyed himself to the area farthest aft, which Miss Rickerby-Carrick's mattress, deflated to the accompaniment of its own improper noises by the boy Tom, had previously occupied.

So Dr. Natouche had offered no opportunity for Mr. Pollock to insult him, and Mr. Pollock had retired, as Caley Bard pointed out to Troy, upon a grumpy alliance with the Hewsons, with whom he could be observed in ridiculously furtive conference, presumably about racial relations.

To these skirmishes and manoeuveres Mr. Lazenby appeared to be oblivious. He swapped philatelic gossip with Mr. Pollock, he discussed the tendencies of art in Australia with Troy when she was unable to escape him, and he made jovial, unimportant small talk with Dr. Natouche.

Perhaps the most effective deterrent to any overt display of racialism from Mr. Pollock was an alliance he had formed with the Tretheways.

To Troy, it appeared that Mr. Pollock, in common, she thought, with every other male in the *Zodiac*, was extremely conscious of Mrs. Tretheway's allure. That was not surprising. What did surprise was Mrs. Tretheway's fairly evident response to Mr. Pollock's offering of homage. Evidently, she found him attractive, but not apparently to an extent that might cause the Skipper any concern, since Troy heard them all planning to meet at a pub in Longminster. They were going to have a bit of an evening, they agreed.

Troy herself was in something of a predicament. She could not, without making a ridiculous issue of it, refuse either to lunch or dine with Caley Bard in Longminster and indeed she had no particular desire to refuse since she enjoyed his company and took his cock-eyed and purely verbal advances with the liberal pinch of salt that she felt sure he expected. So she agreed to dine with him but said she had appointments during the earlier part of the day.

Somehow or another, she must yet again visit a police station and commune with Superintendent Bonney, whose personality, according to Superintendent Tillottson, she would find so very congenial. She could not help but feel that the legend of the lost fur had begun to wear thin but she supposed, unless some likelier device occurred to her, that she must continue to employ it. She told Caley Bard she'd have to make a final inquiry as they'd promised to let the Longminster police know if the wretched fur turned up and she also hinted at visits to the curator of the local gallery and a picture-dealer of some importance.

"All right," he said, "I'll accept your feeble excuses for the day and look forward to dinner. After all, you *are* famous and allowances must be made."

"They are *not* feeble excuses," Troy shouted. Afterwards she determined at least to call on the curator and thus partially salve her conscience. She had arrived at this stage of muddled thinking when Dr. Natouche approached her with an extremely formal invitation.

"You have almost certainly made your own arrangements for today," he said. "In case you have not I must explain that I have invited a friend and his wife to luncheon at the Longminster Arms. He is Sir Leslie Fergus, a biochemist of some distinction, now dedicated to research. We were fellow-students. I would, of course, be delighted if by any fortunate chance you were able to come."

Troy saw that, unlike Caley Bard who had cheerfully cornered and heckled her, Dr. Natouche was scrupulous to leave her the easiest possible means of escape. She said at once that she would be delighted to lunch at the Longminster Arms.

"I am so pleased," said Dr. Natouche with his little bow and withdrew.

"Well!" ejaculated Caley who had unblushingly listened to this exchange. "You *are* a sly-boots!"

"I don't know why you should say that."

"You wouldn't lunch with me."

"I'm dining with you," Troy said crossly.

"Sorry," he said. "I'm being a bore and unfunny. I won't do it again. Thank you for dining. I hope it'll be fun and I hope your luncheon is fabulous."

She now began to have misgivings about Caley Bard's dead set at her.

"At my age," Troy thought, "this sort of thing can well become ridiculous. Am I in for a tricky party, I wonder."

The day, however, turned out to be a success.

They reached Longminster at 10:30. Mr. Lazenby and Mr. Pollock were going straight to the Minster itself and from there planned to follow the itinerary set out in the *Zodiac*'s leaflet. The Hewsons, who had intended to join them, were thrown into a state of ferment when the Skipper happened to remark that it would be half-day closing in Tollardwark on the return journey. They would arrive there at noon.

Miss Hewson broke out in lamentation. The junk shops where she was persuaded she would find the most exciting and delectable bargains! Shut! Now wasn't that just crazy planning on somebody's part? To spend the afternoon in a closed town? In vain did the Tretheways explain that the object of the stay was a visit by special bus to an historic abbey six miles out of Tollardwark. The Hewsons said in unison that they'd seen enough abbeys to last them the rest of their lives. What they desired was a lovely long shop-crawl. Why, Miss Hewson had seen four of the cutest little old shops—one in particular—she appealed to Troy to witness how excited she had been.

They went on and on until at last Caley Bard, in exasperation, suggested that as it was only a few miles by road back to Tollardwark they might like to spend the day there. Mrs. Tretheway said there were buses and the road was a very attractive one, actually passing the abbey. The Skipper said there were good car-hire services, as witness the one that had rung through with Miss Rickerby-Carrick's message.

The Hewsons went into a huffy conference from which they emerged with their chagrin somewhat abated. They settled on a car. They would spend half the day in Tollardwark and half in Longminster. One could see, Troy thought, the timeless charm of the waterways evaporating in the Hewsons' esteem. They departed, mollified and asking each other if it didn't seem kind of dopey to spend two days getting from one historic burg to another when you could take them both in between breakfast and dinner with time left over for shopping.

Caley Bard announced that he was going to have his hair cut and then go to the museum where the lepidoptera were said to be above average. Dr. Natouche told Troy that he would expect her at one o'clock and the two men walked off together.

Troy changed into a linen suit, consulted Mr. Tillottson's

map and found her way to the Longminster central police station and Superintendent Bonney.

Afterwards she was unable to make up her mind whether or not she had been surprised to find Mr. Tillottson there.

He explained that he happened to be in Longminster on a routine call. He did not suggest that he had timed his visit to coincide with Troy's. He merely shook hands with his customary geniality and introduced her to Superintendent Bonney.

Mr. Bonney was another large man but in his case seniority would have seemed to have run to bone rather than flesh. His bones were enormous. They were excessive behind his ears, under and above his eyes and at his wrists. His jaws were cadaverous, and when he smiled, even his gums were knobbly. Troy would not have fallen in with Mr. Tillottson's description of his colleague as a lovely chap.

They were both very pleasant. Troy's first question was as to her husband's return. Was there any chance, did they think, that it might be earlier, because if so—

They said, almost in unison, that Alleyn had rung through last evening; that he would have liked to talk to her this morning but would have missed his connection to New York. And that he hoped he might be home early next week but that depended upon a final conference. He sent his love, they said, beaming at her, and if she was still uneasy she was to abandon ship. "Perhaps a telegram from a sick friend—" Mr. Tillottson here suggested and Troy felt a strong inclination to laugh in his face and ask him if it should be signed "Mavis."

She told them about Miss Rickerby-Carrick.

They listened with great attention saying: "Yerse. Yerse," and "Is that a fact?" and "Fancy that now." When she had finished Mr. Bonney glanced at his desk pad where he had jotted down a note or two.

"The Longminster Car Hire and Taxi Service, eh?" he said. "Now, which would that be, I wonder, Bert? There's Ackroyd's and there's Rutherford's."

"We might make a wee check, Bob," Mr. Tillottson ventured.

"Yerse," Mr. Bonney agreed. "We might at that."

He made his calls while Troy, at their request, waited.

"Ackroyd's Car Hire Service? Just a little item about a

telephone call. Eight-thirty or thereabouts to Crossdyke Lockhouse. Message from a fare phoned by you to the Lock for Tretheway, Skipper, M.V. *Zodiac*. Could you check for us? Much obliged." A pause while Mr. Bonney stared without interest at Mr. Tillottson and Mr. Tillottson stared without interest at nothing in particular.

"I see. No note of it? Much obliged. Just before you go: Fare from Crossdyke Lock, picked up sometime during the night. Lady. Yerse. Well, *any* trips to Crossdyke? Could you check?" Another pause. "Much obliged. Ta," said Mr. Bonney and replaced the receiver.

He repeated his conversation almost word for word on three more calls.

In each instance, it seemed, a blank.

"No trips to Crossdyke," said Mr. Bonney, "between 6:45 last evening and 11 A.M. today."

"Well, well," said Mr. Tillottson, "that's quite interesting, Bob, isn't it?"

All Troy's apprehensions that with the lightened atmosphere of the morning had retired to an uneasy hinterland now returned in force.

"But that means whoever rang gave a false identity," she said.

Mr. Tillottson said it looked a wee bit like that but they'd have to check with the lock-keeper at Crossdyke. He might have mistaken the message. It might have been, he suggested, Miss Rickerby-Carrick herself saying she was hiring a car.

"That's true!" Troy agreed.

"What sort of voice, now, would she have, Mrs. Alleyn?"

"She's got a heavy cold and she sounds excitable. She gabbles and she talks in italics."

"She wouldn't be what you'd call at all eccentric?"

"She would. Very eccentric."

Mr. Tillottson said ah, well, now, there you were, weren't you? Mr. Bonney asked what age Miss Rickerby-Carrick might be and when Troy hazarded, "Fortyish," began to look complacent. Troy mentioned Mavis of Birmingham now in the Highlands and when they asked Mavis who, and where in the Highlands? was obliged to say she'd forgotten. This made her feel foolish and remember some of her husband's strictures upon purveyors of information received.

"I'm sorry," she said, "to be so perfectly hopeless."

They soothed her. Why should she remember these trifles? They would, said Mr. Tillottson, have a wee chin-wag with the lock-keeper at Crossdyke just to get a confirmation of the telephone call. They would ring the telephone department and they would make further inquiries to find out just how Miss Rickerby-Carrick got herself removed in the dead of night. If possible they would discover her destination.

Their manner strongly suggested that Troy's uneasiness rather than official concern was the motive for these inquiries.

"They think I've got a bee in my bonnet," she told herself. "If I wasn't Rory's wife they wouldn't be bothered with me."

She took what she felt had now become her routine leave of superintendents in North Country police stations and, once more reassured by Mr. Tillottson, prepared to enjoy herself in Longminster.

2

She spent the rest of the morning looking at the gallery and the Minster and wandering about the city, which was as beautiful as its reputation.

At noon she began to ask her way to the Longminster Arms. After a diversion into an artist-colourman's shop where she found a very nice old frame of the right size for her signs of the zodiac, she arrived at half-past twelve. Troy was one of those people who can never manage to be unpunctual and was often obliged to go for quite extensive walks round blocks in order to be decently late or at least not indecently early.

However, she didn't mind being early for her luncheon with Dr. Natouche and his friends. She tidied up and found her way into a pleasant drawing-room where there were lots of magazines.

In one of them she at once became absorbed. It printed a long extract from a book written some years ago by a white American who had had his skin pigmentation changed by what, it appeared, was a dangerous but entirely effective process. For some months this man had lived as one of themselves among the Negroes of the Deep South. The author did not divulge the nature of this transformation process and Troy found herself wondering if Dr. Natouche would be able to tell what it was. Could she ask him? Remembering their conversation in the wapentake, she thought she could.

She was still pondering over this and had turned again to the article when she became aware of a presence and found that Dr. Natouche stood beside her, quite close, with his gaze on the printed page.

Her diaphragm contracted with a jolt and the magazine crackled in her hands.

"I am so very sorry," he said, "I startled you. It was stupid of me. The carpet is thick and you were absorbed."

He sat down opposite to her and with a look of great concern said: "I have been unforgivably clumsy."

"Not a bit of it," Troy rejoined. "I don't know why I should be so jumpy. But as you say, I *was* absorbed. Have you read this thing, Dr. Natouche?"

He had lifted his finger to a waiter who approached with a perfectly blank face.

"We shall not wait for the Ferguses," Dr. Natouche said. "You must be given a restorative. Brandy? And soda? Dry ginger? Yes? Two, if you please and may I see the wine list?"

His manner was grand enough to wipe the blank look off any waiter's face.

When the man had gone Dr. Natouche said: "But I have not answered your question. Yes, I have read this book. It was a courageous action."

"I wondered if you would know exactly what was done to him. The process, I mean."

"*Your* colour is returning," he said after a moment. "And so, of course, did his. It was not a permanent change. No, I do not know what was done. Sir Leslie might have an idea, it is more in his line than mine. We must ask him."

"I would have thought—"

"Yes?" he said, when she stopped short.

"You said, when we were at the wapentake, that you didn't think I could say anything to—I don't remember the exact phrase—"

"To hurt or offend me? Something like that was it? It is true."

"I was going to ask, then, if the change of pigmentation would be enough to convince people, supposing the features were still markedly European. And then I saw that your features, Dr. Natouche, are not at all—"

"Negroid?"

"Yes. But perhaps Ethiopians—one is so ignorant."

"You must remember I am a half-caste. My facial structures are those of my mother, I believe."

"Yes, of course," Troy said. "Of course."

The waiter brought their drinks and the wine list and menu and hard on his heels came Sir Leslie and Lady Fergus.

They were charming and the luncheon party was a success, but somehow neither Troy nor her host got round to asking Sir Leslie if he could shed any light on the darkening by scientific methods of the pigmentation of the skin.

3

Troy returned to the *Zodiac,* rested, changed and was taken in a taxi by Caley Bard to dinner with champagne at another hotel.

"I'm not 'alf going it," she thought and wondered what her husband would have to say about these jaunts.

When they had dined, she and Bard walked about Longminster and finally strolled back to the River at half-past ten.

The *Zodiac* was berthed romantically in a bend of the River from which one could see the Long Minster itself against the stars. The lights of the old city quavered and zig-zagged with those of other craft in the black night waters. Troy and Bard could hear quiet voices in the saloon but they loitered on the deserted deck and, before she could do anything about it, Bard had kissed Troy.

"You're adorable," he said.

"Ah, get along with you. Good-night, and thank you for a nice party."

"Don't go away."

"I think I must."

"Couldn't we have a lovely, fairly delicate little affair? Please?"

"We could not," said Troy.

"I've fallen for you in a bloody big way. Don't laugh at me."

"I'm not. But I'm not going to pursue the matter. Don't you, either."

"Well, I can't say you've led me on. You don't know a garden path when you see one."

"I wouldn't say as much for you."

"I like that! What cheek!"

"Look," Troy said, "who's here."

It was the Hewsons. They had arrived on the wharf in a taxi and were hung about with strange parcels. Miss Hewson seemed to be in a state of exalted fatigue and her brother in a state of exhausted resignation.

"Boy, oh boy!" he said.

They had to be helped on board with their unwieldy freight and when this exercise had been accomplished it seemed only decent to get them down the companionway into the saloon. Here the other passengers were assembled and about to go to bed. They formed themselves into a sort of chain gang and by this means assembled the Hewsons' purchases on three of the tables. Newspaper was spread on the deck.

"We just ran crazy," Miss Hewson panted. "We just don't know what's with us when we get loose on an antique spree, do we, Earl?"

"You said it, dear," her brother conceded.

"Where," asked Mr. Pollock, "will you put it?" Feeling, perhaps, that his choice of words was unfortunate, he threw a frightened glance at Mr. Lazenby.

"Well! Now!" Miss Hewson said. "We don't figure we have a problem there, do we dear? We figure if we talk pretty to the Skipper and Mrs. Tretheway we might be allowed to cache it in Miss Rickerby-Carrick's stateroom. We just kind of took a calculated risk on that one, didn't we, dear?"

"Sure did, honey."

"The Tretheways," Pollock said, "have gone to bed."

"Looks like we'll have to step up the calculated risk

some," Mr. Hewson said dryly.

Mr. Lazenby was peering with undisguised curiosity at their booty and so were Troy and Bard. There was an inlaid rosewood box, a newspaper parcel from which horse-brasses partly emerged, a pair of carriage lamps and, packed piecemeal into an open beer carton, a wag-at-the-wall Victorian clock.

Propped against the table was a really filthy roll of what appeared through encrustations of mud to be a collection of prints tied together with an ancient piece of twine.

It was over this trove that Miss Hewson seemed principally to gloat. She had found it, she explained, together with their other purchases, in the yard of the junk shop where Troy had seen them that first night in Tollardwark. Something had told Miss Hewson she would draw a rich reward if she could explore that yard and, sure enough, jammed into a compartment in an Edwardian sideboard, all doubled up, as they could see if they looked, there it was.

"I'm a hound when I get started," Miss Hewson said proudly. "I open up everything that has a door or a lid. And you know something? This guy who owns this dump allowed he never knew he had this roll. He figured it must have been in this terrible little cupboard at the time of the original purchase. And you know something? He said he didn't care if he didn't see the contents and when Earl and I opened it up he gave it a kind of weary glance and said was it worth ten bob? Was it worth one dollar twenty! Boy, I guess when the Ladies Handcraft Guild, back in Apollo, see the screens I get out of this lot, they'll go crazy. Now, Mrs. Alleyn," Miss Hewson continued, "you're artistic. Well, I mean—well, you know what I mean. Now, I said to Brother, I can't wait till I show Mrs. Alleyn and get me an expert opinion. I said: we go right back and show Mrs. Alleyn—"

As she delivered this speech in a high gabble, Miss Hewson doubled herself up and wrestled with the twine that bound her bundle. Dust flew about and flakes of dry mud dropped on the deck. After a moment her brother produced a pocket knife and cut the twine.

The roll opened up abruptly in a cloud of dust and fell apart on the newspaper.

Scraps. Oleographs. Coloured supplements from *Pears'*

Annual. Half a dozen sepia photographs, several of them torn. Four flower pieces. A collection of Edwardian prints from dressmakers' journals. Part of a child's scrapbook. Three lamentable water-colours.

Miss Hewson spread them out on the deck with cries of triumph to which she received but tepid response. Her brother sank into a chair and closed his eyes.

"Is that a painting?" Troy asked.

It had enclosed the roll and its outer surface was so encrusted with occulted dirt that the grain of the canvas was only just perceptible.

It was lying curled up on what was presumably its face. Troy stooped and turned it over.

It was a painting in oil, about 18 by 12 inches.

She knelt down and tapped its edge on the deck, releasing a further accretion of dust. She spread it out.

"Anything?" asked Bard, leaning down.

"I don't know."

"Shall I get a damp cloth or something?"

"Yes, do. If the Hewsons don't mind."

Miss Hewson was in ecstasies over a Victorian scrap depicting an innocent child surrounded by rosebuds. She said: "Sure, sure. Go right ahead." Mr. Hewson was asleep.

Troy wiped the little painting over with an exquisite handkerchief her husband had bought her in Bruges. Trees. A bridge. A scrap of golden sky.

"Exhibit 1. My very, very own face-flannel," said Bard, squatting beside her. "Devotion could go no further. I have added (Exhibit 2) a smear of my very, very own soap. It's called Spruce."

The whole landscape slowly emerged: defaced here and there by dirt and scars in the surface, but not, after all, in bad condition.

In the foreground: water—and a lane that turned back into the middle distance. A pond and a ford. A child in a vermilion dress with a hay-rake. In the middle distance: trees that reflected in countless leafy mirrors the late afternoon sun. In the background: a rising field, a spire, a generous and glowing sky.

"It's sunk," Troy muttered. "We could oil it out."

"What does that mean?"

"Wait a bit. Dry the surface, can you?"

She went to her cabin and came back with linseed oil on a bit of paint-rag. "This won't do any harm," she said. "Have you got the surface dry? Good. Now then."

And in a minute the little picture was clearer and cleaner and speaking bravely for itself.

"'Constables,'" Caley Bard quoted lightly, "'all over the place.' Or did you say 'swarming'?"

Troy looked steadily at him for a moment and then returned to her oiling. Presently she gave a little ejaculation and at the same moment Dr. Natouche's great voice boomed out: "It is a picture of Ramsdyke. That is the lock and the lane and, see, there is the ford and the church spire above the hill."

The others, who had been clustered round Miss Hewson's treasures on the table, all came to look at the painting.

Troy said: "Shall we put it in a better light?"

They made way for her. She stood on the window seat and held the painting close to a wall lamp. She examined the back of the canvas and then the face again.

"It's a good picture," Mr. Lazenby pronounced. "Old-fashioned of course. Early Victorian. But it certainly looks a nice bit of work, don't you think, Mrs. Alleyn?"

"Yes," Troy said. "Yes. It does. Very nice."

She got down from the seat.

"Miss Hewson," she said. "I was in the gallery here this morning. They've got a Constable. One of his big, celebrated, worked-up pieces. I think you should let an expert see this thing because—well because as Mr. Lazenby says it's a very good work of its period and because it might have been painted by the same hand and because—well, if you look closely you will see—it is signed in precisely the same manner."

4

"For pity's sake," Troy said, "don't take my word for anything. I'm not an expert. I can't tell, for instance, how old the actual canvas may be though I do know it's not contemporary and I do know it's the way he signed his major works. 'John Constable. R.A.f.' and the date, 1830, which, I *think,* was soon after he became an R.A."

"R.A.?" asked Miss Hewson.

"Royal Academician."

"Hear that, Earl? What's the 'f' signify, Mrs. Alleyn?"

"Fecit."

There was a considerable pause.

"*Fake* it!" Miss Hewson said in a strangulated voice. "Did you say '*fake*'?"

Dr. Natouche made a curious little sound in his throat. Mr. Lazenby seemed to choke back some furious ejaculation. Troy, with Caley's devilish eye upon her, explained. There was a further silence.

"It's bloody hot down here," said Mr. Pollock.

"Tell us more," Caley invited Troy.

She glared at him and continued. "Of course," she said, "the thing may be a copy of an original Constable. I don't think there's an established work of his that has Ramsdyke Lock as its subject. That doesn't say he didn't paint Ramsdyke Lock when he was in these parts."

"And it doesn't say," Mr. Lazenby added, "that this isn't the Ramsdyke Lock he painted."

Miss Hewson, who seemed never to have heard of Constable until Troy made her remark at Ramsdyke, now became madly excited. She pointed out the excellences of the picture and how you could just fancy yourself walking up that little old-world lane into the sunset.

Mr. Hewson woke up and after listening, in his dead-pan, honest-to-God, dehydrated manner to his sister's ravings asked Troy what, supposing this item was in fact the genuine product of this guy, it might be worth in real money.

Troy said she didn't know—a great deal. Thousands of pounds. It depended upon the present demand for Constables.

"But don't for Heaven's sake go by anything I say. As for forgeries, I am reminded—" She stopped. "I suppose it doesn't really apply," she said. "You'd hardly expect to find an elaborate forgery in a junk-shop yard at Tollardwark, would you?"

"But you were going to tell us a story," Bard said. "Mayn't we have it?"

"It was only that Rory, my husband, had a case quite recently in which a young man, just for the hell of it, forged an Elizabethan glove and did it so well that a top expert was diddled."

"As you say, Mrs. Alleyn," said Mr. Lazenby, "it doesn't really apply. But about forgeries. I always ask myself—"

They were off on an argument that can be depended upon to ruffle more tempers in quicker time than most others. If a forgery was "that good" it could take in the top experts, why wasn't it just as good in every respect as the work of the painter to whom it was falsely attributed?

To and fro went the declarations and aphorisms. Caley Bard was civilized under the heading of "the total oeuvre"; Mr. Hewson said, wryly and obscurely, that every man had his price; Mr. Lazenby upheld a professional view: the forgery was worthless because it was based upon a lie and clerical overtones informed his antipodean delivery. Mr. Pollock's manner was, as usual, a little off-beat. Several times, he interjected: "Oy, chum, half a tick—" only to subside in apparent embarrassment when given the floor. Miss Hewson merely stated, as if informed by an oracle, that she just *knoo* she'd got a genuine old master.

Dr. Natouche excused himself and went below.

And Troy looked at the little picture and was visited once again by the notion that she was involved in some kind of masquerade, that the play, if there was a play, moved towards its climax, if there was a climax, that the tension, if indeed there was any tension, among her fellow-passengers, had been exacerbated by the twist of some carefully concealed screw.

She looked up. Mr. Lazenby's dark glasses were turned on her, Mr. Pollock's somewhat prominent eyes looked into hers and quickly away. Miss Hewson smiled ever so widely at her and Mr. Hewson's dead-pan grin seemed to be plastered over his mouth like a gag.

Troy said good-night to them all and went to bed.

The *Zodiac* left for the return journey before any of the passengers were up.

They had a long morning's cruise, passing through Crossdyke and arriving at Tollardwark at noon.

That evening the Hewsons, Mr. Pollock and Mr. Lazenby played Scrabble. Dr. Natouche wrote letters and Caley Bard suggested a walk but Troy said that she too had letters to write. He pulled a face at her and settled with a book.

Troy supposed that Superintendent Tillottson was in Tollardwark and wondered if he expected her to call. She saw no reason to do so and was sick of confiding nebulous and unconvincing sensations. Nothing of interest to Mr. Tillottson, she thought, had occurred over the past thirty-six hours. He could hardly become alerted by the discovery of a possible "Constable": indeed he could be confidently expected if told about it to regard her with weary tolerance. Still less could she hope to interest him in her own fanciful reactions to an unprovable impression of some kind of conspiracy.

He had promised to let her know by a message to Tollard Lock if there was further news of Alleyn's return. No, there was really no need at all to call on Superintendent Tillottson.

She wrote a couple of short letters to save her face with Caley and at about half-past nine went ashore to post them at the box outside the lockhouse.

The night was warm and still and the air full of pleasant scents from the lock-keeper's garden: stocks, tobacco flower, newly watered earth and at the back of these the cold dank smell of the River. These scents, she thought, made up one of the three elements of night; the next was composed of things that were to be seen before the moon rose: ambiguous pools of darkness, lighted windows, stars, the shapes of trees and the dim whiteness of a bench hard by their moorings. Troy sat there for a time to listen to the third element of night: an owl somewhere in a spinney downstream, the low, intermittent colloquy of moving water, indefinable stirrings, the small flutters and bumps made by flying insects and the homely sound of people talking quietly in the lockhouse and in the saloon of the *Zodiac*.

A door opened and the three Tretheways, who had been spending the evening with the lock-keeper's family, exchanged good-nights and crunched down the gravel path towards Troy.

"Lovely evening, Mrs. Alleyn," Mrs. Tretheway said. The Skipper asked if she was enjoying the cool air and as an afterthought added: "Telegram from Miss Rickerby-Carrick, by the way, Mrs. Alleyn. From Carlisle."

"Oh!" Troy cried, "I *am* glad. Is she all right?"

"Seems so. Er—what *does* she say exactly, dear? Just a minute."

A rustle of paper. Torchlight darted about the Tretheways' faces and settled on a yellow telegram in a brown hand. "'Sorry abrupt departure collected by mutual friends car urgent great friend seriously ill Inverness awfully sad missing cruise cheerio everybody Hay Rickerby-Carrick.'"

"There! *She*'s quite all right, you see," Mrs. Tretheway said comfortably. "It's the friend. Just like they said on the phone at Crossdyke."

"So it wasn't a taxi firm that rang through to Crossdyke," Troy pointed out. "It must have been her friends in the car."

"Unless they were in a taxi and asked the office to ring. Anyway," Mrs. Tretheway repeated, "it's quite all right."

"Yes. It must be," Troy said.

But when she was in bed that night she couldn't help thinking there was still something that didn't quite satisfy her about the departure of Miss Rickerby-Carrick.

"Tomorrow," she thought, "I'll ask Dr. Natouche what he thinks."

Before she went to sleep she found herself listening for the sound she had heard—where? At Tollardwark? At Crossdyke? She wasn't sure—the distant sound of a motor-bicycle. And although there was no such sound to be heard that night she actually dreamt she had heard it.

5

Troy thought: "Today we step back into time." The return journey had taken on something of the character of a recurrent dream: spires, fens, individual trees, locks, even a clod of tufted earth that had fallen away from a bank and was half drowned or a broken branch that dipped into the stream and moved with its flow: these were familiar landmarks that they might have passed, not once, but many times before.

At four in the afternoon the *Zodiac* entered the straight reach of the River below Ramsdyke Lock. Already, drifts of detergent foam had begun to float past her. Wisps of it melted on her deck. Ahead of her the passengers could see an unbroken whiteness that veiled the River like an imponderable counterpane. They could hear the voice of Ramsdyke weir and see a foaming pother where the corrupted fall met the lower reach.

Troy leant on the starboard taffrail and watched their entry into this frothy region. She remembered how she and Dr. Natouche and Caley Bard and Hazel Rickerby-Carrick had discussed reality and beauty. Fragments of conversation drifted across her recollection. She could almost re-hear the voices.

"—in the Eye of the Beholder—"

"—a fish-tin with a red label. Was it the less beautiful—"

"—if a dead something popped up through that foam—"

"—a dead something—"

"—a dead something—"

"—a fish—a cat—"

"—through that foam—"

"—a dead something—"

Hazel Rickerby-Carrick's face, idiotically bloated, looked up: not at Troy, not at anything. Her mouth, drawn into an outlandish rictus, grinned through discoloured froth. She bobbed and bumped against the starboard side. And what terrible disaster had corrupted her river-weed hair and distended her blown cheeks?

The taffrail shot upwards and the trees with it. The voice of the weir exploded with a crack on Troy's head and nothing whatever followed it. Nothing.

VI

RAMSDYKE

"From this point," Alleyn said, "the several elements, if I can put it like that, converge.

"The discovery of this woman's body suddenly threw a complex of apparently unrelated incidents into an integrated whole. You grind away at routine, you collect a vast amount of data ninety-nine per-cent of which is useless, and then something happens and Bingo—the other ten per-cent sits up like Jacky and Bob's your Uncle."

He paused, having astonished himself by this intemperate excursion into jokeyness. He met broad grins from his audience and a startled glance from the man in the second row.

"Oh God, your only jig-maker," thought Alleyn and resumed in a more orthodox style.

"It struck me that there might be some interest—possibly some value—in putting this case before you as it appeared to my wife and as she put it to the county police and in her letters to me. And I wonder if at this juncture you feel you could sort out the evidential wheat from the chaff.

"What, in fact, do you think we ought to have concentrated upon when Inspector Fox and I finally arrived on the scene?"

Alleyn fancied he could detect a certain resentment in the rest of the class when the man in the second row put up his hand.

1

Troy could hear an enormous unlocalized voice in an echo chamber. It approached and enveloped her. It was unalarming.

She emerged with a sickening upward lurch from somewhere that had been like death and for an unappreciable interval was flooded by a delicious surge of recovery. She felt grateful and opened her eyes.

A black face and white teeth were close before her. A recognizable arm supported her.

"You fainted. You are all right. Don't worry."

"I never faint."

"No?"

Fingers on her wrist.

"Why did it happen, I wonder, " said Dr. Natouche. "When you feel more like yourself we will make you comfortable. Will you try a little water?"

Her head was supported. A rim of cold glass pressed her underlip.

"Here are Miss Hewson and Mrs. Tretheway, to help you."

Their faces swam towards her and steadied. Everything had steadied. The passengers stared at her with the greatest concern. Six faces behind Dr. Natouche and Mrs. Tretheway: Miss Hewson with the look of a startled bun, her brother with his hearing-aid and slanted head. Mr. Lazenby's black glasses, Mr. Pollock's ophthalmic stare, like close-ups in a suspense film. And beyond them the Skipper at the wheel.

"Feeling better, honey?" asked Miss Hewson, and then. "Don't look that way, dear. What is it? What's happened?"

"She's frightened," said Mrs. Tretheway.

"Oh God, God, God!" Troy said and her voice sounded in her own ears like that of a stranger: "Oh God, I've remembered."

She turned and clung to Dr. Natouche. "They must stop," she stammered. "Stop. Make them stop. It's Hazel Rickerby-Carrick. There. Back there. In the River."

They broke into commotion. Caley Bard shouted: "You heard what she said. Skipper!"

The *Zodiac* stopped.

Caley Bard knelt beside her. "All right, my dear!" he said. "We've stopped. Don't be frightened. Don't worry. We'll attend to it." And to Dr. Natouche: "Can't we take her down?"

"I think so. Mrs. Alleyn, if we help you, do you think you can manage the stairs? It will be best. We will take it very steadily."

"I'm all right," Troy said. "Please don't worry. I'm perfectly all right. It's not me. Didn't you hear what I said? Back there—in the River."

"Yes, yes. The Captain is attending to it!"

"*Attending* to it!" An ungainly laugh bubbled in Troy's throat. "To *that!* I should hope so! Look, don't fuss about me. I'm all right."

But when they helped her to her feet she was very shaky. Dr. Natouche went backwards before her down the companionway and Caley Bard came behind. The two women followed, making horrified comments.

In the passage her knees gave way. Dr. Natouche carried her into her cabin and put her on her bunk as deftly as if she were a child. The others crowded in the doorway.

"I'm all right," she kept repeating. "It's ridiculous, all this. No—please."

He covered her with the cherry-red blanket and said to Mrs. Tretheway: "A hot-water bottle and tea would not be amiss."

The ladies bustled away in confusion. He stooped his great body over Troy: "You're shocked, Mrs. Alleyn. I hope you will let me advise you."

Troy began to tell them what she had seen. She took a firm hold of herself and spoke lucidly and slowly as if they were stupid men.

"You must tell the police," Troy said. "At once. At once."

Caley Bard said: "Yes, of course. I'm sure the Skipper will know what to do."

"Tell him. It mustn't be—lost—it mustn't be—" she clenched her hands under the blanket. "Superintendent

Tillottson at Tollardwark. Tell the Skipper."

"I'll tell him," Dr. Natouche offered and Caley Bard said: "There now! Don't fuss. And do, like a good girl, stop bossing."

Troy caught the familiar bantering tone and was comforted by it. She and Bard exchanged pallid grins.

"I'll be off," he said.

Dr. Natouche said: "And I. I may be wanted. I think you should stay where you are, Mrs. Alleyn."

He had moved away when Troy, to her own astonishment, heard herself say: "Dr. Natouche!" and when he turned with his calmly polite air, "I—I should like to consult you, please, when you are free. Professionally."

"Of course," he said. "In the meantime these ladies will take care of you."

They did. They ministered with hot-water bottles and with scalding tea. Troy only now realized that she was shivering like a puppy.

Miss Hewson was full of consolatory phrases and horrified speculation.

"Gee," she gabbled, "isn't this just awful? That poor girl and all of us asleep in our beds. What do you figure, Mrs. Tretheway? She was kind of sudden in her reflexes, wasn't she? Now, could it add up this way? She was upset by this news about her girl-friend and she got up and dressed and packed her grip and wrote her little note on the newspaper and lit off for—for wherever she fixed to meet up with her friends and in the dark she—"

Miss Hewson stopped as if jerked to a halt by her listeners' incredulity.

"Well—gee—well, maybe not," she said. "O.K., O.K. Maybe not."

Mrs. Tretheway said: "I don't fancy we do any good by wondering. Not till they know more. Whatever way it turns out, and it looks to me to be a proper mess, it'll bring nothing but worry to us in the *Zodiac;* I know that much."

She took the empty cup from Troy. "You'd best be left quiet," she said. "We'll look in and see how you prosper."

When they had gone Troy lay still and listened. The shivering had stopped. She felt at once drowsy and horrified that she should be so.

By looking up slantways through her open porthole she could see a tree-top. It remained where it was for the most part, only sliding out of its place and returning as the *Zodiac* moved with the River. She heard footfalls overhead and subdued voices and, after an undefined interval, a police siren. It came nearer and stopped. More and heavier steps on deck. More and newer voices, very subdued. This continued for some time. She half-dozed, half-woke.

She was roused by something outside that jarred against the port wall of the *Zodiac* and by the clunk of oars in their rollocks and the dip and drip of the blades.

"Easy as you go, then," said a voice very close at hand. "Shove off a bit." The top of a helmet moved across the porthole. "That's right. Just a wee bit over. Hold her at that, now. Careful now."

Superintendent Tillottson. On the job.

Troy knew with terrible accuracy what was being done on the other side of the cabin wall. She was transfixed in her own vision and hag-ridden by a sick idea that there was some obligation upon her to stand on her bunk and look down into nightmare. She knew this idea was a fantasy but she was deadly afraid that she would obey its compulsion.

"All right. Give way and easy. Easy as you go."

"I can't."

"What? *What?*"

"It's foul of something."

"Here. Hold on."

"Look there, Super. Look."

"All right, all right. Hold steady again and I'll see."

"What is it, then?"

"A line. Cord. Round the waist and made fast to something."

"Will we cut it?"

"Wait while I try a wee haul. *Hold steady,* I said. Now then."

An interval with heavy breathing.

"Coming up. Here she comes."

"*Suitcase?*"

"That's right. Now. Bear a hand to ship it. It's bloody heavy. God, don't do that, man. We don't want any more disfigurement."

A splash and then a thud.

"Fair enough. Now, you can give way. Signal the ambulance, Sarge. Handsomely, now."

The rhythmic clunk, dip and drip, receding.

Troy thought with horror: "They're towing her. It's *Our Mutual Friend* again. Through the detergent foam. They'll life her out, dripping foam, and put her on a stretcher and into an ambulance and drive her away. There'll be an autopsy and an inquest and I'll have to say what I saw and, please God, Rory will be back."

The *Zodiac* trembled. Trees and blue sky with a wisp of cloud moved across the porthole. For a minute or so they were under way and then she felt the slight familiar shock when the craft came up to her mooring.

Miss Hewson opened the door and looked in. She held a little bottle rather coyly between thumb and forefinger and put her head on one side like her brother.

"Wide awake?" she said. "I guess so. Now, look what I've brought!"

She tiptoed the one short space between the door and the bunk and stopped. Her face really was like a bun, Troy thought, with currants for eyes and holes for nostrils and a bit of candy-peel for a mouth. She shrank back a little from Miss Hewson's face.

"I just knew how you'd be. All keyed-up like nobody's business. And I brought you my Trankwitones. You needn't feel any hesitation about using them, dear. They're recommended by pretty well every darn doctor in the States and they just act—"

The voice droned on. Miss Hewson was pouring water into Troy's glass.

"Miss Hewson, you're terribly kind but I don't need anything like that. Really. I'm perfectly all right now and very much ashamed of myself."

"Now, listen dear—"

"No, truly. Thank you *very* much but I'd rather not."

"You know something? Mama's going to get real tough with baby—"

"But, Miss Hewson, I promise you I don't want—"

"May I come in?" said Dr. Natouche.

Miss Hewson turned sharply and for a moment they faced each other.

"I think," he said, and it was the first time Troy had heard him speak to her, "that Mrs. Alleyn is in no need of sedation, Miss Hewson."

"Well, I'm surely not aiming—I just thought if she could get a little sleep—I—"

"That was very kind but there is no necessity for sedation."

"Well—I certainly wouldn't want to—"

"I'm sure you wouldn't. If I may just have a word with my patient."

"Your patient! Pardon me. I was not aware—well, pardon me, *Doctor*," said Miss Hewson with a spurt of venom in her voice and slammed the door on her exit.

Troy said hurriedly: "I want to talk to you. It's about what we discussed before. About Miss Rickerby-Carrick, Dr. Natouche, have you seen—"

"Yes," he said. "They asked me to make an examination—a very superficial examination, of course."

"I could hear them, outside there. I could hear what they found. She's been murdered, hasn't she? Hasn't she?"

He leant over the bunk and shut the porthole. He drew up the little stool and sat on it, leaning towards her. "I think," he said as softly as his huge voice permitted, "we should be careful." His fingers closed professionally on Troy's wrist.

"You could lock the door," she said.

"So I could." He did so and turned back to her.

"Until the autopsy," he murmured, "it will be impossible to say whether she was drowned or not. Externally, in most respects, it would appear that she was. It can be argued, and no doubt it will be argued, that she committed suicide by weighting her suitcase and tying it to herself and perhaps throwing herself into the River from the weir bridge."

"If that was so, what becomes of the telephone call and the telegram from Carlisle?"

"I cannot think of any answer consistent with suicide."

"Murder, then?"

"It would seem so."

"I am going to tell you something. It's complicated and a

bit nebulous but I want to tell you. First of all—my cabin.
You know it was booked—"

"To somebody called Andropoulos? I saw the paragraph
in the paper. I did not speak of it as I thought it would be
unpleasant for you."

"Did any of the others?"

"Not to my knowledge."

"I'll make this as quick and as clear as I can. It has to do
with a case of my husband's. There's a man called
Foljambe—"

A crisp knock on her door and Superintendent Tillottson's voice: "Mrs. Alleyn? Tillottson, here. May I come in."

Troy and Dr. Natouche stared at each other. She
whispered: "He'll have to," and called out: "Come in, Mr.
Tillottson." At the same time Dr. Natouche opened the door.

Suddenly the little cabin was crammed with enormous
men. Superintendent Tillottson and Doctor Natouche were
both over six feet tall and comparably broad. She began to
introduce these mammoths to each other and then relaized
they had been introduced already in hideous formality by
Hazel Rickerby-Carrick. She could not help looking at Mr.
Tillottson's large pink hands which were a little puckered as if
he had been doing the washing. She was very glad he did not
offer one to her, after his hearty fashion, for shaking.

She said: "Dr. Natouche is looking after me on account of
my making a perfect ass of myself."

Mr. Tillottson said, with a sort of wide spread of
blandness, that this was very nice. Dr. Natouche then advised
Troy to take things easy and left them.

Troy pushed back the red blanket, sat up on her bunk, put
her feet on the deck and ran her fingers through her short
hair. "Well, Mr. Tillottson," she said, "what about this one?"

2

With the exception of Chief-Inspector Fox, for whom she
had a deep affection, Troy did not meet her husband's
colleagues with any regularity. Sometimes Alleyn would
bring a few of them in for drinks and two or three times a year
the Alleyns had easy-going evenings when their house, like

Troy's cabin in the *Zodiac,* was full of enormous men talking shop.

From these encounters she had, she thought, learnt to recognize certain occupational characteristics among officers of the Criminal Investigation Department.

They were men who, day in, day out, worked in an atmosphere of intense hostility. They were, they would have said, without illusions and, unless a built-in skepticism by definition includes a degree of illusion, she supposed they were right. Some of them, she thought, had retained a kind of basic compassion: they were shocked by certain crimes and angered by others. They honestly saw themselves as guardians of the peace, however disillusioned they might be as to the character of the beings they protected. Some regarded modern psychiatric theories about crime with massive contempt. Others seemed to look upon the men and women they hunted with a kind of sardonic affection and would strike up what passed for friendships with them. Many of them, like Fox, were of a very kindly disposition, yet, as Alleyn once said of them, if pity entered far into the hunter his occupation was gone. And he had quoted Mark Antony who talked about "pity choked with custom of fell deeds." Some of the men she met were bitter, and with reason, about public attitudes towards the police. "A character comes and robs their tills or does their old Mum or interferes with their kid sister," Mr. Fox once remarked, "and they're all over you. Next day they're among the pigeons in Trafalgar Square advising the gang our chaps are trying to deal with to put in the boot. You could say it's a lonely sort of job."

Very few of Alleyn's colleagues, Troy thought, were natural bullies, but it was to be expected that the Service would occasionally attract such men and that its disciplines would sometimes fail to control them.

At which point in her consideration of the genus of C.I.D. Troy was invariably brought up short by the reflection that her husband fitted into none of these categories. And she would give up generalization as a bad job.

Now, however, she found herself trying to place Superintendent Tillottson and was unable to do so.

How tough was Mr. Tillottson? How intelligent? How impenetrable? And what on earth did he now make of the cruise of the *Zodiac?* If he carried on in his usual way, ironing out her remarks into a featureless expanse of words, she would feel like hitting him.

So. "What do you make of this one?" she asked and heard his "Well, now, Mrs. Alleyn—" before he said it.

"Well, now, Mrs. Alleyn," said Mr. Tillottson and she cut in.

"Has she been murdered? Or can't you say until after the autopsy?"

"We can't say," he admitted, looking wary, "until after the inquest. Not on—er—on—er—"

"The external appearance of her body?"

"That is so, Mrs. Alleyn. That is correct, yes."

"Have you heard that last night the Skipper got a telegram purporting to come from her? From Carlisle? Intimating she was on her way to the Highlands?"

"We have that information, Mrs. Alleyn. Yes."

"Well, then?"

Mr. Tillottson coined a phrase: "It's quite a little problem," he said.

"You," Troy said with feeling, "are telling me." She indicated the stool. "Do sit down, Mr. Tillottson," she said.

He thanked her and did so, obliterating the stool.

"I suppose," she continued, "you want a statement from me, don't you?"

He became cautiously playful. "I see you know all about routine, Mrs. Alleyn. Well, yes, if you've no objection, just a wee statement. Seeing you, as you might say—"

"Discovered the body?"

"That is so, Mrs. Alleyn."

Troy said rapidly: "I was on deck on the port side at the after-end, I think you call it. I leant on the rail and looked at the water which was covered with detergent foam. We were, I suppose, about two chains below Ramsdyke weir and turning towards the Lock. I saw it—I saw her face—through the foam. At first I only thought—I thought—"

"I'm sure it was very unpleasant."

She felt that to concede this understatement would be to give ground before Mr. Tillottson.

"I thought it was something else: a trick of light and colour. And then the foam broke and I saw. That's all really. I

don't think I called out. I'm not sure. Very stupidly, I fainted.
Mr. Tillottson," Troy hurried on, "we know she left the
Zodiac sometime during the night before last at Crossdyke.
She slept on deck, that night."

"Yes?" he asked quickly. "On deck? Sure?"

"Didn't you know?"

"I haven't had the opportunity as yet, to get what you'd
call the full picture."

"No, of course not. She told Dr. Natouche she meant to
sleep on deck. She complained of insomnia. And I think she
must have done so because he and I found a bit of cloth from
the cover of her diary—you know I told you how it went
overboard—on her lie-low mattress."

"Not necessarily left there during the night, though,
would you say?"

"Perhaps not. It was discoloured. I think Dr. Natouche
has kept it."

"*Has* he? Now why would the Doctor do that, I wonder."

"Because I asked him to."

"You *did!*"

"We were both a bit worried about her. Well, *you* know *I*
was, don't you? I told you."

Mr. Tillottson at once looked guarded. "That's so, Mrs.
Alleyn," he said. "You did mention it. Yerse."

"There's one thing I want you to tell me. I daresay I've got
no business to pester you but I hope you won't mind too
much."

"Well, of course not. Naturally not, I'm sure."

"It's just this. If it is found to be homicide you won't, will
you, entertain any idea of her having been set upon by thugs
when she went ashore in the night? That can't be the case,
possibly, can it?"

"We always like to keep an open mind."

"Yes, but you can't, can you, keep an open mind about
that one? Because if she was killed by some unknown thug,
who on earth sent the telegram from Carlisle?"

"We'll have to get you in the Force, Mrs. Alleyn. I can see
that," he joked uneasily.

"I know I'm being a bore."

"Not at all."

"But you see," Troy couldn't resist adding, "it's because of all those silly little things I told you about at the police stations. They don't sound quite so foolish, now. Or do they?"

"Er—no. No. You may be quite sure, Mrs. Alleyn, that we won't neglect any detail, however small."

"Of course. I know."

"I might just mention, Mrs. Alleyn, that since we had our last chat we've re-checked on the whereabouts of the passengers over last weekend. They're O.K. The Hewson couple were in Stratford-upon-Avon. Mr. Pollock did stay in Birmingham. Dr. Natouche *was* in Liverpool, and—"

"But—that's all before the cruise began!"

"Yerse," he said and seemed to be in two minds what to say next. "Still," he said, "as far as it goes, there it is," and left it at that.

"Please, Mr. Tillottson, there's only one more thing. Had she—did you find anything round her neck. A cord or tape with a sort of little bundle on it. Sewn up, I fancy, in chamois leather?"

"No," he said sharply. "Nothing like that. Did she wear something of that nature?"

"Yes," Troy said. "She did. It was—I know this sounds fantastic but it's what she told me—it was an extremely valuable Fabergé jewel representing the signs of the zodiac and given to her grandfather who was a surgeon, by, believe it or not, the Czar of Russia. She told me she never took it off. Except one supposes when she—" Troy stopped short.

"Did she talk about it to anyone else, Mrs. Alleyn?"

"I understood she'd told Miss Hewson about it."

"There you are! The foolishness of some ladies."

"I know."

"Well, now," he said. "This is interesting. This is quite interesting, Mrs. Alleyn."

"You're thinking of motive."

"We have to think of everything," he sighed portentously. "Everything."

"I suppose," Troy said, "you've looked in her suitcase."

She thought how preposterous it was that she should be asking the question and said to herself: "If it wasn't for Rory, he'd have slapped me back long ago."

He said: "That would be routine procedure, wouldn't it, Mrs. Alleyn?"

"You were alongside this cabin when you—when you— were in that boat. The porthole was open. I heard about the suitcase."

He glanced with something like irritation at the porthole.

"There's nothing of the nature of the object you describe in the suitcase," he said and stood up with an air of finality. "I expect you'll appreciate, Mrs. Alleyn, that we'll ask for signed statements from all the personnel in this craft."

"Yes, of course."

"I've suggested they assemble in the saloon upstairs for a preliminary interview. You're feeling quite yourself again—?"

"Quite, thank you."

"That's fine. In about five mintues, then?"

"Certainly."

When he had gone, softly closing the door behind him, Troy tidied herself up. The face that looked out of her glass was pretty white and her hand was not perfectly steady but she was all right. She straightened the red blanket and turned to the washbasin. The tumbler had been half-filled with water and placed on the shelf. Beside it were two capsules.

Trankwitones, no doubt.

Presistent woman: Miss Hewson.

Never in her life, Troy thought, had she felt lonelier. Never had she wished more heartily for her husband's return.

She believed she knew now for certain what had happened to Hazel Rickerby-Carrick. She had been murdered and her murderer was aboard the *Zodiac*.

"But," she thought, "it may stop there. She told Miss Hewson about the jewel and Miss Hewson may well have told—who? Her brother almost certainly and perhaps Mr. Pollock with whom they seemed to be pretty thick. Or the Tretheways? For a matter of that, every man and woman of us may know about the thing and the ones like Dr. Natouche and Caley Bard and me may simply have used discretion and held their tongues.

"And then it might follow that some single one of us," she thought, "tried to steal the jewel when she was asleep on deck and she woke and would have screamed and given him—or her—away and so she got her quietus. But after that—? Here's a nightmarish sort of thing—after that how did poor Hazel get to Ramsdyke weir seven miles or more upstream?"

She remembered that Miss Rickerby-Carrick had been presented with some of Miss Hewson's Trankwitones and that Dr. Natouche had said they were unknown to him.

Now. Was there any reason to suppose that the case didn't stop there but reached out all round itself like a spider to draw in Andropoulos and behind Andropoulos, the shadowy figure of Foljambe? The Jampot? The ultra-clever one?

Was it too fantastic, *now,* to think the Jampot might be on board? And if he was? Well, Troy thought, she couldn't for the life of her name her fancy. Figures, recalled by a professional memory, swam before her mind's eye, each in its way outlandish—black patch, deaf ear, club foot, and with a sort of mental giggle she thought: "If it's Caley I've been kissed by a triple murderer and Rory can put *that* on his needles and knit it."

At this point Mrs. Tretheway's little bell that she rang for meal-times tinkled incisively. Troy opened the door and heard Tillottson's paddy voice and a general stir as of an arrival. While she listened, trying to interpret these sounds, the cabin door on her left opened and Mr. Lazenby came out. He turned and stood on her threshold and they were face-to-face. Even as close to him as she was now Troy could make nothing of the eyes behind the dark glasses and this circumstance lent his face an obviously sinister look as if he were a character out of an early Hitchcock film.

"You are better?" he asked. "I was about to inquire. I'm afraid you were very much upset and distressed. As indeed we all are. Oh, *terribly* distressed. Poor soul! Poor quaint, kindly soul! It's hard to believe she's gone."

"I don't find it so," Troy snapped.

She saw his lips settle in a rather sharp line. There was a further subdued commotion somewhere on deck. Troy listened for a second. A new voice sounded and her heart began to thud against her ribs.

"If a poor parson may make a suggestion, Mrs. Alleyn," Mr. Lazenby said and seemed to peer at her. "I think perhaps you should leave the *Zodiac*. You have had a great shock. You look—" The bell rang again. He turned his head sharply and the spectacles moved. For a fraction of a second Troy caught a glimpse of the left eye-socket behind its dark window. There was no eye in it.

And then she heard a very deep voice at the head of the companionway.

Without thought or conscious effort she was past Mr. Lazenby, out of the cabin, up the stairs and into her husband's arms.

3

Of course it was an extraordinary situation. She could think: "How extraordinary" even while her delight in his return sang so loudly it was enough to deafen her to anything else.

There had been some sort of explanation at large—introductions even—to whoever had been in the saloon followed by a retreat with Alleyn to her cabin. She remembered afterwards that they had encountered Mr. Lazenby in the passage.

Now they sat, side by side, on her bunk and she thought she could cope with Catastrophe itself.

He put his arm round her and swore briefly but violently, asking her what the bloody hell she thought she was doing and giving her a number of hasty but well-planted embraces. This she found satisfactory. He then said they couldn't sit down here on their bottoms all day and invited her to relate as quickly as possible anything she thought he ought to know.

"I've heard your extraordinary spinster's been found in the river and that you were the first to see her. Tillottson seems to think it's a case of foul play. Otherwise I know nothing beyond what you wrote in your last letters which I got the day before yesterday. Look at you. You're as white as a sheet. Troy, my darling."

"It only happened a couple of hours ago, you might remember. Don't fuss. Rory, there's so much to tell and I'm meant to be upstairs being grilled with the others."

"To hell with that. No. Wait a bit. I think we must listen to Tillottson in action. I've thrown him into a fine old tizzy, anyway, by turning up. Tell me quickly, then: what's happened since you posted your last letter at Tollardwark four days ago?"

"It seems more like four weeks. All right. Listen."

She told him about the diary going overboard, the behaviour of Mr. Lazenby, the disappearance of Hazel Rickerby-Carrick, her sense of growing tension and Miss Hewson's discovery of the "Constable."

"There are a lot of other little things that seemed odd to me but those are the landmarks."

"We'll have the whole saga in detail later on. You've put me far enough in the picture for the moment. Come on. Let's give Tillottson a treat. I've arranged to sit in."

So they went upstairs. There were the other passengers in an uneasy row on the semicircular bench at the end of the saloon: the Hewsons, Mr. Pollock, Mr. Lazenby, Caley Bard and, a little apart as always, Dr. Natouche. The Tretheways were grouped together near the bar.

Facing the passengers at a dining table were Superintendent Tillottson and a uniformed sergeant.

Troy sat by Dr. Natouche who, with Caley Bard, rose at her approach. Alleyn stayed at the other end of the saloon. The *Zodiac* was tied up alongside the wapentake side of the river below Ramsdyke Lock, and the shapeless thunder of the weir could be distinctly heard. Scurries of detergent foam were blown past the open windows.

It was easy to see that Mr. Tillottson suffered from a deep embarrassment. He looked at Troy and cleared his throat, he turned and nodded portentously to Alleyn. His neck turned red and he pursed up his lips to show that the situation was child's play to him.

"Yerse, well now," Mr. Tillottson said. "I think if you don't mind, ladies and gentlemen, we'll just have a wee recap. I'll go over the information we have produced about this unfortunate lady and I'll be obliged if you'll correct me if I go wrong."

The Sergeant pushed his book across. Mr. Tillottson put on a pair of spectacles and began to summarize, consulting the notes from time to time.

It was very soon clear to Troy that he refreshed his memory, not only from the Sergeant's notes on what the passengers had divulged, but also from the information she had given him on her three visits to police stations. Particularly was this apparent when he outlined the circumstances of Hazel Rickerby-Carrick's disappearance. Troy sensed her companions' surprise at Mr. Tillottson's omniscience. How, they must surely be asking themselves, had he found time to make so many inquiries? Or would they merely put it all down to the expeditious methods of our county police?

She glanced quickly at Alleyn and saw one eyebrow go up.

Mr. Tillottson himself evidently realized his mistake. His résumé became a trifle scrambled and ended abruptly.

"Well now," he said. "Ladies and gentlemen, since we are all agreed that as far as they go, these are the facts, I won't trouble you any more just now except to say that I hope you will all complete your cruise. The craft will proceed shortly to a mooring above Ramsdyke Lock where she will tie up for the night and she will return to Norminster at about eleven o'clock tomorrow morning. I'm afraid I shall have to ask you to remain within reach for the inquest which will probably be held the following day. In Norminster. If there is any trouble about securing accommodation, my department will be glad to assist."

Upon this the Hewsons broke into vehement expostulation, complaining that they were on a tight schedule and were due next evening to make a connection for Perth, Scotland.

Caley Bard said that with any luck they might meet up with Mavis and everybody but Troy and Dr. Natouche looked shocked. Miss Hewson said if that was a specimen of British humour she did not, for her part, appreciate it, and Mr. Hewson said he did not find himself in stitches either.

Mr. Lazenby asked if—since all their accounts of the affair agreed—it would not be acceptable for them to be represented at the inquest by (as it were) a spokesman, and it was clear that he did not cast himself for this role. He had important appointments with ecclesiastical big-wigs in London and was loath to forgo them. He developed antipodean-type resentment and began to speak of the reactionary conduct of pom policemen. He said: "Good on you," to the Hewsons and formed an alliance.

Caley Bard said it was an unconscionable bore but one didn't, after all, fish corpses out of waterways every day of the week and he would resign himself to the ruling. He grew less popular with every word he uttered.

Mr. Pollock whined. He wanted to know why they couldn't sign a joint statement, for God's sake, and then bugger off if the ladies would excuse the expression.

Everybody except Caley Bard, Troy and Alleyn looked scandalized and Mr. Lazenby expostulated.

Dr. Natouche asked if, since his practice was within reasonable driving distance of Norminster, he might be summoned from thence. He realized, of course, that as he had made the preliminary examination he would be required to give evidence under that heading.

Mr. Tillottson glanced at Alleyn and then said he thought that would be quite in order.

He now asked to see the passports of Mr. Lazenby and the Hewsons and they were produced, Mr. Lazenby taking the opportunity to complain about the treatment of Australian visitors at British Customs. Mr. Tillottson said the passports would be returned and shifted his feet about as a preface to rising.

It was now that Mr. Lazenby suddenly said, "I'm puzzled." And Troy thought, "Here we go."

"I'd like to ask," he said, and he seemed to be looking at her, "just how the police have come by some of their information. When did the Superintendent find the opportunity to make the necessary inquiries? To the best of my belief, from the time he got here until this present moment, the Superintendent has been on the river or here in this boat. If you don't object, Superintendent, I think this calls for an explanation. Just to keep the record straight."

"Blimey, chum, you're right!" Mr. Pollock exclaimed and the Hewsons broke into a little paean of agreement. They all stared at Troy.

Mr. Tillottson made an almost instant recovery. He looked straight before him and said that he happened to receive information about Miss Rickerby-Carrick's mode of departure and had thought it unusual enough to warrant a routine inquiry.

And from whom, if the Superintendent didn't mind, Mr. Lazenby persisted, had he received this information.

Troy heard herself, as if it were with somebody else's voice saying: "It was from me. I think you all know I called at the police station at Tollardwark. I happened in the course of conversation to say something about Miss Rickerby-Carrick's unexpected departure."

"Quite so," said Mr. Tillottson. "That is correct."

"And I imagine," Caley Bard said angrily, "you have no objections to that perfectly reasonable explanation, Mr. Lazenby."

"Certainly not. By no means. One only wanted to know."

"And now one does know, one may as well pipe down."

"There's no call to take that tone," Mr. Pollock said. "We didn't mean anything personal."

"Then what the hell did you mean?"

"Gentlemen!" Mr. Tillottson almost shouted and they subsided. "A statement," he said, "will be typed on the lines of your information. You will be asked to look it over and if you find it correct, to sign it. I have only one other remark to make, ladies and gentlemen. As you have already been informed, we have Superintendent Alleyn, C.I.D., with us. Mr. Alleyn came, you might say, on unofficial business." Here Mr. Tillottson ducked his head at Troy, "But I don't have to tell him we'll be very glad of his advice in a matter which I'm sure everybody wants to see cleared up to the satisfaction of all concerned. Thank you."

Having wound himself into a cocoon of generalities Mr. Tillottson added that as the afternoon was rather close he was sure they would all like a breath of air. Upon this hint the passengers retired above. Troy after a look from Alleyn went with them. She noticed that Dr. Natouche remained below.

It seemed to her that the Hewsons and Mr. Lazenby and Mr. Pollock were in two minds as to what attitude they would adopt towards her. After a short and uncomfortable silence, Mr. Lazenby settled this problem by bearing down upon her with his widest smile.

"Happy now, Mrs. Alleyn?" he fluted. "I'll bet! And I must say, without, I hope, being uncharitable, we all ought to congratulate ourselves on your husband's arrival. Really," Mr. Lazenby said, looking—or seeming to look—about him. "It would almost seem that he was Sent."

It was from this moment that Troy began to suspect Mr.
Lazenby, in spite of the Bishop of Norminster, of not being a
clergyman.

He had sparked off a popularity poll in favour of Troy.
Miss Hewson said that maybe she wasn't qualified to speak
but she certainly did not know what was with this cop and for
her money the sooner Alleyn set up a regular investigation
the better she'd feel and Mr. Pollock hurriedly agreed.

Caley Bard watched this demonstration with a scarcely
veiled expression of glee. He strolled over to Troy and said:
"We don't know yet, though, or do we, if the celebrated
husband *is* going to act."

"I'm sure *I* don't," she said. "They have to be asked. They
don't just waltz in because they happen to be on the spot."

"I suppose you're enchanted to see him."

"Of course I am."

"That monumental creature seemed to indicate a
collaboration, didn't you think?"

"Well, yes. But it'd all be by arrangement with head
office."

"Hullo," he said, "we're going through the lock."

"Thank God!" Troy ejaculated.

It would be something—it would be a great deal—to get
out of that region of polluted foam. Troy had been unable to
look at the River since she came on deck.

They slipped into the clear dark waters, the sluice-gates
were shut, the paddles set, and the familiar slow ascent
began. She moved to the after-end of the *Zodiac* and Caley
Bard joined her there.

"I don't know if it has occurred to you," he said, "that
everybody is cutting dead, the obvious inference."

"Inference?"

"Well—question if you prefer. Aren't we all asking
ourselves whether the ebullient Hay has been made away
with?"

After a pause, Troy said: "I suppose so."

"Well, of course we are. We'd be certifiable if we didn't.
Do you mind talking about it?"

"I think it's worse not to do so."

"I couldn't agree more. Have you heard what they
found?"

"In the River?"

"Yes."

"I *did* hear a good deal. In my cabin."

"I was on deck. I saw."

"How horrible," said Troy.

But she was not as deeply horrified as she might have been because her attention was rivited by a pair of large, neat and highly polished boots and decent iron-grey trousers on the rim of the lock above her. They looked familiar. She tilted her head back and was rewarded by a worm's-eye view in violent perspective of the edge of a jacket, the modest swell of a stomach and the underneath of a massive chin, a pair of nostrils and the brim of a hat.

As the *Zodiac* quietly rose in the lock, these items resolved themselves into an unmistakable whole.

"Well," Troy thought, "this settles it. It's a case," and when she found herself sufficiently elevated to do so without absurd contortion, she addressed herself to the person now revealed.

"Hullo, Br'er Fox," she said.

4

"What was *said,*" Fox explained, "was this. Tillottson's asked for us to come in. He rang the department on finding the body. The A.C. said that as you've been in on this Jampot thing from the time it came our way, the only sensible course is for you to follow it up. Regardless, as it were. And I've been shot up here by plane to act as your support and to let you know how things stand on my file. Which is a nice way of saying how big a bloody fool I've been made to look by this expert."

"But who says this is a Jampot affair, may I ask?" Alleyn crossly interjected.

"The A.C. works it out that this job up here, this river job, ought properly be regarded as a possible lead on Foljambe. On account of the Andropoulos connection. Having been made a monkey of," Fox added with feeling, "by a faked-up false scent to Paris, I don't say I reacted with enthusiasm to his theories, but you have to look at these things with what

I've heard you call a disparate eye."

"I entirely agree. And that, under the circumstances, is something I cannot be expected to do. Look here, Fox. Here's Troy, one of a group of people who, if this woman was murdered, and I'll bet she was, come into the field of police investigation: right?"

"The A.C. says it'll be nicer for you to be here with her."

"That be damned! What? Me? Needle my wife? Give her the old one-two treatment if she doesn't provide all the answers? *Nicer?*"

"It won't," Fox said, "be as bad as that now, will it?"

"I can't tell you how much I dislike having her mixed up in any of our shows. I came here to get her out of it. Not to take on a bloody homicide job."

"I know that. It's a natural reaction," Mr. Fox said. "Both of you being what you are."

"I don't know what you mean by that."

"Suppose you didn't take the case, Mr. Alleyn. What's the drill on that one? Somebody else comes up from the Yard and you hand him the file. And is his face red! He goes ahead and you clear out leaving Mrs. Alleyn here to get through the routine as best she can."

"You know damn' well that's grotesque."

"Well, Mr. Alleyn, the alternative's not to your fancy either, is it?"

"If you put it like that the only thing that remains for me to do is to retire in a hurry and to hell wih the pension."

"Oh, now! Come, come!"

"All right. *All* right. I'm unreasonable under this heading and we both know it."

Fox mildly contemplated his superior officer. "I can see it's awkward," he said. "It's not what we'd choose. You're thinking about her position and how it'll appear to others and what say the Press get on to it, I daresay. But if you ask me it won't be so bad. It's only until the inquest."

"And in the meantime what's the form? We've issued orders that they're all to stay in that damned boat tonight, one of them almost certainly being the Rickerby-Carrick's murderer and just possibly the toughest proposition in homicide on either side of the Atlantic. I can't withdraw my wife and insist on keeping the others here. Well, can I? Can I?"

"It might be awkward," said Fox. "But you could."

They fell silent and as people do when they come to a blind wall in a conversation, stared vaguely about them. A lark sang, a faint breeze lifted the long grass, and in the excavation below the wapentake, sand and gravel fell with a whisper of sound from the grassy overhang.

"That's very dangerous," Fox said absently. "That place. Kids might get in there. If they interfered with those props, anything could happen." He stood up, eased his legs and looked down at the River. It was masked by a rising mist.

The *Zodiac* was moored for the night some distance above Ramsdyke Lock. The passengers were having their dinner, Mr. Tillottson and his sergeant being provided for at an extra table. Alleyn had had a moment or two with Troy and had suggested that she might slip away and join them if an opportunity presented itself. If, however, she could not do so without attracting a lot of attention she was to go early to bed and lock her door. He would come to her later and she was to unlock it to nobody else. To which she had replied: "Well, naturally," and he had said she knew damned well what he meant and they had broken into highly inappropriate laughter. He and Fox had then walked up to the wapentake where at least they were able to converse above a mutter.

"There is," Alleyn said, "a vacant cabin, of course. Now."

"That's right."

"I tell you what, Fox. We'll have a word with the Skipper and take it over. We'll search and we'll need a warrant."

"I picked one up on my way from the beak at Tollardwark. He didn't altogether see it but changed his mind when I talked about the Foljambe connection."

"As well he might. One of us could doss down in the cabin for the night if there's any chance of a bit of kip which is not likely. It'd be a safety measure."

"You," said Fox, "if it suits. I've dumped a homicide bag at the Ramsdyke Arms."

"Tillottson kept his head and had the cabin locked. He says it's full of junk. We'll get the key off him. Look who's here."

It was Troy, coming into the field from Dyke Way by the top gate. Alleyn thought: "I wonder how rare it is for a man's heart to behave as mine does at the unexpected sight of his wife."

Fox said: "I'll nip along to the pub, shall I, and settle for my room and bring back the kit and something to eat. Then you can relieve Tillottson and start on the cabin. Will I ring the Yard and get the boys sent up?"

"Yes," Alleyn said. "Yes. Better do that. Thank you, Br'er Fox." By "the boys" Mr. Fox meant Sergeants Bailey and Thompson, fingerprint and photograph experts who normally worked with Alleyn.

"We'll need a patrol," Alleyn said, "along the river from Tollard Lock to where she was found, and we'll have to make a complete and no doubt fruitless search of the towpath and surroundings. You'd better get on to that, Fox. Take the Sergeant with you. Particular attention to the moorings at Crossdyke and the area round Ramsdyke weir."

"Right, I'll be off, then."

He started up the hill towards Troy looking, as always, exactly what he was. An incongruous figure, was Mr. Fox in that still mediaeval landscape. They met and spoke and Fox moved on to the gate.

Alleyn watched Troy come down the hill and went out of the wapentake to meet her.

"They've all gone ashore," she said. "I *think* to talk about me. Except Dr. Natouche who's putting finishing touches to his map. They're sitting in a huddle in the middle distance of the view that inspired the original remark about Constables. I expect you must push on with routine, mustn't you? What haven't I told you that you ought to know? Should I fill you in, as Miss Hewson would say, on some of the details?"

"Yes, darling, fill me in, do. I'll ask questions, shall I? It might be quickest. And you add anything—anything at all— that you think might be, however remotely, to the point. Shall we go?"

"Fire ahead," said Troy.

During this process Troy's answers became more and more staccato and her face grew progressively whiter. Alleyn watched her with an attentiveness that she wondered if she dreaded and knew that she loved. She answered his final question and said in a voice that sounded shrilly in her own ears: "There. Now you know as much as I do. See."

"What is it?" he asked. "Tell me."

"She scratched on my door," Troy said. "And when I opened it she'd gone away. She wanted to tell me something and I let Mr. Lazenby rescue me because I had a migraine and because she was such a bore. She was unhappy and who can tell what might have been the outcome if I'd let her confide? Who can tell *that!*"

"I *think* I can. I don't believe that it would, and I promise you this, it wouldn't have made the smallest difference to what happened to her. And I'll promise you as well, that if it turns out otherwise I shall say so."

"I can't forgive myself."

"Yes, you can. Is one never to run away from a bore for fear she'll be murdered?"

"Oh Rory."

"All right, darling. I know. And I tell you what—I'm glad you had your migraine and I'm bloody glad she didn't talk to you. Now, then. Better?"

"A bit."

"Good. One more question. That junk shop in Tollardwark where you encountered the Hewsons. Did you notice the name of the street?"

"I think it was Ferry Lane."

"You wouldn't know that name of the shop?"

"No," Troy said doubtfully. "It was so dark. I don't think I saw. But—wait a bit—yes: on a very dilapidated little sign in Dr. Natouche's torchlight. 'Jno. Bagg: Licensed Dealer.'"

"Good. And it was there they made their haul?"

"That's right. They went back there from Longminster. On Wednesday."

"Do you think it might be a Constable?"

"I've no idea. It's in his manner and it's extremely well painted."

"What was the general reaction to the find?"

"The Hewsons are going to show it to an expert. If it's genuine I think they plan to come back and scour the district for more. I rather fancy Lazenby's got the same idea."

"And you've doubts about him being a parson?"

"Yes. I don't know why."

"No eye in the left socket?"

"It was only a glimpse but I don't think so. Rory—?"

"Yes?"

"The man who killed Andropoulos—Foljambe—the Jampot. Do you know what he looks like?"

"Not really. We've got a photograph but Santa Claus isn't more heavily bearded, and his hair, which looks fairish, covers his ears. It was taken over two years ago and is not a credit to the Bolivian photographer. He had both his eyes then but we *have* heard indirectly that he received some sort of injury after he escaped and lay doggo with it for a time. One report was that it was facial and another that it wasn't. There was a third rumour thought to have originated in the South that he'd undergone an operation to change his appearance but none of this stuff was dependable. We think it likely that there is some sort of physical abnormality."

"Please tell me, Rory. *Please*. Do you think he's on board?"

And because Alleyn didn't at once protest, she said: "You do. Don't you? Why?"

"Before I got here, I would have said there was no solid reason to suppose it. On your letters and on general circumstances. Now, I'm less sure."

"Is it because of—have you seen—?"

"The body? Yes, it's largely because of that."

"Then—what—?"

"We'll have to wait for the autopsy. I don't think they'll find she drowned, Troy. I think she was killed in precisely the same way as Andropoulos was killed. And I think it was done by the Jampot."

VII

ROUTINE

"And so," Alleyn said, "we set up the appropriate routine and went to work in the usual way. Tillottson was understaffed—the familiar story—but he was able to let us have half-a-dozen uniformed men. He and the Super at Longminster—Mr. Bonney—did all they could to cooperate. But once we'd caught that whiff of the Jampot it became essentially our job with strong European and American connections.

"We did a big line with Interpol and the appropriate countries but although they were dead keen they weren't all that much of a help. Throughout his lamentable career the Jampot had made only one blunder; and that, as far we could ferret out, was because an associate at the Bolivian end of his drug racket had grassed. The associate was found dead by quick attack from behind on the carotids: the method that Foljambe had certainly employed in Paris and was later to employ upon the wretched Andropoulos. But for reasons about which the Bolivian police were uncommonly cagey, the Jampot was not accused by them of murder but of smuggling. Bribery is a little word we are not supposed to use when in communication with our brothers in anti-crime.

"It's worth noticing that whereas other big-shots in his world employ their staffs of salaried killers, the Jampot believes in the do-it-yourself kit and is unique in this as in many other respects.

"Apart from routine field-work, the immediate task, as I saw it, was to lay out the bits of information as provided by my wife and try to discover which fitted and which were extraneous. I suggest that you treat yourselves to the same exercise."

The man in the second row could almost be seen to lay back his ears.

"We found nothing to help us on deck," continued Alleyn. "Her mattress had been deflated and stowed away and so had her blankets and the deck had been hosed down in the normal course of routine.

"But the towpath and adjacent terrain turned up a show of colour. At the Crossdyke end, and you'll remember it was during the night at Crossdyke that the murdered woman disappeared, Mr. Fox's party found on the river-bank, at the site of the *Zodiac*'s moorings, a number of indentations made by either a woman's Cuban heels or those of the kind of 'gear' boots currently fashionable in Carnaby Street. They overlapped and their general type and characteristics suggested that the wearer had moved forwards with ease and then backwards under a heavy load. Here's a blow-up of Detective-Sergeant Thompson's photographs.

"There had either been some attempt to flatten these marks or else a heavy object had been dragged across them at right angles to the riverbank.

"The towpath was too hard to offer anything useful, and the path from there up to the road was tar-sealed and provided nothing. Nor did a muddy track along the waterfront. If the heels had gone that way we would certainly have picked them up so the main road must have been the route. Mr. Fox, who is probably the most meticulous clue-hound in the Force, had a long hard look at the road. Here are some blown-up shots of what he found: footprints. A patch of oil on the verge under a hedgerow not far from the moorings. Accompanying tyre marks suggest that a motor-bike had been parked there for some time. He found identical tracks on the road above Ramsdyke. At Crossdyke on an overhanging hawthorn twig—look at this close-up—there was a scrap of a dark blue synthetic material corresponding in colour and type with deceased's pyjamas.

"Right. Question now arose: if deceased came this way was she alive or dead at the time of transit? Yes, Carmichael?"

The man in the second row passed his paddle of a hand over the back of his sandy head.

"Sir," he said. "It would appear from the character of the

footprints, the marks on the bank, the evidence at the braeside and the wee wispies of cloth, that the leddy was, at the least of it, unconscious and carried from the craft to the bike. Further than that, sir, I would not care to venture."

The rest of the class stirred irritably.

"By and large," Alleyn said, "you would be right. To continue—"

1

Alleyn and Troy returned together to the *Zodiac*. They found Dr. Natouche reading on deck and the other passengers distantly visible in a seated group on the far hillside above the ford.

Natouche glanced up for a moment at Troy. She walked towards him and he stood up.

"Rory," Troy said, "you've not heard how good Dr. Natouche has been. He gave me a lovely lunch at Longminster and he was as kind as could be when I passed out this afternoon."

Alleyn said: "We're lucky, on all counts, to have you on board."

"I have been privileged," he replied with his little bow.

"I've told him," Troy said, "how uneasy you were when she disappeared and how we talked it over."

"It was not, of course, that I feared that any violence would be done to her. There was no reason to suppose that. It was because I thought her disturbed."

"To the point," Alleyn said, "where she might do violence upon herself?"

Dr. Natouche folded his hands and looked at them. "No," he said. "Not specifically. But she was, I thought, in a very unstable condition: a condition that is not incompatible with suicidal intention."

"Yes," Alleyn said. "I see. Oh dear."

"You find something wrong, Mr. Alleyn?"

"No, no. Not wrong. It's just that I seem to hear you giving the opinion in the witness box."

"For the defence?" he asked calmly.

"For the defence."

"Well," said Dr. Natouche, "I daresay I should be obliged to qualify it under cross-examination. While I am about it, may I give you another opinion? I think your wife would be better away from the *Zodiac*. She has had a most unpleasant shock, she is subject to migraine and I think she is finding the prospect of staying in the ship a little hard to face."

"No, no," Troy said. "Not at all. Not now."

"You mean not now your husband is here. Of course. But I think he will be very much occupied. You must forgive me for my persistence but—why not a room at the inn in Ramsdyke? Or even in Norminster? It is not far."

"I couldn't agree more," Alleyn said, "but there are difficulties. If my wife is given leave—"

"Some of us may also demand it? If you will allow me I'll suggest that she should go immediately and I'll say that as her medical adviser, I insisted."

"Rory—would it be easier? It would, wouldn't it? For you? For both of us?"

"Yes, darling, it would."

"Well, then?"

She saw Alleyn give Natouche one utterly noncommittal look of which the doctor appeared to be perfectly unaware. "I think you are right," Alleyn said. "I have been in two minds about it but I think you are right. How far is it by road to Norminster?"

"Six miles and three-eighths," Natouche said.

"How very well-informed!"

"Dr. Natouche is a map-maker," Troy said. "You must see what he's doing."

"Love to," Alleyn agreed politely. "Where did you stay in Norminster, Troy? The Percy, was it?"

"Yes."

"All right?"

"Perfectly."

"I'll ring up from the lockhouse. If they've got a room I'll send for a taxi. We'll obey doctor's orders."

"All right. But—"

"What?"

"I'll feel as if I'm ratting. So will they."

"Let them."

"All right."

"Would you go down and pack, then?"

"Yes. All right." They could say nothing to each other, Troy thought, but "all right."

She went down to her cabin.

Natouche said: "I hope you didn't mind my making this suggestion. Your wife commands an unusual degree of self-discipline, I think, but she really has had as much as she should be asked to take. I may say that some of the passengers would not be inclined to make matters any easier for her if she stayed."

"No?"

"They are, I think, a little suspicious of the lost fur."

"I can't blame them," Alleyn said dryly.

"Perhaps," Natouche continued, "I should say this. If you find, as I think you will, that Miss Rickerby-Carrick was murdered, I fully realize that I come into the field of suspects. Of course I do. I only mention this in case you should think that I try to put myself in an exclusive position by speaking as a doctor in respect of your wife."

"Do you suppose," Alleyn asked carefully, "that any of the others think it may be a case of homicide?"

"They do not confide in me, but I should undoubtedly think so. Yes."

"And they suspect that they will come into the field of inquiry?"

"They would be extremely stupid if they did not expect to do so," he said. "And by and large I don't find they are stupid people. Although at least three of them will certainly begin to suspect me of killing Miss Rickerby-Carrick."

"Why?"

"Briefly: because I am an Ethiopian and they would prefer that I, rather than a white member of the company, should be found guilty."

Alleyn listened to the huge voice, looked at the impassive face and wondered if this was a manifestation of inverted racialism or of sober judgement.

"I hope you're mistaken," he said.

"And so, of course, do I," said Dr. Natouche.

"By the way, Troy tells me you found a scrap of material on deck."

"Ah, yes. You would like to see it? It's here."

He took out his pocket-book and extracted an envelope. "Shall I show you where it was?" he asked.

"Please."

They went to the after-end of the deck.

"The mattress was inflated," Natouche explained, "and lying where it had been when she used it. Mrs. Alleyn noticed this fragment. It was caught under the edge of the pillow pocket. You will see that it is stained presumably with river water. It seemed to me that Miss Rickerby-Carrick had probably taken her diary with her when she came up here to bed and that this piece of the cover, if it is that, became detached. The book was of course saturated. I noted the cloth of its cover was torn when Lazenby rescued it. Your wife thought we should keep the fragment."

"Yes, she told me. Thank you. I must get on with my unlovely job. I am very much obliged to you, Dr. Natouche, for having taken care of Troy."

"Please! I was most honoured that she placed a little confidence in me. I think," he added, "that I shall stroll up to the wapentake. If you'll excuse me."

Alleyn watched him take an easy stride from the gunwale of the *Zodiac* to the grassy bank and noticed the perfect coordination of movement and the suggestion of unusual strength. Alleyn was visited by an odd notion: "Suppose," he thought, "he just went on. Suppose he became an Ethiopian in a canary-coloured sweater striding over historic English fens and out of our field of inquiry. Ah well, he's extremely conspicuous, after all."

He looked downstream towards the weir and could see Fox and the local sergeant moving about the towpath. Fox stooped over a wayside patch of bramble and presently righted himself with an air that Alleyn, even at that distance, recognized as one of mild satisfaction. He turned, saw Alleyn and raised a hand, thumb up.

Alleyn went ashore, telephoned the Percy hotel at Norminster, booked a room and ordered a taxi for Troy. When he returned to the *Zodiac* he found it deserted except for Troy, who had packed her bags and was waiting for him in her cabin.

Half an hour later he put her in her taxi and she drove away from Ramsdyke. Her fellow-passengers, except for Dr. Natouche, were sitting round an outdoor table at the pub. The Hewsons, Mr. Lazenby and Mr. Pollock had their heads together. Caley Bard slouched back dejectedly in his chair and gazed into a beer pot.

She asked the driver to stop and got out. As she approached the men stood up, Caley Bard at once, the others rather mulishly.

Troy said: "I've been kicked out. Rory thinks I'll be an embarrassment to the Force if I stay and I think he's got something so I'm going to Norminster."

Nobody spoke.

"I would rather have stayed," she said, "but I do see the point and I hope very much that all of you do, too. Wives are not meant to muscle-in on police routine."

Caley Bard put his arm across her shoulders and gave her a little shake. "Of course we do," he said. "Don't be a donkey. Off you go to Norminster and good riddance."

"Well!" Troy said. "That *is* handsome of you."

Mr. Lazenby said: "This is the course I suggested, if you remember, Mrs. Alleyn. I said I thought you would be well advised to leave the *Zodiac*."

"So you did," Troy agreed.

"For *your* sake, you know. For your sake."

"For whatever reason, you were right."

Pollock said something under his breath to Mr. Hewson who received it with a wry grin that Troy found rather more disagreeable than a shouted insult would have been. Miss Hewson laughed.

"Well," Troy said. "We'll all meet, I suppose. At the inquest. I just felt I'd like to explain. Goodbye."

She went back to the taxi. Caley Bard caught her up. "I don't know if your old man thinks this is a case of murder," he said, "but you can take it from me I'd cheerfully lay that lot out. For God's sake don't let it hurt you. It's not worth a second thought."

"No," Troy said. "Of course not. Goodbye."

The car drove through the Constable landscape up the hill. When they got to the crest they found a policeman on duty at the entry to the main road. Troy looked back. There, down below, was the River with the *Zodiac* at her moorings. Fox had moved from the weir and Alleyn and Tillottson had met him. They seemed to examine something that Fox had in his hand. As if he felt her gaze upon him, Alleyn lifted his head and, across the Constable picture, they looked at each other and waved their hands.

Above the River on the far side was the wapentake and alone in its hollow like a resident deity sat a figure in a yellow sweater with a black face and hands.

It would be getting dark soon and the passengers would stroll back to the ship. For the last time they would go to bed in their cabins. The River and trees and fields would send up their night-time voices and scents, and the countryside, after its quiet habit, would move into night. The seasonal mist, which the Skipper had told them was called locally the Creeper, had increased, and already the River looked like a stream of hot water threading the low country.

How strange, Troy thought as they drove away, that she should so sharply regret leaving the River. For a moment she entertained a notion that because of the violence that threaded its history there was something unremarkable, even appropriate, in the latest affront to the River. Poor Hazel Rickerby-Carrick, she thought, has joined a long line of drowned faces and tumbled limbs: Plantagenets and Frenchmen, Lancastrians and Yorkists, cropped, wigged and ringleted heads: bloated and desecrated bodies. They had drenched the fields and fed the River. The landscape had drawn them into itself and perhaps grown richer for them.

"I shall come back to the waterways," Troy thought. She and Alleyn and their son and his best girl might hire a longboat and cruise, not here, not between Tollardwark and Ramsdyke, but further south or west where there was no detergent on the face of the waters. But it was extremely odd, all the same, that she would want to do so.

2

While Fox and Tillottson stooped over footprints on the bank at Crossdyke and Sergeants Bailey and Thompson sped northwards, Alleyn explored the contents of Miss Rickerby-Carrick's cabin.

The passengers were still up at the pub and if Dr. Natouche had returned he had not come below. The Tretheways were sitting in a family huddle near the bar. Out in the darkling landscape the Creeper rose stealthily and police constables patrolled the exits from Ramsdyke into the main roads and the towpath near the *Zodiac*.

The cabin, of course, had been swept out and the berth stripped of its bed-clothes. The Hewsons had made use of it not only for their purchases but for their camera equipment and some of their luggage.

Alleyn found that their cameras—they had three—were loaded with partially used film. They were expensive models, one of them being equipped with a phenomenally powerful lens of the sort used by geologists when recording rock-faces.

Their booty from Tollardwark was bestowed along the floor, most of it in a beer carton. The prints and scraps had been re-rolled, pretty roughly, into a bundle tied up with the original string.

The painting of Ramsdyke Lock was laid between sheets of newspaper in an empty suitcase.

He took it out and put in on the bunk.

Troy and Caley Bard had made a fairly thorough job of their cleaning and oiling but there were still some signs of dirt caught under the edge of brush strokes, but not, he thought, incorporated in the print. It was a glowing picture and, as Troy had said, it was well-painted. Alleyn was not an expert in picture forgery but he knew that the processes were refined, elaborate and highly scientific, involving in the case of seventeenth-century reproductions the use of specially manufactured pigments, of phenolformaldehyde and an essential oil, of baking and of old paintings scraped down to the ground layer. With nineteenth-century forgeries these techniques might not be necessary. Alleyn knew that extremely indifferent forgeries had deceived the widows and close associates of celebrated painters and even tolerable authorities. He had heard talk of "studio sweepings" and arguments that not every casual, unsigned authentic sketch bore the over-all painterly "signature" of the master. One much-practised trick, of course, was to paint the forgery over an old work. An X-ray would show if this had been done.

Outside, presenting itself for comparison, was the subject of the picture: Ramsdyke Lock, the pond, the ford, the winding lane, the hazy distance. Nothing could be handier, he thought, and he did in fact compare them.

He made an interesting discovery.

The trees in the picture were in the right places, they were elms, they enclosed the middle distance just as the real elms did in the now darkling landscape outside. Undoubtedly, it was a picture of Ramsdyke Lock.

But they were not precisely the same elms.

The masses of foliage, painted with all the acute observation of Constable's school, were of a different relationship, one to another. Would this merely go to show that when the picture was painted the trees were a great deal smaller—No, he thought not. These *were* smaller but the major branches sprang from their trunks at different intervals. But might not this be a deliberate alteration made by the artist for reasons of composition? He remembered Troy saying that the painter has as much right to prune or transplant a tree as the clod who had planted it in the wrong place.

All the same . . .

Voices and footfalls on the upper deck announced the return of the passengers. Alleyn restored the painting to its suitcase and the suitcase to its position against the wall. He opened the cabin door, shut his working-kit, took out his pocket-lens, squatted at the head of the bunk and waited.

Not for long. The passengers came below, Mr. Lazenby first. He paused, looked in and fluted: "Busy, Superintendent?"

"Routine, sir."

"Ah! Routine!" Lazenby playfully echoed. "That's what you folk always say, isn't it, Superintendent? Routine!"

"I sometimes think it's all we ever do, Mr. Lazenby."

"Really? Well, I suppose I mustn't ask what it's all about. Poor girl. Poor girl. She was not a happy girl, Mr. Alleyn."

"No?"

"Emotionally unstable. A type that we parsons are all too familiar with, you know. Starved of true, worthwhile relationships, I suspect, and at a difficult, a trying time of life. Poor girl."

"Do I take it, you believe this to be a case of suicide, Mr. Lazenby?"

"I have grave misgivings that it may be so."

"And the messages received after her death?"

"I don't profess to have any profound knowledge of these matters, Superintendent, but *as* a parson, they *do* come my way. These poor souls can behave very strangely, you know. She might even have arranged the messages, hoping to create a storm of interest in herself."

"That's a very interesting suggestion, sir."

"I throw it out," Mr. Lazenby said with a modest gesture, "for what it's worth. I mustn't be curious," he added, "but—you hope to find some—er, help—in here? Out of, as it were, Routine?"

"We'd be glad to know whether or not she returned to her cabin during the night," Alleyn said. "But to tell you the truth, there's nothing to show, either way."

"Well," said Mr. Lazenby, "good on you, anyhow. I'll leave you to it."

"Thank you, sir," Alleyn said, and when Mr. Lazenby had gone, whistled, almost inaudibly, the tune of "Yes, we have no bananas," which for some reason seemed to express his mood.

He was disturbed almost immediately by the arrival of the Hewsons and Mr. Pollock.

Miss Hewson came first. She checked in the open doorway and looked, as far as an inexpressive face allowed her to do so, absolutely furious. Alleyn rose.

"Pardon *me*. I *had* gotten an impression that this stateroom had been allocated to our personal use," said Miss Hewson.

Alleyn said he was sure she would find that nothing had been disturbed.

Mr. Hewson, looking over his sister's shoulder like a gaunt familiar spirit said he guessed that wasn't the point, and Mr. Pollock, obscured, could be heard to say something about search warrants.

Alleyn repeated his story. Without committing himself in

so many words he contrived to suggest that his mind was running along the lines of suicide as indicated by Mr. Lazenby. He semsed an easing off in antagonism among his hearers. The time had come for what Troy was in the habit of referring to as his unbridled comehithery, which was unfair of Troy. He talked about the Hewsons' find and said his wife had told him it might well prove to be an important Constable.

He said, untruthfully, that he had had no police experience in the realms of art forgery. He believed, he said, and he had, in fact, been told by a top man, that it was most important for the canvas to be untouched until the experts looked at it. He wasn't sure that his wife and Mr. Bard hadn't been naughty to oil the surface.

He would love to see the picture. He said if he could afford it he would be a collector. He had the mania. He gushed.

As soon as he broached the matter of the picture Alleyn was quite sure that the Hewsons did not want him to see it. They listened to him and eyed him and said next to nothing. Mr. Pollock, still in the background, hung off and on and could be heard to mutter.

Finally, Alleyn fired point-blank. "Do show me your 'Constable,'" he said. "I'm longing to see it."

Miss Hewson with every appearance of the deepest reluctance seemed to be about to move into the cabin when her brother suddenly ejaculated: "Now, isn't this just too bad! Sis, what do you know!"

From the glance she shot at him, Alleyn would have thought that she hadn't the remotest idea what he was driving at. She said nothing.

Mr. Hewson turned to Alleyn with a very wide smile.

"Just too bad," he repeated. "Just one of those darn things! It sure would've been a privilege to have your opinion, Superintendent, but you know what? We packaged up that problem picture and mailed it right back to our London address not more'n half an hour before we quit Crossdyke."

"Did you really? I *am* disappointed," said Alleyn.

3

"Funny way to carry on," said Tillottson.

"So funny that I've taken it upon myself to lock the cabin door, keep the key and make sure there is not a duplicate. And if the Hewsons don't fancy that one they can lump it. What's more I'm going to rouse up Mr. Jno. Bagg, licensed dealer of Tollardwark. I think you'd better come, too, Bert," said Alleyn who had arrived at Mr. Tillottson's first name by way of Fox.

"Him! Why?"

"I'll explain on the way. Warn them at the lock, will you, Bert, to hold anything from the *Zodiac* that's handed in for posting. After all, they could pick that lock. And tell your chaps to watch like lynxes for anything to go overboard. It's too big," he added, "for them to shove it down the loo and if they dropped it out of a porthole I think it'd float. But tell your chaps to watch. We'll take your car, shall we?"

They left the mist-shrouded *Zodiac* and drove up the lane through the Constable landscape. When they reached the intersection a policeman on a motor-cycle saluted.

"My chap," Tillottson said.

"Yes. I'm still uneasy, though. You're sure this specimen can't break for the open country and lie doggo?"

"I've got three chaps on the intersections and two down at the lock. No one'll get off that boat tonight: I'll guarantee it."

"I suppose not. All right. Press on," Alleyn said.

The evening had begun to close in when they reached Tollardwark and Ferry Lane. They left their car in the Market Square and followed Troy's route downhill to the premises of Jno. Bagg.

"Pretty tumbledown dump," Tillottson said. "But he's honest enough as dealers go. Not a local man. Southerner. Previous owner died and this chap Jo Bagg bought the show as it stood. We've nothing against him in Records. He's a rum character, though, is Jo Bagg."

The premises consisted of a cottage, a lean-to and a yard, which was partly sheltered by a sort of ramshackle cloister pieced together from scrap iron and linoleum. The yard gate was locked. Through it Alleyn saw copious disjecta membra of Mr. Bagg's operations. A shop window in the cottage wall dingily faced the lane. It was into this window that Troy had found the Hewsons peering last Monday night.

Tillottson said: "He'll be in bed as like as not. They go to bed early in these parts."

"Stir him up." Alleyn rejoined and jerked at a cord that dangled from a hole near the door. A bell jangled inside. No response. "Up you get," Alleyn muttered and jerked again. Tillottson banged on the door.

"If you lads don't want to be given in charge," bawled a voice within, "you better 'op it. Go on. Get out of it. I'll murder you one of these nights, see if I don't."

"It's me, Jo," Tillottson shouted through the keyhole. "Tillottson. Police. Spare us a moment, will you?"

"*Who?*"

"Tillottson: Toll'ark Police."

Silence. A light was turned on somewhere behind the dirty window. They heard shuffling steps and the elaborate unchaining and unbolting of the door which was finally dragged open with a screech to reveal a small, dirty man wearing pyjamas and an unspeakable overcoat.

"What's it all about?" he complained. "I'm going to bed. What's the idea?"

"We won't keep you, Jo. If we can just come in for half a sec."

He muttered and stood aside. "In there, then," he said and dragged and banged the door shut. "In the shop."

They walked into what passed for a shop: a low room crammed to its ceiling and so ill-lit that nothing came out into the open or declared itself in its character of table, hatrack or mouldering chair. Rather, everything lurked in menacing anonymity and it really was going too far in the macabre for Jno. Bagg to suspend a doll from one of the rafters by a cord round its broken neck.

"This," said Mr. Tillottson, "is Superintendent Alleyn of the C.I.D., Jo. He wonders if you can help him."

"'Ere," said Mr. Bagg, "that's a type of remark I never expected to have thrown at me on me own premises. Help the police. We all know what that one leads to."

"No, you don't, Jo. Listen, Jo—"

Alleyn intervened. "Mr. Bagg," he said, "you can take my

word for it there is no question of anything being held against you in any way whatever. I'll come to the point at once. We are anxious to trace the origin of a picture which was sold by you yesterday to an American lady and her brother. We have reason to believe—"

"Don't you start making out I'm a fence. Don't you come at that one, Mister. Me! A fence—!"

"I don't for one moment suggest you're anything of the sort. Do pay attention like a good chap. I have reason to believe that this picture may have been dumped on your premises and I want to find out if that could be so."

"Dumped! You joking?"

"Not at all. Now, listen. The picture, as you will remember, was in a bundle of old prints and scraps and the lady found it when she opened the door of a cupboard in your yard. The bundle was rolled up and tied with string and very dirty. It looked as if it hadn't been touched for donkey's years. You told the lady you didn't know you had it and you sold it to her unexamined for ten bob and nobody's complaining or blaming you or suspecting you of anything."

"Are you telling me," Mr. Bagg said with a change of manner, "that she struck it lucky? Is that the lay?"

"It may be a valuable painting and it may be a forgery."

"I'll be damned!"

"Now, all I want to know, and I hope you'll see your way to telling me, is whether, on thinking it over, you can remember seeing the roll of prints in that cupboard before yesterday."

"What I meantersay, no. No, I can't. No."

"Had you never opened the cupboard, or sideboard is it, since you bought it?"

"No. I can't say fairer than that, Mister, can I? No. Not me, I never."

"May I look at it?"

He grumbled a little but finally led them out to his yard where the very dregs of his collection mouldered. The sideboard was a vast Edwardian piece executed in pitchpine with the cupboard in the middle. Alleyn tried the door, which had warped and only opened to a hard wrench and a screech that compared favourably with that of the front door.

"She was nosey," Mr. Bagg offered. "Had to open

everything she saw. Had a job with that one. Still nothing would do—nosey."

"And there it was."

"That's correct, Mister. There it was. And there it wasn't, if you can understand, three days before."

"*What?*"

"Which I won't deceive you, Mister. While my old woman was looking over the stock out here, Monday, she opened that cupboard and she mentions the same to me when them two Yanks had gone and she says it wasn't there then."

"Why couldn't you tell us at once, Jo?" Mr. Tillottson asked more in resignation than in anger.

"You arst, you know you did, or this gentleman which is all one, arst if *I* never opened the cupboard and I answered truthfully that I never. Now then!"

"All right, Jo, all right. That's all we wanted to know."

"Not quite," Alleyn said. "I wonder, Mr. Bagg, if you've any idea of how the bundle could have got there. Have you anybody working for you? A boy?"

"Boy? Don't mention Boy to me. Runaway knockers and ringers, the lot of them. I wouldn't have Boys on me property, not if *they* paid *me*."

"Is the gate from this yard to the road unlocked during the day?"

"Yes, it is unlocked. To oblige."

"Have many people been in over the last two days, would you say?"

Not many, it appeared. His customers, as a general rule, came into the shop. All the stuff in the yard was of a size or worthlessness that made it unpilferable. It was evident that anybody with a mind to it could wander round the yard without Mr. Bagg being aware of their presence. Under persuasion he recalled one or two locals who had drifted in and bought nothing. Alleyn delicately suggested that perhaps Mrs. Bagg—?

"Mrs. Bagg," said Mr. Bagg, "is in bed and asleep which game to rouse her, I am not. No more would you be if you knew how she can shape up."

"But if your wife—"

"Wife? Do me a favour! She's my Mum."

"Oh."

As if to confirm the general trend of thought a female voice like a saw screamed from inside the cottage that its owner wanted to know what the hell Mr. Bagg thought he was doing creating a nuisance in the middle of the night.

"There you are," he said. "Now, see what you done." He approached a window at the rear of the cottage and tapped on it. "It's me," he mumbled. "It's not the middle of the night, Mum, it's early. It's Mr. Tillottson of the Police, Mum, and a gentleman friend. They was inquiring about them Yanks what bought that stuff."

"I can't hear you. Police! Did you say Police? 'Ere! Come round 'ere this instant-moment, Jo Bagg, and explain yourself: *Police*."

"I better go," he said and re-entered the cottage.

"The old lady," Mr. Tillottson said, "is a wee bit difficult."

"So it would seem"

"They make out she's nearly a hundred."

"But she's got the stamina?"

"My oath!"

The Baggs were in conversation beyond the window but at a subdued level and nothing could be made of it. When Mr. Bagg re-emerged he spoke in a whisper.

"Do me a favour, gents," he whispered. "Move away!"

They withdrew into the shop and from thence to the front door.

"She's deaf," Mr. Bagg said, "but there are times when you wouldn't credit it. She don't know anything about nothing but she worked it out that if this picture you mention is a valuable antique it's been taken off us by false pretences and we ought to get it back."

"Oh."

"That's the view she takes. And so," Mr. Bagg added loyally, "do I. Now!"

"I daresay you do," Mr. Tillottson readily conceded. "Very natural. And she's no ideas about how it got there?"

"No more nor the Holy Saints in Heaven, and she's a Catholic," Mr. Bagg said unexpectedly.

"Well, we'll bid you good-night, Jo. Unless Mr. Alleyn has anything further?"

"Not at the moment, thank you, Mr. Bagg."

Mr. Bagg wrenched open the front door to the inevitable

screech which was at once echoed from the back bedroom.

"You ask them Police," screamed old Mrs. Bagg, "why they don't do something about them motor-biking Beasts instead of making night hijjus, on their own accounts."

"What motor-biking beasts?" Alleyn suddenly yelled into the darkness.

"You know. And if you don't you ought to. Backfiring up and down the streets at all hours and hanging round up to no good. Jo! Show them out and get to bed."

"Yes, Mum."

"And another thing," invisibly screamed Mrs. Bagg. "What was them two Americans doing nosey-parkering about the place last week was a month back, taking photers and never letting on they was the same as before."

Alleyn set himself to bawl again and thought better of it. "What does she mean?" he asked Mr. Bagg.

"You don't have to notice," he said. "But it's correct, all right. They been here before, see, taking photographs, and Mum recognized them. She wouldn't have made nothink of it only for suspecting they done us."

"When were they here? Where did they stay?"

"In the Spring. May. Late April: I wouldn't know. But it was them all right. They made out, when I says weren't they here before, they was that taken with the place they come back for more."

"You're sure about this?"

"Don't be funny," Mr. Bagg said. "'Course I'm sure. This way, for Gawd's sake."

They went out. Mr. Bagg had re-addressed himself to the door when Alleyn said: "Can you tell us anything about these motor-cyclists?"

"Them? Couple of mods. Staying up at the Star in Chantry Street. Tearing about the country all hours and disturbing people. Tuesday evening Mum 'eard something in our yard and caught the chap nosing round. Looking for old chain he said, but she didn't fancy him. She took against him very strong, did Mum, and anyway, we ain't got no old chain. *Chain!*"

"Why," began Mr. Tillottson on a note of anguish, "didn't you mention—"

"I never give it a thought. You can't think of everything."

"Nor you can," Alleyn hurriedly intervened. "But now you have thought, can you tell us what drew Mrs. Bagg's attention to the chap in the yard?"

"Like I said, she 'eard something."

"What, though?"

"Some sort of screech. I 'eard it too."

"You did!"

"But I was engaged with a customer," Mr. Bagg said majestically, "in my shop."

"Could the screech have been made by the door in the sideboard?"

Mr. Bagg peered into Alleyn's face as if into that of an oracle. "Mister," he said, "it not only could but it did." He took thought and burst into protestation. "Look," he said. "I want an explanation. If I been done I want to know how I been done. If I been in possession of a valuable article and sold this article for a gift without being fully informed I want to get it back, fair and proper. Now."

They left him discontentedly pursuing this thought but not loudly enough to arouse the curiosity of old Mrs. Bagg. The door shrieked and slammed and they heard the bolts shoot home on the inside.

"Star Inn," Alleyn said as they got in the car but when they reached the inn it was to find that the motor-bicyclists had paid their bill the previous evening and set off for an unknown destination. They had registered as Mr. and Mrs. Smith.

4

The motor-bicycle had been parked in a dampish yard behind the pub and the tyre-tracks were easy enough to pick up. Alleyn took measurements, made a sketch of the prints and had them covered, pending the arrival of Bailey and Thompson. He thought that when they examined Fox's find under the hedgerow above Crossdyke they would find an exact correspondence. An outside man at the Star remembered the make of vehicle—Route-Rocket—but nobody could give the number.

Alleyn telephoned Troy at the Percy Arms in Norminster

and asked her if by any chance she could recall it.

She sat on the edge of her bed with the receiver at her ear and tried to summon up her draughtsman's memory of the scene on the quay at Norminster last Monday morning. Miss Rickerby-Carrick squatted on her suitcase, writing. Caley Bard and Dr. Natouche were down by the River. Pollock limped off in a sulk. The Bishop's car was in the lane with Lazenby inside. The two riders lounged against their machine, their oiled heads and black leather gear softly glistening in the sun. She had wanted to draw them, booted legs, easy, insolent pose, gum-chewing faces, gloved hands. And the machine. She screwed her memory to the sticking point, waited and then heard her own voice.

"I think," said her voice, "it was XKL-460."

"Now there!" Alleyn ejaculated. "See what a girl I've got! Thank you, my love, and good-night." He hung up. "All right," he said. "We set up a general call. They'll be God knows where by now but they've got to be somewhere and by God we'll fetch them in."

He, Fox and Tillottson were in the Superintendent's office at the Tollardwark police station where, on Monday night, Troy had first encountered Mr. Tillottson. The Sergeant set up the call. In a matter of minutes all divisions throughout the country and all police personnel were alerted for a Route-Rocket, XKL-460, black, with either one or two riders, mod-types, leather clothes, dark, long hair, calf-boots. Retain for questioning and report in.

"And by now," Fox observed, "they've repainted their bike, cut their hair and gone into rompers."

"Always the little sunbeam," Alleyn muttered, absently. He had covered a table in the office with newspaper and now very carefully they laid upon it an old-fashioned hide suitcase, saturated with river-water, blotched, disreputable, with one end of its handle detached from its ring. A length of cord had been firmly knotted through both rings.

"We opened it," Tillottson said, "and checked the contents as they lay. You can see what happened. The other end of the cord was secured round her waist. The slack had been passed two or three times under the handle and round the case. When the handle came away at one end the slack paid out and instead of being anchored on the river-bed, the

body rose to the surface but remained fastened to the
weighted case. As it was when we recovered it."

"Yes," Alleyn agreed. "You can see where the turns of
rope bit into the leather."

Fox, who was bent over the cord, said: "Clothes-line. Did
they pinch it or had they got it?" and sighed heavily.

"We'll inquire." he said.

"They might have had it," Tillottson said. "In their kit,
you know. Easily they might. Or what say," he added,
brightening, "they picked it up in Jo's yard? How's that?"

"That might or might not argue premeditation," Alleyn
said. "For the moment it can wait. We'd better take another
look inside."

The case was unlocked but fastened with strong old-
fashioned hasps and a strap. The saturated leather was slimy
to the touch. He opened and laid back the lid.

A jumble of clothes that had been stuffed into the case.
Three pairs of shoes which spoke with dreadful eloquence of
the feet that had distorted them. A seedy comb and hairbrush
with straggles of grey hairs still engaged in them.

"And the whole lot stowed away in a hurry and not by her.
No hope of prints, he's a damn' sight too fly for that, but we'll
have to try. Hullo, what's here?"

Five stones of varying sizes. A half brick. Two handfuls of
gravel. Underneath all these, a sponge-bag containing a half-
empty bottle of aspirins (Troy's, thought Alleyn), a
toothbrush and a tube of paste, and, in a state of
disintegration, Hazel Rickerby-Carrick's "self-propelling
confessional."

"The diary," Alleyn said. "And to misuse a nastily
appropriate line: 'lift it up tenderly, treat it with care.' You
never know: it may turn out to be a guidebook."

VIII

ROUTINE CONTINUED

"At this point," Alleyn said, "I'm going to jump the gun and show you a photograph of post-mortem marks across the back at waist level and diagonally across the shoulder blades of the body. Here are her wrists, similarly scarred. These marks were classed as having been inflicted after death. As you see they have all the characteristics of post-mortem scarring. What do they suggest? Yes?"

"The cord, sir," ventured Carmichael in the second row. "The cord that attached the bawdy to the suitcase."

"I'm afraid that's not quite accurate. These grooves are narrow and deep and only appear on the back. Now look at this. That's the cord, laid beside the marks. You can see it tallies. So far you are right, Carmichael. But you see that the higher marks cross each other in the form of an X with a line underneath. Have another shot. What are they?"

From somewhere towards the back a doubtful voice uttered the word "flagellation" and followed it with an apologetic little cough. Someone else made the noise "gatcha" upon which there was a muffled guffaw.

"You'll have to do better than that," Alleyn said. "However: to press on with Mr. Fox's investigations. He found nothing else of interest at the Crossdyke end and moved to the stretch of river below Ramsdyke weir where the body was found. Above Ramsdyke near the hollow called Wapentake Pot, the road from Crossdyke and Tollardwark was undergoing repairs. There were loose stones and rubble. It crosses Dyke Way and Dyke Way leads down to a bridge over the river where the Roman canal joins it. Downstream from here is the weir with its own bridge, a narrow affair with a single handrail. It's here that the effluent from a factory enters the mainstream and brews a great mass of detergent foam over the lower reaches.

"The weir bridge is narrow, green, wet and slithery with foam blown back from the fall. It is approached from the road by concrete steps and a cinder path.

"Along this path, Mr. Fox again found a thread or two of dark blue synthetic caught on a bramble. Here's the photograph. And I may tell you that a close search of the pyjamas revealed a triangular gap that matched the fragment from Crossdyke. Classic stuff.

"The path is bordered on one side by a very old wall from which a number of bricks had worked loose.

"Now for the weir bridge. Nearly three days had passed between the night she disappeared and our work on it. A pretty dense film of detergent had been blown back and it was a particularly awkward job to examine it without destroying any evidence there might be. However, there was a notice warning people that it was dangerous to use the bridge and the lock-keeper said he didn't think anyone had been on it for at least a week.

"Mr. Fox found some evidence of recent, gloved handholds on the rail. No prints were obtainable. For a distance of about twelve feet from the bank the actual footway looked to be less thickly encrusted than the remaining stretch of the bridge. Mr. Fox reckoned that there was a sort of family resemblance between the appearance of the bridge and the drag over the heel-prints on the bank at Crossdyke. Here are Thompson's blow-ups for comparison. You can see how bad, from our point-of-view, the conditions were on the bridge.

"Now, out of all this, what sort of picture do you begin to get. Yes? All right, Carmichael?"

Carmichael rose, fixed Alleyn with his blue stare and delivered.

"To re-cap, sir," Carmichael began ominously. "As a wur-r-rking hypothesis, it could be argued that the bawdy of the deceased had been passed from the deck of the vessel into the possession of the persons who received it and that it had maybe been drawped and dragged in the process, sir, thus pairtially obleeterating the heel-prints. Furthermore it could be reasonably deduced, sir, that the bawdy was transpotted by means of the motorbike to Ramsdyke where it was conveyed by hand to the weir bridge, dragged some twelve feet along and consigned to the watter."

He stopped, cleared his throat and raised his hand. "As a rider to the above, sir, and proceeding out of it," he said. "A suitcase, being the personal property of deceased, and packed with her effects, was removed from her cabin and transferred by the means already detailed, *with* the bawdy, *to* the said weir and there, weighted with stones and gravel and a half-brick, attached to the bawdy by the cord produced. The bawdy and the suitcase were then as detailed consigned to the watter."

He resumed his seat and gave Alleyn a modest smile.

"Yes, Carmichael, yes," Alleyn said, "and what about the post-mortem marks of the cord?"

Carmichael rose again.

"For want of an alternative," he said with the utmost complacency, "I would assume as a working premiss, sir, that the deed bawdy was lashed to the person of the cyclist thus rendering the spurious appearance of a pillion-rider."

"Revolting as the picture you conjure up may be," Alleyn said, "I'm afraid you're right, Carmichael."

"Shall we say *deed* right, sir?" Carmichael suggested with an odiously pawky grin.

"We shall do nothing of the sort, Carmichael. Sit down."

1

"It's a horrid picture that begins to emerge, isn't it?" Alleyn said as he eased the diary out of the sponge-bag and laid it with elaborate care on a folded towel. "The body is lashed to the cyclist's back and over it is dragged the dull magenta gown, hiding the cord. The arms are pulled round his waist and the wrists tied. The head, one must suppose, lolls forward on the rider's shoulder.

"And if anyone was abroad in the night on the road from Crossdyke to Ramsdyke they might have seen an antic show:

a man on a Route-Rocket with what seemed to be either a very affectionate or a very drunken rider on his pillion: a rider whose head lolled and jerked preposterously and who seemed to be glued to his back."

"What about the suitcase?" asked Tillottson.

"Made fast. It's not weighted at this stage. The stones were collected at the weir."

"Roadside heap," Fox put in. "Loose brick. Shingle. We've got all that."

"Exactly, Br'er Fox. Fish out a sponge from my bag, would you?"

Fox did so. Alleyn pressed it over the surfaces of the diary, mopping up the water that seeped out. "It's when he gets to Ramsdyke," he went on, "that the cyclist's toughest job begins. Presumably he's single-handed. He has to dismount, carry his burden, a ghastly pick-a-back, presumably, down to the weir. He unlooses and dumps it, returns for the case, puts in the stones and shingle, humps the case to the body, adds a loose half-brick, ties the body to the case and pushes both of them far enough along the footbridge to topple them into the weir."

"Do I," Fox blandly inquired, "hear the little word conjecture?"

"If you do you can shut up about it. But you don't hear it all that clearly, old boy. Find me another theory that fits the facts and I'll eat the dust."

"I won't give you the satisfaction, Mr. Alleyn."

"Find something to slide under the diary, will you? I want to turn it over. A stiff card will do. Good. Here we go. Now, the sponge again. Yes. Well, from here, the sinister cyclist and his moll begin to set up their disappearing act. All we know is that they had paid their bill at the Star and that they lit off some time that night or early next morning. Presumably with a fabulous Fabergé bibelot representing the signs of the zodiac in their possession."

"Hi!" Tillottson ejaculated. "D'you reckon?"

"This really *is* conjecture," Alleyn said. "But I don't mind betting we do *not* find the damned jewel on board the *Zodiac*."

"River-bed? Swept off the body, like?"

"I don't see him leaving it on the body, you know."

"I suppose not. No."

"It may have been the motive," Fox said. "If it's all that fabulous."

"Or it may have been a particularly lush extra: a kind of bonus in the general scheme of awards."

Tillottson said: "You don't lean to the notion that this cyclist character—"

"Call him Smith," Fox suggested sourly. "I'll bet nobody else ever has."

"This Smith, then. You don't fancy he did the killing?"

"No," Alleyn said. "I don't. I think she was killed on board the *Zodiac*. I think the body was handed over to Smith together with the suitcase and probably the Fabergé jewel. Now dare we take a look inside this diary."

It had deteriorated since poor Hazel Rickerby-Carrick had examined it after its first immersion. The block of pages had parted company with the spine and had broken into sections. The binding was pulpy and the paper softened.

"Should we dry it out first?" Fox asked.

"I'll try one gingerly fiddle. Got a broadish knife in the station?"

Tillottson produced a bread knife. With infinite caution Alleyn introduced it into the diary at the place where the condition of the edges suggested a division between the much-used and still-unused sections. He followed the knife blade up with a wider piece of card and finally turned the top section back.

Blotched, mottled, in places blistered and in others torn, it was still for the most part legible.

"Waterproof ink," Alleyn said. "God bless the self-propelling pencil."

And like the writer, when she sat in her cabin on the last day of her life, Alleyn read the final entry in her diary.

"I'm at it again. Trying too hard, as usual—"

And like her, having read it, he turned the page and drew a blank.

2

"So there it is," Alleyn said. "She writes that she returned from compline at St. Crispin-in-the-Fields to the motor-vessel *Zodiac*. She doesn't say by what road but as Troy followed the same procedure and returned by Ferry Lane and did not encounter her, it may be that she took a different route."

"She could," Tillottson said. "Easily. Weyland Street, it'd have to be."

"All right. She was wearing rubber-sole shoes. At some stage in her return trip she retired into a dark shop-entry to remove a pebble or something from one of her sneakers. From this position, she overheard a conversation between two or more—from the context I would think more—people that, quote, 'froze' and 'riveted' her. One of the voices—it was a whisper—she failed to identify. The other—or others—she no doubt revealed on the subsequent page which has been torn out of the diary. Now. My wife has told me that after Lazenby rescued the diary she thought she saw, for a fractional moment, paper with writing on it clutched in his left hand. That evening at Crossdyke, Miss Rickerby-Carrick, who was in a state of violent excitement, intimated that she wanted urgently to confide in Troy, to ask her advice. No doubt she would have done so but Troy got a migraine and instead of exploring Crossdyke went early to bed. Miss R.-C. joined the others and inspected the ruins and was shown how to catch butterflies by Caley Bard. Troy, who was feeling better, saw this episode through her porthole.

"She also saw Miss Rickerby-Carrick peel off from the main party, run down the hill and excitedly latch on to Dr. Natouche who was walking down the lane. She seemed to show him something that she held in the palm of her hand. Troy couldn't see what it was."

"That's interesting," said Fox.

"Dr. Natouche has subsequently told Troy that she asked him about some sort of tranquilizer pill she'd been given by Miss Hewson. He did not, I think, actually say that she showed him this pill when they were in the lane; Troy simply supposes that was what it was."

"Might it," Tillottson ventured, "have been this whatyoucallit—furbished jewel?"

"Fah-ber-zhay," murmured Mr. Fox who spoke French. "And she wore that round her neck on a cord, Bert."

"Yes."

"Well," Alleyn said, leaving it, "that night she disappeared, and in my opinion, that night, very late, she was murdered.

"The next day, Natouche told Troy he was concerned about Miss Rickerby-Carrick. He didn't say in so many words that he thought she might commit suicide but Troy got the impression that he did in fact fear it.

"I'll round up the rest of the bits and pieces gleaned by my wife, most of which, but I think not all, you have already heard, Tillottson."

"Er—well—yerse."

"Here they are, piecemeal. Pollock started life as a commercial artist and changed to real estate. He does a beautiful job of lettering when told exactly what's wanted.

"Natouche makes pretty maps.

"Miss Hewson was shown the Fabergé bibelot by its owner.

"Miss Hewson seems to be very keen on handing out pills.

"The Hewsons were disproportionately annoyed when they heard that the return visit to Tollardwark would be on early-closing day. They hired a car from Longminster to do their shop-crawl in Tollardwark and on that trip bought their stuff at Jo Bagg's in Ferry Lane.

"In their loot was an oil painting, purporting to be a signed Constable. Hewson said they'd posted it on to their address in London but I saw it in one of their suitcases.

"The cyclists watched the *Zodiac* sail from Norminster and reappeared that evening at Ramsdyke. Troy thought she heard them—but says of course she might be wrong—during the night in Tollardwark.

"Mrs. Bagg complains about cyclists hanging round their yard on Tuesday. A screech, as of the cupboard door, attracted her attention.

"The Baggs say the roll of prints was not in the cupboard a few days before the Hewsons found it there.

"Lazenby is a one-eyed man and conceals the condition. Troy, who can give no valid reason, thinks he's not a parson, an opinion that evidently is not shared by the Bishop of Norminster who had him to stay and sent him in the episcopal car to the *Zodiac*. He says he's an Australian. We send his prints and a description to the Australian police. We also send the Hewsons' over to the F.B.I. in New York."

Fox made a note of it.

"The Hewsons," Alleyn continued, "are expensively equipped photographers.

"Pollock irritates Caley Bard. Miss Rickerby-Carrick irritates everybody. Caley Bard irritates the Hewsons, Pollock, and possibly, Lazenby.

"Pollock and the Hewsons are racially prejudiced against Natouche. Bard and Lazenby are not.

"A preliminary examination of the body in question supports the theory that she was killed by an attack from behind on the carotids.

"Andropoulos would have been a passenger on the *Zodiac* if Foljambe hadn't killed him—by sudden and violent pressure from behind on the carotids."

Alleyn broke off, stared absently at the diary, waited for a moment and then said: "Some of these items are certainly of the first importance, others may be of none at all. Taken as a whole do you think they point to any one general conclusion?"

"Yes," Fox said. "I do. I certainly do."

"What?" Tillottson asked.

"Conspiracy."

"I agree with you," said Alleyn. "Between whom?"

"You mean—what's the gang?"

"Yes."

"Ah. Now." Fox dragged his great palm across his mouth. "Why don't we say it?" he asked.

"Say what? That the real question is not only one of conspiracy but of who's running the show? And more particularly: is it the Jampot?"

"That's right. That's it. Cherchez," said Mr. Fox with his customary care, "le Folichon. Ou," he added, "le Pot á Confitures, which is what they're beginning to call him in the Sureté."

"You made your mark, evidently, in Paris."

"Not so's you'd notice," Fox said heavily. "But let it pass. Yes, Mr. Alleyn. I reckon it's the Jampot on this job."

"Why," Tillottson asked, "are you so sure, Teddy?"

"Well, take a look at it, Bert. Take a look at the lot Mr. Alleyn's just handed us. Three items point to it, you know, now don't they?"

"Yerse," Mr. Tillottson concurred after a long pause. "I get you. Yerse."

Alleyn was bent over the diary. His long forefinger touched the rag of paper that was the remnant of the last entry. He slipped his nail under it and disclosed another and then another torn marginal strip still caught in the binding. "Three pages gone," he said, "and it's not unreasonable to suppose they would have told us what she overheard from her dark entry in Tollardwark. Wrenched out in a hurry, and, I suppose, either burnt or thrown overboard. The latter almost certainly. They were wet and pulpy. Torn out whether purposely or accidentally, and into the River with *them*."

"That'll be the story," Fox agreed heavily. "And the inference is—by Lazenby."

"If Troy's right. She's not certain."

Mr. Tillottson who had been in a hard, abstracted stare since his last utterance now said: "So it's a field of five—six if you count the Skipper and that'd be plain ridiculous. I've known Jim Tretheway these five years, decent wee man."

"He's not all that wee," Fox said mildly.

"The doctor, Mr. Bard, Mr. Hewson, the Reverend and Pollock. And if you're right one of them's the toughest proposition in what they call the international crime world. You wouldn't credit it, though, would you? Here!" Mr. Tillottson said, struck by a new thought. "You wouldn't entertain the idea of the whole boiling being in cahoots, would you? If so: why? Why go river-cruising if they're a pack of villains in a great big international racket. Not for kicks you'd think, now, would you?"

"Of the lot that remains on board, excluding the Tretheways," Alleyn said, "I incline to think there's only one non-villain. I'll give you my reasons, such as they are, and I fully admit they wouldn't take first prize in the inescapable logic stakes. But still. Here they are."

His colleagues listened in massive silence. Fox sighed heavily when he had finished. "And that," he said, "followed out, leaves us with only one guess for the identity of the Jampot. Or does it?"

"I think it does. If, if, if and it's a hell of a big if."

"I'll back it," Fox said. "What's our next bit of toil?"

"We don't wait for the report on the P.M. I think, Br'er Fox, we cut in and use our search warrant. What's the time? Five past nine. If they've gone to bed it's just too bad. Back to Ramsdyke Lock with us. Did you pick up a bit of nosh, by the way?"

"Pickle and beef sandwiches and a couple of half-pints."

"We'll sink them on the trip. Hark bloody forrard away."

3

If events do, as some would have us believe, stamp an intangible print upon their surroundings, this phenomenon is not instantaneous. Murder doesn't scream instantly from the walls of a room that may be drenched in blood. Clean the room up and it is just a room again. If violence of behaviour or of emotion does, in fact, project itself upon its immediate surroundings, like light upon photographic film, the process seems to be cumulative rather than immediate. It may be a long time after the event that people begin to think: this is an unhappy house. Or room. Or place. Or craft.

The saloon in that most pleasant of water-wanderers, the *Zodiac,* wore its usual after-dark aspect. Its cherry-coloured window-curtains were drawn and its lamps were lit. It was cosy. The more so, perhaps, because the river mist known as the Creeper had now shut the craft off from her surroundings.

The six remaining passengers occupied themselves in much the same way as they had done before Hazel Rickerby-Carrick disappeared in the night. The Hewsons, Mr. Lazenby, and Mr. Pollock played Scrabble. Caley Bard read. Dr. Natouche, a little removed as always, put some finishing touches to his map of the River. Behind the bar, Mrs. Tretheway read a magazine. The Skipper was on shore and the boy Tom was in bed.

Troy's zodiac picture with its vivid impersonations of the passengers was now framed and had replaced its begetter above the bar. There they all were, preposterously masquerading as Heavenly bodies, skipping round Mr. Pollock's impeccable lettering.

> The Hunt of the Heavenly Host begins
> With the Ram, the Bull and the Heavenly Twins.
> The Crab is followed by the Lion
> The Virgin and the Scales,
> The Scorpion, Archer and He-Goat
> The Man that carries the Watering-Pot
> And the Fish with the Glittering Tails.

The Virgin was gone for good and the Goat, as Troy had thought of herself, was removed to Norminster, but there, Alleyn thought, were all the others, mildly employed, with a killer among them.

When Alleyn and Fox arrived in the saloon, the Scrabble players became quite still, Miss Hewson's forefinger, pushing a lettered tile into place, stopped and remained, pointed down, like an admonitory digit on a monument. Pollock's head, bent over the Scrabble board, was not raised though his eyes were and looked at Alleyn from under his brows, showing rims of white. Lazenby, who had been attending to the score, let his pencil remain in suspended action. Hewson, pipe gripped in teeth, held the head of a match against the box but did not strike it.

For a few seconds this picture was presented like an unheralded still at the cinema; then it animated as if there had been no hitch in its mild progression.

"I'm sorry," Alleyn said, "that we have to make nuisances of ourselves again but there it is. In police work it's a case of set a nuisance to catch a nuisance."

"Well!" Caley Bard ejaculated. "I must say that as reassuring remarks go, I don't think much of that one. If it was meant to reassure."

"It was meant as a sort of apology," Alleyn said, "but I see your point. Please don't let us disturb anybody. We've come to tidy up a loose end of routine and I'm afraid we shall have to ask you all to be very patient and stay out of your cabins until we've done so. We won't be long about it, I hope."

After a considerable silence Mr. Hewson predictably said:
"Yeah?" and leant back in his chair with his thumbs in the
armholes of his waistcoat. He turned his left ear with its
hearing-aid towards Alleyn.

"'Stay out of our cabins,'" he quoted with what seemed to
be intended as a parody of Alleyn's voice. "Is that so? Now,
would that be a kind of polite indication of a search,
Superintendent?"

"I'm glad it sounded polite," Alleyn rejoined cheerfully.
"Yes. It would."

"You got a warrant?" Pollock asked.

"Yes, indeed. Would you like to see it?"

"Of course we don't want to see it," Caley Bard wearily
interjected. "Don't be an ass, Pollock."

Pollock muttered: "I'm within my rights, aren't I?"

Alleyn said: "Miss Hewson, I'll start with your cabin, if
that suits you, and as soon as I've finished, you will be free to
use it. At the same time Inspector Fox will take a look at
yours, Mr. Hewson."

"A second look," Mr. Hewson sourly amended.

"If," Alleyn said, "you now count the deceased's cabin as
yours. I meant your very own cabin, Mr. Hewson. A
formality, you might call it."

"You might," Mr. Hewson conceded. "I wouldn't."

Miss Hewson said: "Gee, Earl, if I hadn't clean forgotten!
Gee, how crazy can you get? Look, Mr. Alleyn, look.
Superintendent, I got to 'fess up' right now, about that
problem-picture. There's a kind of misunderstanding
between Brother and me. *He* calculated *I'd* sent it off and *I*
calculated *he* had."

"Just the darnedest thing," Mr. Hewson put in with a
savage glance at his sister.

"Certainly is," she agreed, "and so what do you know?
There it is just exactly where it's been all this time. In the
bottom of a grip in my stateroom."

"Fancy," said Alleyn. "I shall enjoy taking a second look.
Last time I saw it, it was in an otherwise empty case in your
brother's borrowed cabin, which, by the way, I locked."

A fairly long silence was decorated with a stifled giggle
from Caley Bard.

Miss Hewson said breathlessly: "Well, pardon me, again. I guess I'm kind of nervously exhausted. I meant to say Brother's cabin. Brother's other cabin," she wildly amended.

Mr. Hewson said angrily: "O.K. O.K. So it wasn't posted. So we acted like it was. Why? I'll tell you just precisely why, Superintendent. This picture's a work of art. Ask your lady-wife. And this work of art maybe was executed by this guy Constable which would make it a very, very interesting proposition commercially. And we paid out real money, real British money, if that's not a contradiction in terms, for this work of art and we don't appreciate the idea of having it removed from our possession by anybody. Repeat: anybody Period. Cops or whoever. Period. So whadda-we-do?" Mr. Hewson asked at large and answered himself with perhaps a slight loss of countenance. "We anticipate," he said, "the event. We make like this picture's already on its way."

"And so I'm sure it would be," Alleyn said cheerfully, "if it wasn't for a large and conspicuous constable on duty outside the Ramsdyke Lock post-office."

Mr. Hewson's face became slightly pink but his gaze which was directed at Alleyn did not shift. His sister coughed with refinement, said: "Pardon me," and looked terrified.

"You can't win," Mr. Pollock observed to nobody in particular and added after a moment's reflection: "It's disgusting."

"If we're not going to keep you up till all hours," Alleyn said, "we'd better begin. Anybody really want to see the search warrant, by the way?"

"I certainly do," Mr. Hewson announced. "It may be a very crude notion but I certainly do want that thing."

"But, not at all," Alleyn rejoined. "Very sensible of you. Here it is."

Fox displayed the warrant and the Hewsons and Mr. Pollock looked upon it with distaste. Mr. Lazenby said generally that it was a fair go and he had no complaints. Caley Bard tipped Alleyn one of his cock-eyed winks but offered no comment and Dr. Natouche interrupted his work on the map to produce a key of his cabin and lay it on the table. This action seemed to rattle everybody but Caley Bard who merely remarked that his own cabin was unlocked.

"Thank you so much," Alleyn said. "We do carry one or

two of those open-sesame jobs but this will be quicker." He picked up the key. "Any more?" he asked.

"You know something?" Mr. Hewson said. "If you hadn't gotten those other honest-to-God cops around I'd say you were some kind of phoney laugh with the pay-off line left out."

"You would?" Alleyn said absently. "Sorry. There's no joke anywhere that I can see, I promise you that."

It turned out that the only other locked cabin apart from Natouche's and the Hewsons' was Mr. Pollock's. He handed over his key with as bad a grace as he could muster, turned his back on the company and sucked his teeth.

Before he left, Alleyn walked over to the corner table where Dr. Natouche still concerned himself with his map of the waterways. He drew back, rested his dark hands and looked placidly at what he had done. "I am an amateur of maps," he said, perhaps by way of excuse.

If this was a true example of his work he was right. The chart with its little tentative insets and its meticulous lettering was indeed the work of a devoted amateur. It was so fine and so detailed that it almost needed a lens to examine it. Alleyn followed the line of the River to Longminster. There he saw, predictably, the Minster itself, but there, too, was an inn sign and beside it a thin, gallant and carefully drawn female figure with a dark cropped head.

He looked down at Dr. Natouche's head with its own short-cropped fuzz and at the darkish scalp beneath. The two men did not speak to each other.

Alleyn and Fox embarked on their search.

They found the "Constable" still in place, took possession of it, and having found nothing of interest in her brother's very own cabin, moved into Miss Hewson's and methodically emptied the drawers and luggage.

"Funny," Mr. Fox remarked, laying out a rather dreary nightgown with infinite care upon Miss Hewson's bed. "I always expect American ladies' lingerie to be more *troublante* than this type of stuff."

Alleyn stared at him. "I am speechless," he said.

"Why do you make out they were so anxious we wouldn't get a look at that picture?"

"You tell me."

"Well," Fox said. "I've been trying to set up a working theory. Suppose it was all on the level. Suppose this picture was in the cupboard when this Jo Bagg bought the sideboard."

"Which it wasn't, if his story's right."

"Quite so. Suppose, then, it'd been on the premises and somebody shoved it in the cupboard and the Baggs hadn't taken any notice of it and suppose the Hewsons just happened to pick it up like they said and pay for it all fair and aboveboard. In that case what's wrong with letting us have a look at it? They showed it off willingly enough by all accounts. *He* kind of hinted they were afraid we might confiscate. They *may* have been looking at British telly exports in the States, of course, and taken some fanciful notion of how we go to work, but personally I didn't think their yarn stood up."

"I agree. Playing it by ear, they were, I don't mind betting."

"All right, then. Why? People only go on in that style because they've got something to hide. What would they have to hide about this picture? I can only think of one answer. What about you, Mr. Alleyn?"

"That it's a racket and they're in on it."

"Just so. The thing's a forgery and they know it. From that it's a short step to supposing Jo Bagg never had it. The Hewsons brought it with them and planted it in the cupboard when the Baggs weren't looking."

"I don't think so, Br'er Fox. Not from the account Bagg gave of the sale."

"No? I wasn't there, of course, when he gave it," Fox admitted.

"How do you like the possibility of motor-cyclists planting it? They were hanging about Bagg's yard on Tuesday and the screech of the cupboard door seems to have drawn old Mrs. B.'s baleful attention to them."

"Could be. Could well be. Come to that, they might be salting the district with carefully planted forgeries."

"They might, at that. Look at these, Fox."

Alleyn had drawn out of a pocket in Miss Hewson's

dressing-case a folder of colour photographs and film. He laid the prints out on the lid of the suitcase. Three of them were of Ramsdyke Lock. He put the painting on the deck beside them.

"Same thing," Fox said.

"Yes. Taken from precisely the same spot and, by the look of the trees, in spring. Presumably on the previous visit that old Mrs. Bagg went on about. But look. There's that difference we noticed."

"The trees. Yes. Yes. In the painting they're smaller and—well—different."

"Very thorough. Wouldn't do, you see, to have them as they are now. They had to go back to the Constable era. I wouldn't mind betting," Alleyn said, "that those trees have been copied from an actual Constable or a reproduction of one."

"Who by?"

Alleyn didn't reply at once. He restored the photographs to the dressing-case and after another long look at the picture, rolled it carefully and tied it up. "We'll take possession of this," he said, "and thus justify the Hewsons' worst forebodings. I'll write a receipt. Everything in order here? We'll move on. Br'er Fox, to the other locked cabin; I simply can't wait to call, in his absence, on Mr. Pollock."

4

Thompson and Bailey had arrived. They went quietly round the cabins collecting prints from tooth glasses and were then to move to the sites of the motor-cycle traces. Tillottson was in his station in Tollardwark hoping for news of the cyclists and, optimistically, for reports from America and Australia to come through London. Meanwhile the appropriate department was setting up an exhaustive check on the deceased and on the two passengers, Natouche and Caley Bard, who lived in England. Caley had given a London address and his occupation as: "Crammer of ill-digested raw-material into the maws of unwilling adolescents." In other words, he was a free-lance coach to a tutorial firm of considerable repute.

Troy was in bed and asleep at the Percy Arms in Norminster and Alleyn and Fox had completed their search of the cabins.

"A poor, thin time we've had of it," Alleyn said. "Except for that one small thing."

"The Pollock exhibit?"

"That's right."

In Mr. Pollock's cabin they had found in the breast pocket of his deplorable suit a plastic wallet containing a print of the Hewson photograph of Ramsdyke Lock and several envelopes displaying trial sketches for the words with which he had subsequently embellished Troy's picture. He had evidently taken a lot of trouble over them, interrupting himself from time to time to doodle. It was his doodling that Alleyn had found interesting.

"Very neat, very detailed, very meticulous," he had muttered. "Not the doodles of a non-draughtsman. No. I wonder what the psychiatric experts have to say under this heading. Someone ought to write a monograph: "Doodling and the Unconscious' or: 'How to—.'" And he had broken off in the middle of the sentence to stare at the last of Mr. Pollock's trial efforts. He held it out to Fox to examine.

"The Crab is followed—" Mr. Pollock had printed and then repeated, with slight changes, several of the letters. But down one side of the envelope he had made a really elaborate doodle.

It was the drawing of a tree, for all the world twin to the elm that overhung the village pond in Miss Hewson's oil painting.

"Very careless," Alleyn had said as he put it in his pocket. "I'm surprised at him."

When they returned to the saloon they found the Hewsons, and Mr. Pollock and Mr. Lazenby, still up and still playing Scrabble. Caley Bard and Dr. Natouche were reading. Mrs. Tretheway had gone to bed.

Bailey and Thompson passed through, carrying their gear. The passengers watched them in silence.

When they had gone Alleyn said: "We've done our stuff down there and the cabins are all yours. I'm very sorry if we've kept you up too late. Here are the keys." He laid them on the table. "And here," he said, holding up the rolled canvas, "is your picture, Miss Hewson. We would like to take charge of it for a short time, if you please. I'll give you this receipt. I assure you the canvas will come to no harm."

Miss Hewson had turned, as Fox liked to say, as white as a turnip and really her skin did have something of the aspect of that unlovely root. She looked from Alleyn to her brother and then wildly round the group of passengers as if appealing against some terrible decision. She rose to her feet, pulled at her underlip with uncertain fingers and had actually made a curious little whining sound when her brother said: "Take it easy, Sis. You don't have to act this way. It's O.K.; take it easy."

Mr. Hewson had very large, pale hands. Alleyn saw his left hand clench and his right hand close round his sister's forearm. She gave a short cry of pain, sank back in her chair and shot what seemed to be a look of terror at her brother.

"My sister's a super-sensitive girl, Superintendent," Mr. Hewson said. "She gets nervous very, very easy."

"I hope there is no occasion for her to do so now," Alleyn said. "I understand this is not your first visit to this district, Mr. Hewson. You were here in the spring, weren't you?"

Dr. Natouche lowered his book and for the first time seemed to listen to what was being said: Caley Bard gave an ejaculation of surprise. Miss Hewson mouthed inaudibly and fingered her arm and Mr. Lazenby said: "Really? Is that so? Your second visit to the River? I didn't realize," as if they were all making polite conversation.

"That is so," Mr. Hewson said. "A flying visit. We were captivated and settled to return."

"When did you book your passages in the *Zodiac?*" Alleyn asked.

A silence, broken at last by Mr. Hewson.

"Pardon me, I should have put that a little differently, I guess. We made our reservations before we left the States. I should have said we were enchanted to learn when we got here that the *Zodiac* cruise would cover this same territory."

"On your previous visit, did you take many photographs?"

"Some. Yes, sir; quite some."

"Including several shots here at Ramsdyke, of exactly the

same subject as the one in this picture?"

Mr. Hewson said: Maybe. I wouldn't remember offhand. We certainly do get around to taking plenty of pictures."

"Have you seen this particular photograph, Mr. Pollock?"

Mr. Pollock lounged back in his seat, put his hands in his trouser pockets and assumed a look of cagey impertinence with which Alleyn was very familiar.

"Couldn't say, I'm sure," he said.

"Surely you'd remember. The photograph that is taken from the same place as the painting?"

"Haven't the vaguest."

"You mean you haven't seen it?"

"Know what?" Mr. Pollock said. "I don't get all this stuff about photos. It doesn't mean a thing to me. It's silly."

Mr. Pollock's tree doodle and the Hewsons' photograph of Ramsdyke Lock dropped on the table in front of him.

"These were in the pocket of your suit."

"What of it?"

"The drawing is a replica of a tree in the painting."

"Fancy that."

"When did you make this drawing?"

For the first time he hesitated but said at last: "After I see the picture. It's kind of recollection. I was doodling."

"While you practised your lettering?"

"That's right. *No!*" he said quickly. "After."

"It would have to be after, wouldn't it? Because you'd done the lettering on the zodiac drawing before you saw the picture. A day or more before. Hadn't you?"

"That's your idea; I didn't say so."

"Mr. Pollock: I suggest that your first answer is the true one. I suggest you did in fact 'doodle' this very accurate drawing when you were practising your lettering a couple of days ago and that you did it, subconsciously or not, out of your knowledge of the picture. Your very vivid and accurate recollection of the picture with which you were already as familiar as if—" Alleyn paused. Mr. Pollock had gone very still. "—as if you yourself had painted it," said Alleyn.

Dr. Natouche rose, murmured, "Excuse me, please," and went up on deck.

"You don't have to insult me," Pollock said, "in front of that nigger."

Caley Bard walked over and looked at him as if he was something nasty he'd caught in his butterfly net.

"You *bloody* little tit," he said. "Will you shut up, you perfectly bloody little tit?"

Pollock stared at him with a kind of shrinking defiance that was extremely unpleasant to see.

"Sorry," Caley said to Alleyn and returned to his seat.

"—as if you yourself had painted it," Alleyn repeated. "Did you paint it, Mr. Pollock?"

"No. And that's it. No."

And that *was* as far as Mr. Pollock was concerned. He might have gone stone deaf and blind for all the response he made to anything else that was said to him.

"It's very hot in here," said Mr. Lazenby.

It was indeed. The summer night had grown sultry. There were rumours of thunder in the air and sheet-lightning made occasional irrelevant gestures somewhere a long way beyond Norminster.

Mr. Lazenby pulled the curtain back from one of the windows and exposed a white blank. The Creeper had risen.

"Very close," Mr. Lazenby said and ran his finger under his dog-collar. "I think," he said in his slightly parsonic, slightly Australian accents, "that we're entitled to an explanation, Superintendent. We've all experienced a big shock, you know. We've found ourselves alongside a terrible tragedy in the death and subsequent discovery of this poor girl. I'm sure there's not one of us doesn't want to see the whole thing cleared up and settled. If you reckon all this business about a painting picked up in a yard has something to do with the death of the poor girl, well: good on you. Go ahead. But, fair dinkum, I don't myself see how there can be the remotest connection."

"With which observation," Mr. Hewson said loudly, "I certainly concur. Yes, *sir*."

"The connection," Alleyn said, "if there is one, will I hope declare itself as the investigation develops. In the meantime, if you don't mind, we'll push along with preliminaries. Will you cast your minds back to Monday night when you all explored Toll'ark?"

The group at the table eyed him warily. From behind his book Caley said: "O.K. I've cast mine, such as it is, back."

"Good. What did you do in Toll'ark?"

"Thwarted of my original intention which was to ask your wife if she'd explore the antiquities with me, I sat in the Northumberland Arms drinking mild-and-bitter and listening to the dullest brand of Mummerset-type gossip it would be possible to conceive. When the pub closed I returned, more pensive than pickled, to our gallant craft."

"By which route?"

"By a precipitous, rather smelly and cobbled alley laughingly called Something Street—wait—. It was on a shop wall. I've got it. Weyland Street."

"Meet any of the other passengers?"

"I don't think so. Did we?" Caley asked them.

They slightly shook their heads.

"You Mr. Lazenby, attended compline in the church. Did you return alone to the *Zodiac?*"

"No," he said easily. "Not all the way. I ran into Stan and we went back together. Didn't we, Stan?"

Mr. Pollock, answering to his first name, nodded glumly.

"We know that Mr. and Miss Hewson, followed by my wife and then by Dr. Natouche returned to the River by way of Ferry Lane where they all met, outside Bagg's second-hand premises. We also know," Alleyn said, "that Miss Rickerby-Carrick returned alone, presumably not by Ferry Lane. As Weyland Street is the only other direct road down to the River it seems probable that she took that way home. Did either of you see her?"

"No," Pollock said instantly and very loudly.

"No," Lazenby agreed.

"Mr. Lazenby," Alleyn said, taking a sudden and outrageous risk, "what did you do with the papers you tore out of Miss Rickerby-Carrick's diary?"

A gust of misted air moved the curtain over an open window on the starboard side and the trees above Ramsdyke Lock soughed and were silent again.

"I don't think that's a very nice way of talking," said Mr. Lazenby.

Miss Hewson had begun quietly to cry.

"There are ways and ways of putting things," Mr.

Lazenby continued, "and that way was offensive."

"Why?" Alleyn asked. "Do you say you didn't tear them out?"

"By a mishap, I may have done something of the sort. Naturally. I rescued the diary from a watery grave," he said, attempting some kind of irony.

"Which was more than anybody did for its owner," Caley Bard remarked. They looked at him with consternation.

"It was a very, very prompt and praiseworthy undertaking," said Mr. Hewson stuffily. "She was very, very grateful to the Reverend. It was the Action of a Man. Yes, sir. A man."

"As we could see for ourselves," Caley remarked and bowed slightly to Mr. Lazenby.

"It was nothing, really," Mr. Lazenby protested. "I'm a Sydneysider, don't forget, and I *was* in my bathers."

"As I have already indicated," Caley said.

"The pages," Alleyn said, "were in your left hand when you sat on the bank just before the *Zodiac* picked you up. You had turned the leaves of the diary over while you waited."

Mr. Pollock broke his self-imposed silence. "Anybody like to make a guess where all this information came from?" he asked. "Marvellous, isn't it? Quite a family affair."

"Shut up," Caley said and turned to Alleyn. "You're right, of course, about this. I remember—I expect we all do—that the Padre had got a loose page in his hand. But, Alleyn, I do think there's a very obvious explanation—the one that he has in fact given you. The damn' diary was soaked to a sop and probably disintegrating in his hands."

"It's not in quite as bad shape as that."

"Well—all right. But it *had* opened in the water, you know. And when he grabbed it, surely he might have loosened a couple of pages or more."

"But," Alleyn said mildly, "I haven't for a moment suggested anything else. I only asked Mr. Lazenby what he did with the loose page or pages."

"Mr. Bard is right. I did not tear them out. They came out."

"Cometer pieces in 'is 'ands, like," Caley explained.

"Very funny," said Mr. Pollock. "I don't think."

"I do not know," Mr. Lazenby announced with hauteur, "what I did with any pieces of pulpy paper that may or may not have come away in my hand. I remember nothing about it."

"Did you read them?"

"That suggestion, Superintendent, is unworthy of you."

Alleyn said: "Last Monday night on your way to the *Zodiac* you and Mr. Pollock stopped near a dark entry in Weyland Street? What did you talk about?"

And now, he saw with satisfaction, they were unmistakably rattled. "They're asking themselves," he thought, "just how much I am bluffing. They know Troy couldn't have told me about this one. They're asking themselves where I could have picked it up and the only answer is the Rickerby-Carrick diary. I'll stake my oath, Lazenby read whatever was on the missing pages and Pollock knows about it. What's more they probably know the diary was in the suitcase and that we must have seen it. They're dead scared we've found the missing pages which I wish to hell we had. If they're as fly as I believe they are, there's only one line for them to take and I hope they don't take it."

They took it, however. "I'm not making any more bloody statements," Mr. Pollock suddenly shouted, "till I've seen a lawyer and that's my advice to all and sundry."

"Dead right," Mr. Lazenby applauded. "Good on you." And feeling perhaps that his style was inappropriate, he added: "We shall be absolutely within our rights to adopt this attitude. In my opinion it is entirely proper for us to do so."

"Reverend Lazenby," Mr. Hewson said with fervour, "you said it, boy, you certainly said it."

Miss Hewson, who had been furtively dabbing at her eyes and nose gave a shatteringly profound sob.

"Ah, for Pete's sake, Sis," said Hewson.

"No! No! No!" she cried out on a note of real terror. "Don't touch me. I'm not staying here. I'm going to my room. I'm going to bed."

"Do," Alleyn said politely. "Why not take one of your own pills?"

She caught her breath, stared at him and then blundered

down the companionway to the lower deck.

"Poor girl," said Mr. Lazenby. "Poor dear girl."

"There's one other question," Alleyn said. "In view of your decision of a moment ago you may not feel inclined to answer it. Unless—?" he smiled at Caley Bard.

"At the moment," Caley said, "I'm not sending for my solicitor or taking vows of silence."

"Good. Well, then, here it is. Miss Rickerby-Carrick wore, on a cord round her neck, an extremely valuable jewel. She told Miss Hewson and my wife about it. It has not been found."

"Washed off?" Caley suggested.

"Possible, of course. If necessary we'll search the riverbed."

Caley thought for a moment. "Look," he then said. "She was a pretty scatty individual. I gather she was sleeping on deck, or trying to sleep. She said she suffered from insomnia. My God, if she did, it was fully orchestrated but that's by the way. Suppose in the dead of night she *was* awake and suppose she took a hike along the towpath in her navy pijams and her magenta gown with her bit of Fabergé tat around her neck? Grotesque it may sound but it would be entirely in character."

"How," Alleyn said, "do you know it was Fabergé, Mr. Bard?"

"Because, for God's sake, she told me. When we thundered about the Crossdyke ruins, butterfly hunting. I daresay she told everybody. She was scatty as a hen, poor wretch."

"Well?"

"Well, and suppose she met an unsavoury character who grabbed the bauble and when she cut up rough, throttled her and shoved her in the river?"

"First collecting her suitcase from her cabin in the *Zodiac*?"

"Damn!" said Caley. "You would bring that up, wouldn't you."

"All the same," Alleyn said, turning to the group round the table, "we can't overlook the possibility of interference of some sort from outside."

"Like who?" Hewson demanded.

"Like, for instance, a motor-cyclist and his girl who seem to have rather haunted the course of the Zodiac. Do you all know who I mean?"

Silence.

"Oh *really!*" Caley exclaimed. "This is too much! Of course we all know who you mean. They've turned up from time to time like prologues to the omens coming on in an early Cocteau film." He addressed his fellow-passengers. "We've seen them, we've remarked upon them, why the hell shouldn't we say so?"

They stirred uneasily. Lazenby said: "You're right, of course, Mr. Bard. No reason at all. A couple of young mods—we used to call them bodgies in Aussie—with I daresay no harm in them. They seem to be cobbers of young Tom's."

"Have any of you ever spoken to them?"

Nobody answered.

"You better ask the coloured gentleman," Hewson said and Alleyn thought he heard a note of fear in his voice.

"Dr. Natouche has spoken to them, you think?"

"I don't think. I know. The first day when we went through the lock here. They were on the bridge and he came down from this helluva whatsit in the hillside. These two hobos shouted something and he walked up to them and said something and they kinda laughed and kicked up their machine and roared off."

"Where were you?"

"Me? Walking up the hill with the mob."

Hewson shifted his position slightly and continued, with considerable finesse, to emphasize the already richly offensive tone of his behaviour. "Mrs. Alleyn," he said, "was in the whatsit with the deceased. She'd been there for quite some time before the deceased got there. So'd he. Natouche. Yes, sir. Quite some time."

This was said so objectionably that Alleyn felt the short hair rise on the back of his scalp. Fox, who had performed his usual trick of making his bulk inconspicuous while he took notes, let out a slight ejaculation and at once stifled it.

Hewson, after a look at Alleyn's face said in a great hurry:

"Don't get me wrong. Take it easy. Hell, Superintendent, I didn't mean a thing."

Alleyn raised his eyebrows at Fox who soundlessly formed the word "Tom?" and went below. Alleyn climbed the companionway leading to the upper deck and looked over the half-door. Dr. Natouche leant on the port taffrail. He was wreathed in mist. His hands were clasped and his head bent as if he stared at them.

"Dr. Natouche, can I trouble you again for a moment?"

"Certainly. Shall I come down?"

"If you please."

When he had come down, blinking a little in the light, Alleyn, watching Pollock and the Hewsons and Lazenby, was reminded of Troy's first letter. These passengers, she had written, eyed Natouche with something that seemed very like fear.

He asked Natouche what had passed between him and the motor-cyclists. He waited for a moment or two and then said the young man had asked him if he was a passenger in the *Zodiac*. He thought from his manner that the question was intended as a covert insult of some sort, Dr. Natouche said tranquilly, but he had answered that he was and the girl had burst out laughing.

"I walked away," he said, "and the young man gave one of those cries—I think they are known as cat-calls. It was not an unusual incident."

"Can you remember them clearly? They sound sufficiently objectionable to be remembered."

"They were dressed in black leather. The man was rather older than one expected. They both had long, very dark hair falling from their helmets to their shoulders. The man's hair was oily. He had a broad face, small, deepset eyes and a slightly prognathic jaw. The girl was sallow. She had large eyes and an outbreak of acne on her chin."

Pollock made his standard remark. "Isn't it marvellous?" and gave his little sneering laugh.

"Thank you," Alleyn said. "That's very useful."

Pollock now took action. He got up from the table, lounged across the saloon and stood with his hands in his pockets and his head on one side, quite close to Natouche.

"'Ere," he said. "You! 'Doctor.' What's the big idea?"

"I don't understand you. I'm sorry."

"You don't? I think you do. I see you talking to the ton-up combo and I never took the impression they was slinging off at you. I think that's just your story like you lot always trot out: 'O dear, aren't they all insultin' to us noble martyrs.' I took a different impression. I took the impression you knew them two before. See?"

"You are mistaken."

Alleyn said: "Did anyone else get such an impression?"

Hewson said: "Yeah! Yeah. I guess I did. Yeah, sure did."

"Mr. Lazenby?"

"I'm very loath to jump to conclusions. I'm not prepared to say positively. I must confess—"

"Well?"

"We were some way away, Superintendent, on the wapentake slope. I don't think an impression at that distance has much value. But—well, yes, I thought—vaguely, you know—that perhaps the Doctor had found some friends. Only a vague idea."

"Mr. Bard? What about you?"

Caley Bard drove his fingers through his hair and swore under his breath. He then said "I agree that any impression one may have taken at that remove is absolutely valueless. We could hear nothing that was said. Dr. Natouche's explanation fits as well as any other."

"If he never seen them before how's he remember all this stuff about jaws and pimples?" Pollock demanded. "After half a minute! Not likely!"

"But I fancy," Alleyn said, "that, in common with all the rest of you, Dr. Natouche had ample opportunity to observe them at Norminster on the morning you embarked."

"Here!" Pollock shouted. "What price this for a theory? What price he and them knocked it up between them? What price they did the clobbering and he handled the suitcase? Now then!"

He stared in front of him, sneering vaingloriously and contriving at the same time to look frightened. Natouche's face was closed like a wall.

"I thought," Caley said to Pollock, "you'd settled to keep

your mouth shut until you got a solicitor. Why the devil can't you follow your own advice and belt up?"

"Here, 'ere, 'ere!"

Fox returned with young Tom who, tousled with sleep and naked to the waist, looked very young indeed and rather frightened.

"Sorry to knock you up like this, Tom," Alleyn said. "Mr. Fox will have told you what it's all about."

Tom nodded.

"We just want to know if you can tell us anything about the ton-up couple. Friends of yours?"

Tom showed the whites of his eyes and said not to say friends exactly. He shifted his feet, curled his toes, looked everywhere but at Alleyn and answered in monosyllables. The passengers listened avidly. Alleyn wondered if he was wise to conduct this one-sided interview in front of them and thought that, on the whole, it would probably pay off. He extracted, by slow degrees, that Tom had hobnobbed with the ton-up pair some time ago in a coffee-bar in Norminster. When? He couldn't say exactly. Some time back. Early in the cruising season? Yes. Early on. He hadn't seen them again until this cruise. Names? He wouldn't know the surnames. The chap got called Pluggy and his girl-friend was Glenys. Did they live in the district? He didn't think so. He couldn't say where they lived.

This was heavy going. Caley sighed and took up his book. Dr. Natouche had the air of politely attending a function that did not interest him. Pollock bit his nails. Lazenby assumed a tolerant smile and Hewson stared at Tom with glazed intensity.

Alleyn said: "Did they talk to you first or did you make up to them? In the coffee-bar?"

"They did," Tom mumbled. "They wanted to know about places."

"What sort of places?"

"Along the River. Back of the River."

"Just any old places?"

No. It appeared, not quite that. They were interested in the second-hand trade. They wanted to know where there were junk shops or yards or used-parts dumps. Yes, he'd told them about Jo Bagg.

The passengers shifted their feet.

By a tortuous process something like a coherent story began to emerge. Alleyn thought he recognized the symptoms. The ton-ups had been adventurous figures to young Tom. They had a buccaneering air about them. They were cool. They were with it. They had flattered him. Troy had noticed, when the *Zodiac* sailed, something furtive in their exchange of signals. Alleyn asked Tom abruptly what his parents thought of the acquaintanceship. He flushed scarlet and muttered indistinguishably. They had, it seemed, not approved. The Skipper's attitude to ton-ups was evidently regrettably square. Alleyn gathered that he had asked Tom if he hadn't got something better to do than hang round the moorings with a couple of freaks.

"Did they ever ask you to talk about any of the passengers?"

Tom was silent.

"This is important, Tom," Alleyn said. "You know what's happened, don't you? You know why we're here?"

He nodded.

"You wouldn't want to see someone wrongfully accused, would you?"

He shook his head.

"Did they talk about any of the passengers?"

Tom's dark eyes slewed round until they looked at Dr. Natouche and then at the floor.

"Did they talk about Dr. Natouche?"

He nodded again.

"What did they say?"

"They—. They said to—give him a message."

"What message? Come along. As far as you can remember it, in their own words: What message?"

Tom, looking as if he was about to cry, blurted out. "They said to tell him from them he could—"

"Could what?"

A stream of obscenity quoted in the broken voice of an adolescent boy, jetted into the quiet decency of the little saloon.

"You asked," Tom said miserably. "You asked. I can't help it. It's what they said. They don't like—they don't like—" He jerked his head at Natouche.

"Very well," Alleyn said. "We'll leave it at that." He turned to Natouche. "I take it," he said, "the message was not delivered?"

"No."

"I should bloody well hope not," said Caley Bard.

"Did they talk about any of the other passengers?" Alleyn pursued.

At Norminster they had asked, it appeared, about Troy. Only, Tom said, twisting himself about in a quite astonishing manner, only who she was and when she booked her passage.

"Did you know the answer?"

He knew she'd booked a cancellation that morning. He didn't know then—. Here Tom boggled and shuffled and was finally induced to say he didn't know until later that she was the celebrated painter or who her husband was.

"And Miss Rickerby-Carrick—did they talk about her?"

Only, Tom mumbled, to say she was some barmy old tart.

"When did you last see them?"

This provoked another unhappy reaction. The dark, uncertain face whitened, the lips opened and moved but no sound came from them. Tom looked as if for tuppence he'd bolt.

Caley said: "This is getting a bit tough, Alleyn, isn't it?" and Pollock at once began to talk about police methods. "This is nothing," he said. "Nothing to what goes on in the cells. Don't you answer 'im, kid. Don't give 'im the satisfaction. They can't make you. Don't put yourself in wrong."

Tom turned aside, ducked his head into the crook of his arms and gave way to ungainly tears. There were sounds of indignation from the passengers.

The Skipper had returned. His voice could be heard on deck and in a moment he came nimbly down the companionway followed by the Sergeant from Tollardwark.

The Skipper looked at his son. "What's all this?" he asked.

Tom raised a tear-blubbered face, tried to say something and incontinently bolted to the lower deck.

Alleyn said: "I'll have a word with you about this in a moment, Skipper," and turned to the Sergeant.

"What is it?"

"Message from the Super at Toll'ark, sir." He looked at the assembly and produced a note which he handed to Alleyn.

"Motor-bike couple picked up near Pontefract. Bringing them to Tollardwark at once. With article of jewellery."

IX

THE CREEPER

"I pause here," Alleyn said, "to draw your attention to a matter of technique.

"You'll have noticed that at this point I questioned the passengers in a group instead of following the more orthodox line of seeing them separately, taking notes and getting a signed statement. This was admittedly a risky thing to do and I didn't take that risk without hesitation. You see, by now we were sure we had a case of conspiracy on our hands and I felt that, interviewed separately, they would have time to concoct some kind of consistent tarradiddle, whereas, if we caught them all together and on the hop, they would have to improvise and in doing so might give themselves away. We felt certain they were under orders from Foljambe and that Foljambe was one of them, and Mr. Fox and I had a pretty good notion which. You will, I daresay, have a pretty good notion yourselves."

Carmichael, in the second row, showed signs of becoming active.

"I won't, however," Alleyn said, "ask what they are. We're not playing a guessing game, or are we? Well—never mind. I'll press on.

"In the due course, we came, as you will hear, to a point in the investigation where we could draw only one conclusion. The 'alibis,' to call them so, for the earlier case would be established, in that suspects of given names would be proved to be in given places at given times. The only conclusion, as I hope you will see as the case develops, could be that one of these suspects was operating under what might be called the double identity lay. This is, in fact, what Foljambe was doing.

He had adopted, for purposes of the cruise, the identity of another and a living person whom he knew to be out of England. This meant that in the event of an inquiry the police would check this person's background, see that it was impeccable, look up his address, find that he was away, make further inquiries and discover he could not possibly be fitted into the Foljambe file. And so turn elsewhere for a culprit. It is an extremely risky but not unusual gimmick and is only effective for a short time, but the Jampot is a tip-and-run expert and had decided to give it a go. Bear this in mind as we go on.

"We come now to the point when the investigation went grievously, indeed tragically, wrong and it went wrong because a police officer neglected a fundamental rule. Police officers, like the rest of mankind, are vulnerable creatures and like the rest of mankind they sometimes slip up. In this case a simple, basic rule of procedure was ignored. The chap who ignored it was a middle-aged provincial P.C., not all that familiar with the type of job in hand and not as alert as he needed to be. He had his dim moment and the result was a death that could have been avoided. I don't mind telling you, it still, as people say, haunts me. There's one such case at least in the lives of most investigating officers and sooner or later every man jack of you is liable to encounter it. Ours is a job, let's face it, for which one has to grow an extra skin. In some of us, under constant irritation this becomes a rhinoceros hide. We are not a starry-eyed lot. But at the risk of getting right off the track—a most undesirable proceeding—I would like to say this. You won't be any worse at your job if you can keep your humanity. If you lose it altogether you'll be, in my opinion, better out of the force, because with it you'll have lost your sense of values and that's a dire thing to befall any policeman.

"Sorry. I'll push on. Following the signal about the motor-bike pair, Mr. Fox and I returned in the Yard car to Tollardwark. But first of all I talked to the Skipper—"

1

"Now get this straight," Alleyn said. "I'm not suggesting the boy's implicated in any way whatever. I am suggesting that they've appealed to his imagination and to the instinct for rebellion that rumbles in any normal chap of Tom's age. Now, after what's happened, he's scared. He knows something but he won't talk. I'm not going to sit him down and grill him. I don't want to and I haven't time. If you can get him to tell you whether he saw, or spoke to, or knows anything about, this precious pair *after* he saw them on the bridge here at Ramsdyke on Monday afternoon—well, it may help us and it may not. We've caught them in possession of a valuable jewel which when last seen was slung round Miss Rickerby-Carrick's neck. That's the picture, Skipper, and as far as Tom's concerned it's over to you."

"I told him. I told him to keep clear of that lot. If I thought it'd do any good I'd belt him."

"Would you? He's left school, hasn't he? What does he do week in, week out? Norminster to Longminster and back with a turn at the wheel if he's in luck on the straight reaches? What did you do at his age, Skipper?"

"Me?" The Skipper shot a look at Alleyn. "I shipped cabin boy aboard a Singapore tramp. All right, I get the point. I'll talk to him."

Alleyn walked to the starboard side and looked at the River.

It almost seemed as if the field of detergent foam that had closed over Hazel Rickerby-Carrick had supernaturally climbed the weir, invested the upper reaches and closed in upon the *Zodiac*. "Is that what you call the Creeper?" Alleyn said.

"That's right. You get her at this time of year. Very low-lying country from Norminster to Crossdyke."

"Thick," Fox said. "Fog, more like."

"And will be more so before dawn. She's making."

"We'll push on," Alleyn said. "You know the drill, don't you, Skipper? As soon as they're all in bed put your craft in the lock and empty the lock. Give them a bit of time to settle. Watch for their lights to go out. It's twenty to eleven. You won't have long to wait."

"It is O.K. with the Authority, isn't it? I wouldn't want—"

"Perfectly. It's all fixed."

"A man could scramble out of it, you know."

"Yes, but only with a certain amount of trouble. It wouldn't be so simple in this fog, whereas at her moorings it would be extremely easy to jump or, if necessary, swim. It'll confine the escape area, in effect. You'll be relieved as soon as possible after first light. We're very much in your debt over this, Skipper. Thank you for helping. Good-night."

With Fox and the constable he went ashore. The Skipper removed the gangplank.

"Good-night, then," said the Skipper softly.

The Creeper had already begun to move about the towpath and condense on a green hedge near the lockhouse. It was threading gently into the trees and making wraiths of those that could be seen. The night smelt dank. Small sounds were exaggerated and everything was damp to the touch.

"Damn," Alleyn whispered. "We don't want this. Where's that chap—oh, there you are."

The considerable bulk of Tillottson's P.C. on duty, loomed out of a drift of mist.

"Sir," said the shape.

"You know what you've got to do, don't you? Nobody to leave the *Zodiac*."

"Yes, sir."

"Where's your nearest support?"

"T'other bank, sir."

"And then?"

"This side, sir, up beyond Wapentake Pot at th' crossroads. T'other side, sir, above pub at main road crossing."

"Yes. Well, you'd better keep well down by the craft, with the mist rising. The Skipper's putting her in the lock before long. If there's an attempt you should be able to spot it. If anyone tries to come ashore, order them back and if they try to bolt, get them."

"Sir."

"Watch it, now."

"Sir."

"A dull-sounding chap," Alleyn muttered.

They climbed up to the road and crossed the main bridge below the lock to the left bank. The formless voice of the weir obliterated other sounds. Blown flecks of detergent mingled with the rising mist.

"We'll have a bloody tiresome drive back to Toll'ark, if this is the form. Where's that car? And where—oh—here you are."

Thompson and Bailey loomed up. They'd completed their job along the riverside and were told to come back to Tollardwark. The London police car gave a discreet hoot and turned on its fog lamps. They piled into it. Alleyn called up Tollardwark on the sound system and spoke to Tillottson.

"They won't talk," Tillottson said. "Not a peep out of them."

"We're on our way. I hope. Over and out."

The local man gave them a lead on his motor-bike. When they reached the crest of the hill they found the mist had not risen to that level. The man at the crossroads flashed his torch, they turned into the main road and in eight minutes arrived once again at Tollardwark.

In the office where Troy had first encountered Mr. Tillottson, he sat behind his desk with a telephone receiver at his ear and a note-pad under his hand. He repeated everything that was said to him, partly, it seemed, for accuracy's sake and partly for Alleyn's information.

"Ta," he said and signalled to Alleyn. "Yes. Ta. Mind repeating that? Description tallies with that of 'Dinky Dickson,' con man 1964. Sus. drug contact Kings Cross, Sydney. Place of origin unknown but claims to be Australian. Believed to be—Here! What's that? Oh! Oh, I get you! Unfrocked clergyman. Australian police got nothing on him since May '67 when heavy sus. drug racket but no hard proof. Very plausible type. Ta. And the U.S. lot? Two hundred and seven left-ear-deficients on F.B.I. records. No Hewsons. Might be Deafy Ed Moran, big-time fix, heroin, Chicago, undercover picture-dealing. Expatriated Briton but speaks with strong U.S. accent. Sister works with him; homely, middle-aged, usually known as Sis. No convictions since 1960 but heavy sus., Foljambe—here, wait a sec. This is important—heavy sus., Foljambe—accomplice. Message ends. Ta. What about Pollock, then? Anything come through? Pardon?"

Mr. Tillottson's pen hovered anxiously. "Pardon?" he repeated. "Oh. Wait a wee, till I get it down. One-time commercial artist. No present known occupation but owns property, is in the money and living well. Nothing in Records? O.K. And the other two? Natouche and Bard? Nothing. What's that? Yes, we've got that stuff about his practice in Liverpool. What? Laurenson and Busby, London? Tutorial Service? Spends his vacations chasing butterflies. Known to *who?* British Lepi—Oh. Given his name to *what?* Spell it out. L-a-p-a-z-b-a-r-d-i-i. What's that when it's at home? A *butterfly?* Ta. Yes. Yes. Mr. Alleyn's come in. I'll tell him, then. Thanks."

Alleyn said: "Don't hang up. Let me have a word." He took the receiver. "Alleyn here," he said. "Look, I heard all that but I'd like men to call immediately at all the addresses. Yes. Liverpool, too. Yes, I know. Yes, but nevertheless— right. And ring us back, will you? Yes."

He hung up. "Well, Bert," he said, "what have you got in your back parlour? Let's take a look, shall we?"

"Better see this first, hadn't you?"

Tillottson unlocked a wall safe and from it took an object like a miniature pudding tied up in chamois leather and attached to a cord. "I haven't opened it," he said.

Alleyn opened it, cautiously. "Good God!" he said.

There it lay, on a police officer's desk in an English market town: an exotic if ever there was one: a turquoise enamel ovoid, starred with diamonds and girt with twelve minuscule figures decked out in emeralds and rubies and pearls, all dancing in order round their jewelled firmament. Aries, Taurus, Gemini—. "The old gang," Alleyn said. "It's an Easter egg by Fabergé, Fox, and the gift of an Emperor. And now—what a descent!—we've got to try it for dabs." He looked at Thompson and Bailey. "Job for you," he said.

"Do you mean to say she charged about the place with this thing hung round her neck!" Fox exclaimed. "It must be worth a fortune. And it's uncommonly pretty," he added. "Uncommonly so."

"That, unless we're on the wrong track altogether, is what the Jampot thought. Go ahead, you two. Dabs and pictures."

They were about to leave the room when the telephone rang. Tillottson answered it. "You'd better report to Mr. Alleyn," he said. "Hold on." He held out the receiver. "P.M. result," he said.

Alleyn listened. "Thank you," he said. "What we expected." He hung up. "She didn't drown, Fox. Pressure on the carotids and vagus nerve. The mixture as before and straight from the Jampot. All right, Bert. Show us your captives."

They were in the little charge-room, lounging back on a couple of office chairs and chewing gum. They were as Natouche had described them and their behaviour was completely predictable: the quarter sneer, the drooped eyelid, the hunched shoulder and the perpetual complacent chew. The girl, Alleyn thought, looking at her hands, was frightened: the man hid his hands in his pockets and betrayed nothing but his own insolence.

"They've been charged," Tillottson said, "with theft. They won't make a statement."

Alleyn said to the young man: "I'm going to put questions to you. You've been taken into custody and found to be in possession of a jewel belonging to a lady into whose death we are inquiring. Driving license?" He looked at Tillottson who slightly nodded. The young man, sketching boredom and impertinence in equal parts, raised his eyebrows, dipped his fingers into a pocket and threw a license on the table. He opened his mouth, accelerated his chewing and resumed his former pose.

The license was made out in the name of Albert Bernard Smith and seemed to be in order. It gave an address in Soho.

"This will be checked. The night before last," Alleyn said, "you were on the towpath at Crossdyke alongside the *Zodiac* wearing those boots. You had parked your bicycle under a hedge on the left-hand side of the road above the Lock. Later that night you were here at Ramsdyke. You arrived here, with a passenger. Not:" he looked at the girl, "this lady. You carried your passenger—a dead weight—" For two seconds the slightly prognathic jaw, noticed by Dr. Natouche, stopped champing. The girl suddenly recrossed her legs.

"—a dead weight," Alleyn repeated, "down to the weir. Her pyjamas caught on a briar. You did what you'd been instructed to do and then picked up your present companion and made off for Carlisle where you arrived yesterday in time to send a telegram to the Skipper of the *Zodiac*. It was signed Hay Rickerby-Carrick which is not much like Albert

Bernard Smith. Having executed this commission you turned south and were picked up by the police at Pontefract."

The young man yawned widely, displaying the wad of gum on his tongue. He stretched his arms. The girl gave a scarey giggle and clapped her hand over her mouth.

"You've been so busy," Alleyn said, "on your northern jaunt that you can't have heard the news. The body has been found and the woman was murdered. I shall now repeat the usual warning which you've already had from Superintendent Tillottson. At the moment you are being held for theft."

The young man, now very white about the side whiskers, heard the usual warning with a sneer that seemed to have come unstuck. The girl watched him.

"Any statement?"

For the first time the young man spoke. His voice was strongly cockney.

"You can contact Mr. C. D. E. Struthers," he said. "I'm not talking."

Mr. C. D. E. Struthers was an extremely adroit London solicitor whose practice was confined, profitably, to top-level experts in mayhem.

"Really?" Alleyn said. "And who's going to pay for that?"

"Mention my name."

"If I knew it, I would be delighted to do so. Good evening to you."

When the couple had swaggered unconvincingly to the cells Tillottson said: "'Smith' they may be, but not for my money."

"Ah," Fox agreed. "They'd have done the virtuous indignation stuff if they were."

"Well, Smith or Montmorency," Alleyn said, "we'd better let them talk to Mr. C. D. E. Struthers. He may wish them onto one of his legal brethren in the North or he may come up here himself. It's a matter of prestige."

"How d'you mean? Prestige?" asked Tillottson.

"The other name for it is Foljambe. Get your sergeant here to trace the license, will you, Bert? And a description to Records. And Dabs."

"Yes, O.K. I'll see to it."

But before he could do so the Sergeant himself appeared looking perturbed.

"Call for you, sir," he said to Alleyn. "P.C. Cape on duty at Ramsdyke Lock. Very urgent."

"What the hell's this," Alleyn said. But when he heard the voice, he guessed.

"I'm reporting at once, sir," gabbled P.C. Cape. "I'm very sorry, sir, but there's been a slip-up, sir. In the fog, sir."

"Who?"

"The lady, sir. The American lady."

"What do you mean—slip-up?"

"She's gone, sir."

2

Six minutes with their siren wailing brought them back to the Ramsdyke. Tillottson kept up an uninterrupted flow of anathemas against his P.C. Cape. Alleyn and Fox said little, knowing that nothing they could offer would solace him. There was still no fog to speak of on the main road but when they turned off into the lane above Ramsdyke Lock they looked down on a vague uniform pallor of the sort that fills the valleys in a Japanese landscape. Their fog-lamps isolated them in a moving confinement that closed as they descended.

"A likely night for it," Tillottson kept repeating. "My Gawd, a likely night."

He was driving his own car with Alleyn and Fox as passengers. The London C.I.D. car followed with a driver, a local constable and Sergeants Thompson and Bailey who had been pressed in as an emergency measure.

Sirens could be heard without definition as to place or distance. Road blocks and search parties from Longminster, Norminster and Crossdyke were being established about the landscape.

With that dramatic suddenness created by fog, a constable flashing an amber torchlight stood in their path.

"Well!" Tillottson said, leaning out of the window.

"This is as far as you can drive, sir."

"Where's Cape?"

"T'other side, sir."

They got out. Close on their left hand the fog-masked weir kept up its anonymous thunder. They followed the constable along the towpath to the flight of steps that led up to the main bridge.

"All right," Tillottson said. "Get back to your point."

As they groped their way over the bridge a car crept past them filled with revellers engaged in doleful song.

The constable stepped into its path and waved his torch.

"Hullo-'ullo-'ullo," shouted the driver. "Anything wrong, Officer?"

"Just a minute, if you please, sir."

"Our Breath is as the Breath of Spring," someone in the back seat sang dismally.

"May I see your license, sir?"

When this formality was completed Alleyn and Tillottson moved in. Had they, Alleyn asked, seen a solitary woman? They replied merrily that they'd had no such luck and emitted wolf-like whistles. Alleyn said: "If we weren't so busy we'd have something to say to you. As it is, will you pull yourselves together, proceed on your silly journey, stop if you see a solitary woman and address her decently. If she's got a strong American accent, offer her a lift, behave yourselves and drive her to the nearest police stop or police station, whichever comes first. Do you understand?"

"Er—yes. Righty-jolly-ho. Fair enough," said the driver, taken aback as much by Alleyn's manner and voice as by what he said. The passengers had become very quiet.

"Repeat it, if you please."

He did.

"Thank you. Drive carefully. We've got your number. Good-night."

They crawled away.

Bailey and Thompson and their driver loomed up and the whole party inched along until they found the top of a flight of steps going down to the lock.

"What can have got into her?" Fox mused, not for the first time.

"Fear," said Alleyn. "She was terrified. She's tried to do a bolt. *And* succeeded, blast it. The Skipper must have delayed—hullo, here we are. That's the roof of the lockhouse down there. Come on and for God's sake don't let's have any falling into the lock. Easy as we go, now."

They felt their way down the steps to the towpath.

"*Cape!*" Tillottson shouted in a terrible voice.

"Here, sir."

He was wretchedly waiting where he had been told to wait: between the lock and the lockhouse. The fog down here was dense indeed and they were upon him almost before they saw him. He seemed to be standing to attention and expecting the worst.

"Ever heard of a Misconduct Form?" Tillottson ominously began.

"Sir."

"Superintendent Alleyn's got something to say to you."

"Sir."

Alleyn said: "What happened, Cape?"

There had, he said, been a commotion on board the *Zodiac*. He couldn't see anything much because of the Creeper but he heard the Skipper's voice asking what was wrong and a woman taking on a fair treat, shrieking: "Let me go. Let me go." He went down to the moorings and called out: "What seems to be wrong there?" but as far as he could make out the happening was on the far side. And then one of the gentlemen on board came round the deck and asked P.C. Cape where he was and said he'd better come on board and get things under control like. He could hardly see a thing except that there was a gap between the edge and the gunwale. He couldn't see the gentleman either but said he had a very loud voice.

"Go on."

The loud voice said he could jump for it and as he could just make out enough for that he did jump and came aboard in a flounder and nearly lost his helmet. Alleyn gathered that a sort of blind search had set in under circumstances of the greatest possible confusion. Cape had proceeded with outstretched arms doing a breast-stroke action, to the starboard side which was the farthest removed from the towpath. He had bumped into a number of persons and had loudly demanded that everybody should keep calm.

A strange disordered mêlée now took place in the greatest possible confusion. Presently it occurred to Cape that the woman's voice could no longer be heard. He had got alongside the Skipper and they had, between them, rounded up the passengers and herded them into the saloon where after a good deal of milling about and counting of heads, Miss Hewson's head was found to be missing.

By this time the policeman on the pub side of the river had become alerted and started to cross the bridge.

Cape and the Skipper went through the cabins and searched the craft. All available lights were switched on but were not much help on deck where the fog was now of the pea-soup variety.

Caley Bard and Dr. Natouche bore a hand and the Skipper had evidently behaved very sensibly. When it was certain that Miss Hewson was not in the *Zodiac,* Cape got himself ashore and blew his whistle. He and his colleague now met, poked uselessly about in the fog and settled that while Cape got through to Tollardwark his mate should alert by walky-talky the other men on duty in the vicinity.

Alleyn said: "Very well. Where's the *Zodiac?*"

"The boat, sir?" Cape ejaculated. "I beg pardon, sir?"

"Where's the bloody *lock,* for pity's sake."

"The lock, sir?"

"Find the lockhouse and stay by it, all of you."

Alleyn inched along the towpath. A lighted window loomed up on his left. The lockhouse. He faced right, stood still, listened and peered down into a blanket.

"Hullo? *Zodiac?*" he said very quietly.

"Hullo," said a muted voice below his feet.

"Skipper?"

"That's right."

"Show a light, can you?"

A yellow globe swam into being far below.

"You did it, then? You and Tom?"

"And the Lock himself. Talk about stable doors! It was a job in this muck but here we are."

"All present?"

"Except for her."

"Sure?"

"Dead sure."

"No idea, of course, which way she went?"

"No idea."

"And Mrs. Tretheway's sleeping at the lockhouse?"

"Yes."

"Good. You're very quiet down there."

"They've gone to bed. I waited for it."

"Do they know where they are?"

"Not when I saw them. They will."

"They could scramble up and out, of course."

"They're in their cabins and they can't get ashore from there. Have to come up on deck and young Tom and I are keeping watch."

"Splendid. Stay put till you hear from us, won't you?"

"Don't make it too long," the voice murmured.

"Do our best. Good-night."

Alleyn returned to the lockhouse. He and the other six men were admitted by the keeper and crowded into the parlour.

"Well," Alleyn said. "Search we must. Any chance of this lifting?"

Not before dawn, most likely, said the lock-keeper, but you never knew. If a wind got up, she'd drift.

"It's essentially a river mist, isn't it?" Alleyn said. "Miss Hewson may still be milling round in it or lying doggo. If she managed to get above it she'll be on the move. All we can do is follow the usual procedure." He looked at the Tollardwark constable. "You'd better keep within hailing distance of Mr. Tillottson, Mr. Fox and me. You've got radar and we haven't. We're going to find our way up to the wapentake. Br'er Fox, would you work out to my right? Bert, if you'd keep going beyond that and take the driver out on your own right wing. Bailey and Thompson, you take the left wing. Near the roadside hedge if you could see it. She may be anywhere: under the hedge, in the Wapentake Pot or a quarter of a mile away. As little noise and talk as possible. The rest of this unspeakable terrain we leave to the men already alerted."

He looked at the wretched Cape.

"Oh, yes. You," he said. "You move up the hill on my left." And to the two remaining men: "And you watch the *Zodiac*. She's in the lock and the lock's at its lowest. Nobody can leap ashore in seconds but that doesn't say they can't make it."

Tillottson said: "The *Zodiac?* In the lock?"

"Yes," Alleyn said. He looked at the keeper, who was grinning. "By arrangement. Like it or lump it with any luck and a good watch they're there till we want them. Come on."

3

Seven hours ago he and Fox had climbed this hill and Troy, a little later, had come to him in the wapentake. Four days ago Troy and the other passengers had met there and Troy had sat in the Wapentake Pot and talked with Dr. Natouche.

Alleyn tried to recall the lie of the land. This was the first grassy slope under his feet, now, and ahead of him must be the tufted embankment below the wapentake field. He had begun to think he must have veered and now walked parallel with the embankment when it rose at his feet. He climbed it and could hear the others breathe and the soft thud of their feet. They used torches to show their whereabouts. The insignificant yellow discs floated and bobbed, giving an occasional glimpse of a leg or coat or a few inches of earth and grass.

The ascent felt steeper and more uneven under these blindfold conditions than it had in the afternoon. They had only climbed a few paces when, suddenly and inconsequently, there was less mist. It drifted and eddied and thinned out and now they waded rather than swam through it and appeared to each other as familiar phantoms.

"Clearing," Fox murmured.

Alleyn sniffed. "Rum!" he said, "I seem to smell dust."

The hillside was before them, living its own life under the stars. A blackness vaguely defined the wapentake itself. Alleyn moved his torchlight slowly across to his right and gave a stifled ejaculation.

"Come in on this, all of you," he said.

Their lights met at a dishevelment of earth, gravel and pieces of half-buried timber.

"It's that old digging," Fox exclaimed. "I said it wasn't safe. It's caved in."

"Come in, all of you."

The seven men collected round him and used their

torchlights. The crazy structure had collapsed. A fang of broken timber stuck out of the rubble and the edge of an old door that had supported an overhanging roof of earth now showed beneath a landslide of earth and gravel.

Alleyn said: "And there's still a smell of dust in the air. Don't go nearer, any of you. Stay where you are. Give me all the light you can raise. Here."

Their lights concentrated round his on a patch of ground near his feet and came to a halt again at the edge of the rubble.

"Bailey," Alleyn said.

Bailey and he knelt together, their heads bowed devotedly over slurs, indentations and flattened grass.

"Here's a good one. A patch of bare soil. Take a look at this," Alleyn said. Bailey took a long hard look.

"Fair enough," he said. "She was wearing them and there's another pair in her cabin."

"American type, low-heeled walking jobs."

"That's right, sir."

"Good Gawd!" Tillottson loudly exclaimed. "She went in there to hide and—. Good Gawd!"

But Alleyn and Bailey paid no attention to Tillottson and Fox said: "Wait on, Bert."

The wapentake field had turned towards a rising moon and was illuminated. The mist had now retired upon its source and wound like a cottonwood snake between the riverbanks. The landscape had changed and lightened.

Alleyn had thrown off his overcoat and was working at the rubble with his gloved hands.

"Bear a hand," he said. "We're too late but bear a hand."

The other men joined him. They mounted their torches where they shone on the rubble and went hard to work.

"Very painstaking," Alleyn grunted. "But not quite painstaking enough. Something—a stone, a bit of broken wood from the rubble—something—has been scuffed over the ground. Prints of the woman's shoes have been left. Right up to where the rubble has lapped over them and pointing towards the excavation. But the surrounding patches of soil have been scuffed. We are meant to think what you thought, Bert."

Superintendent Tillottson peered sideways at P.C. Cape

as if longing for a better view.

"You hear that?" he said. "You understand what's been said? You know what you've allowed to be done, you disgusting chap?"

Alleyn said: "All right, Cape, you'll have to take what's coming, won't you?"

He squatted back on his heels. "This is no good," he said and turned to the two constables. "Go down to the lockhouse and get spades. There's not a hope, now, but we've got to act as if there was. And bring something—pieces of wood—galvanized iron—anything to cover these prints. Quick as you can. Thompson, have you got a flash? All right. Go ahead."

Sergeant Thompson moved in with the hand-held camera he used in emergencies. His light flashed intermittently. The wretched Cape and his opposite number thundered downhill.

"We'd better continue to go through the motions," Alleyn said: "As I recollect there were two props. One may have been used to knock away the other. He'd have a second or two to jump clear. Or there may have been a spare timber lying round."

Fox said: "What's the form, Mr. Alleyn? About that lot down there in the lock? There's nobody missing?" He jerked his head at the rubble. "Apart from her?"

"The Skipper says not but we'll have to see them. Look Bert, will you go down there? Ring your local police surgeon. My compliments and he'll be needed again, with the ambulance and the usual equipment. Give him the story and tell him it's suspected homicide. Then get yourself aboard the *Zodiac*. We won't raise her until we've checked and then only when we can muster a closer guard. We've got a tough little clutch of villains down there and the big double-barrel himself."

"I'll go, then. And if they *are* all there?"

"Call off the general search and bring the men in to Ramsdyke."

"See you in a wee while, then," Tillottson said.

Bailey and Thompson went back to the car to fetch their heavy gear and Alleyn and Fox were left together: a tall elegant figure and a large thickset one incongruously moonlit

in the wapentake field and scraping like dogs with their
forepaws at gravelly rubble.

"This is quite a big case," Fox remarked.

"You are the king of meiosis. Take an international triple
murderer fresh from his latest kill, and pen him up with his
associates in a pleasure-craft at the bottom of a lock. Flavour
with at least three innocent beings and leave to explode. And
you call it quite a big case."

"I suppose," Fox said, disregarding this, "it was all done
under—" He stopped short. "How do you work it out?" He
said. "A put-up job, the whole thing? What?"

"She was blowing up for trouble when we had that last
interview. She may have threatened to grass on them.
Perhaps the Jampot saw how she shaped up, offered to get
her away. Or—" Alleyn panted as he shifted a largish
boulder, "or she may simply have bolted. Whichever way it
was, she raised a rumpus—screeching and on-going. When
that ass Cape flung himself aboard, off she lit in the fog,
pursued, I don't mind betting, by the Jampot. In a matter of
minutes they were over the embankment and into the pit.
And that was it."

"I like that one best."

"It has a Foljambe smack about it, you think?"

"Suppose," Fox said, "she's not here. Suppose she and
whoever-it-was came up here this afternoon and she poked
into this excavation and came out again and it collapsed
later?"

"No prints to suggest a return. And why did whoever-it-
was try to obliterate his own prints?"

"There's that, of course. And you make out that while the
commotion in the *Zodiac* still continued he went straight
back and was all present and correct when that silly chump
Cape and the Skipper started counting heads in the saloon?"

"That's it."

They worked for some time in silence.

"I don't know," Fox said presently. "I don't somehow feel
too certain she's here."

"Don't you?" Alleyn said with a change of voice.

Fox let out an oath and drew back his hand.

From under a counterpane of soil that might have been

withdrawn by a sleeping hand, a foot stuck up, rigid in its well-made American walking shoes.

The two constables came up the hill, swinging a lantern and carrying shovels. Bailey and Thompson returned with their gear. In a very little while they had uncovered Miss Hewson. Her print dress was up round her neck and contained her arms. Her body and legs clad in their sensible undergarments were shockingly displayed and so was her face: open eyes and open mouth filled with sandy soil and the cheekbones cut about with gravel.

"But not congested," Fox said and added loudly: "That's not a suffocated face. Is it?"

"Oh, no," Alleyn said. "No. Did you expect it would be, Br'er Fox? It's hopeless but we'll try artificial respiration."

One of the local men took off his helmet and knelt down.

"The old carotid job?" Fox mused.

"That's what I expect. We'll see what the doctor says."

Fox made a movement of his head towards the hidden *Zodiac*.

"Not, of course—him?"

"No. No. And yet—After all, why not? Why not, indeed." He thought for a moment. "Perhaps better not," he said and turned to Bailey and Thompson. "The lot," he said. "Get going."

He and Fox moved to where the roof had originally overhung the excavation. Here they looked down on the whole subsidence. Tiny runnels of friable soil trickled and started at their footfall. They found no footprints or traces of obliteration.

Alleyn said: "I think you'd better take over here, Br'er Fox, if you will. Meet the doctor when he comes and when he's finished bring him down to the lock."

As he went down the hill Thompson's flash-lamp blinked and blinked again.

The River was still misted but when Alleyn looked into the lock, there was the roof of the *Zodiac*'s wheelhouse, her deck and the tarpaulin cover, the top of a helmet, shoulders, a stomach and a pair of regulation boots.

Light from the saloon shone on the wet walls of the lock. He could hear voices.

"Hullo," he said. The constable looked up and saluted. He was the man who had been on duty by the pub.

"There's a ladder at the lockhouse, sir," he said.

"I'll drop, thank you."

He managed this feat and for what turned out to be the last time, met the *Zodiac* passengers in the *Zodiac* saloon.

4

They were in what Fox liked to call *déshabillé* and looking none the better for it with the exception of Dr. Natouche who wore a dressing gown of sombre grandeur, scarlet kid slippers and a scarf that bore witness, as did none of his other garments, to an exotic taste for colour. He was indeed, himself an exotic, sitting apart at a corner table, upright, black and without expression. Troy would have liked to paint him, Alleyn thought, as he was now. What a pity she couldn't.

The Skipper also sat apart, looking watchful. Mr. Tillottson was back at his former table and the passengers were in the semi-circular seat under the windows. Hewson at once began a heated protest. His sister! Where was his sister! What was the meaning of all this! Did Alleyn realize that he and his sister were American citizens and as such were entitled to protest to their Ambassador in London? Did he appreciate—"

Alleyn let it run for a minute and then clamped down.

"I think," he said, "that we do have a rough idea of the situation, Mr. Hewson. We're in touch with the Federal Bureau in New York. They've been very helpful."

Hewson changed colour, opened his mouth and shut it again.

Alleyn said: "Do you really not know where your sister has gone?"

"I know," he said, "she's been real scared by you guys acting like you thought—" he stopped, got to his feet and looked from Tillottson to Alleyn. "Say, what is all this?" he said. "What's with you guys? What's happened to Sis?" He fumbled with his hearing-aid and thrust his deaf ear towards

Alleyn. "C'mon," he said. "C'mon. Give, can't you?"

Alleyn said clearly: "Something very bad, I'm afraid."

"Like what? Hell, can't you talk like it makes sense? What's happened?" And then, it seemed with flat incredulity, he said: "Are you telling me she's dead? Sis? Dead? Are you telling me that?"

Lazenby walked over to Hewson and put his arm across his shoulders: "Hold hard, old man," he fluted. "Stick it out, boy. Steady. Steady."

Hewson looked at him. "You make me sick," he said. "Christ Almighty, you make me sick to my stomach." He turned on Alleyn. "Where?" he said. "What was it? What happened?"

Alleyn told him where she had been found. He listened with his head slanted and his face screwed up as if he still had difficulty in hearing.

"Smothered," he said. "Smothered, huh?"

Alleyn said nothing. There was an immense stillness in the saloon as if everybody waited for a climax.

"Why don't you all say something?" Hewson suddenly demanded. "Sitting round like you were dumbbells. God damn you. Say something."

"What can we say?" Caley Bard murmured. "There's nothing we can say."

"You!" Hewson said. And as if he had to find some object upon which to focus an undefined misery and resentment he leant forward and shook his finger at Caley Bard. "You sit round!" he stammered. "You act like nothing mattered! For Pete's sake, what sort of a monster do you figure *you* are?"

"I'm sorry," Caley said.

"Pardon me?" Hewson shouted angrily with his hand cupped round his ear. "What's that? Pardon?"

"I'm sorry," Caley shouted in return.

"Sorry? *Sorry,* hell! He says he's sorry!"

Pollock intervened. "There you are," he said. "That's what happens. That's the way our wonderful police get to work. Scare the daylights out of some poor woman so she scarpers and gets herself smothered in a gravel-pit. All in the day's work."

"In our opinion," Alleyn said, "Miss Hewson was not smothered in the gravel-pit. She was buried there."

"My dear Superintendent—" Lazenby exclaimed, "what *do* you mean by that? That's a shocking statement."

"We think that she was murdered in the same way as Miss Rickerby-Carrick was murdered on Tuesday night and a man called Andropoulos was murdered last Saturday. And we think it highly probable that one of you is responsible."

"Do you know," Caley said, "I had a strong premonition you were going to say that. But *why?* Why should you suppose one of *us*—? I mean we're a cross-section of middle-class people from four different countries of origin who have never met before. We none of us knew that unfortunate eccentric before she, to speak frankly, bored the pants off us in the *Zodiac*. With the exception of her brother we'd none of us ever set eyes on Miss Hewson. Earlier tonight, Alleyn, you seemed to be suggesting there was some kind of conspiracy at work among us. All this carry-on about people being overheard muttering together in a side street in Tollardwark. And then you started a line about Miss Rickerby-Carrick having been robbed of a Fabergé bibelot. And what's the strength of the bit about Pollock and his doodles? I must apologize," Caley said with a change of tone. "I didn't mean to address the meeting at such length, but really, Alleyn, when you coolly announce that one of us is a murderer it's bloody frightening and I, for one, want to know what it's all about."

Alleyn waited for a little and then said: "Yes. Of course, I'm sure you do. Under ordinary conditions it wouldn't be proper for me to tell you but in several ways this is an extraordinary case and I propose to be a damn sight more candid than I daresay I ought to be."

"I'm glad to hear it," Caley said wryly.

Alleyn said: "Here goes, then. Conspiracy? Yes. We think there is a conspiracy at work in the *Zodiac* and we think all but one of the passengers is involved. Murder? Yes. We think one of you is a murderer and hope to prove it. His name? Foljambe, alias the Jampot. At present, however, known by the name of another person. And his record? International bad-lot with at least five homicides to his discredit."

The silence that followed was broken by Pollock. "You must be barmy," he said.

"Conspiracy," Alleyn went on. "Briefly, it involves the

painting by you, Mr. Pollock, of extremely accomplished Constable forgeries. The general idea, we think, went something like this. You made the forgeries. Your young friends on the motor-bike, working under Foljambe's orders, were to plant them about this countryside where Constable once painted. The general principle of 'salting' the nonexistent mine. The first discovery by Mr. and Miss Hewson (if that is their name) in Bagg's yard was to be given exactly the right amount of publicity. If necessary the circumstances surrounding the lucky find would be authenticated by Bagg himself, by my wife and Miss Rickerby-Carrick and the only other unimplicated passenger. There was to be an immediate bogus hunt throughout the countryside by: (A) Mr. Lazenby, better known in the Antipodes, we incline to believe, as Dinky Dickson. (B) Mr. and Miss Hewson or Ed and Sally-Lou Moran as the case may be, and (C)—ineffable cheek—by you yourself, Mr. Pollock, in hot pursuit of your own forgeries."

"You got to be dreaming," said Mr. Pollock.

"The result of this treasure-hunt would be—surprise! surprise!—a tidy haul of 'Constables' and a general melting away of the conspirators to sell them in the highest market. The whole operation, was, we believe, in the nature of a trial run, observed by the key figures and designed for expansion, with appropriate modifications, into world-wide operations."

"All of this," said Lazenby breathlessly, "is untrue. It is wickedly and scandalously untrue."

"Meanwhile," Alleyn continued, "the terrain would have been thoroughly explored for the subsequent disposal (or we don't know anything about our Jampot) of hard drugs by means of what is laughingly known in the racket as aerial top-dressing. The collectors would be at large among a swarm of Constable-seekers and would be accepted by the locals, with however marked a degree of exasperation, as such."

"How do you like this fella? Do we have to sit around and take this?" Mr. Hewson asked of no one in particular.

"You haven't got much choice, have you?" Caley Bard said. And to Alleyn: "Go on, please."

"Almost from the first, things went askew. I again draw

your attention to Mr. L. G. Z. Andropoulos who was to be a passenger in Cabin 7. He was a bit of wreckage from Greece who had a picture-dealing shop in Soho which may have been intended as a dispersal point for some of the forgeries. He turned nark on Foljambe, madly tried a spot of blackmail, and was murdered, in exactly the same way as the women. By the Jampot himself, about thirty-eight hours before he embarked in the *Zodiac*."

The three men broke into simultaneous ejaculations. Alleyn raised his hand.

"We'll come to alibis," he said, "in due course. They have been checked."

"All I can say," Caley said, "is, thank God, and perhaps I'm being premature, at that."

"Yes, and perhaps you bloody well are," Pollock burst out. "Sitting there, like Jacky. How do we know—"

"You don't," Caley said. "So shut up." He turned to Alleyn. "But about this—about Miss Hewson. Why, to begin with, are you so sure there's been foul play?"

Alleyn said: "We are waiting for an official medical opinion. In the meantime, since we have a doctor among us, I think I shall ask him to describe the post-mortem appearances of suffocation by earth and gravel. As opposed to those following an attack from behind involving abrupt and violent pressure on the carotid arteries."

"Ah *no!*" Caley cried out. "Alleyn, I mean—*surely!*" He looked at Hewson who leant on the table, his face in his hands. "I mean." Caley repeated: "I mean—well—there *are* decencies."

"As far as possible," Alleyn rejoined, "we try to observe them. Mr. Hewson will be asked to identify. He may prefer to know, if he doesn't know already, what to expect."

"*Know!*" Hewson sobbed behind his fingers. "*Know.* My God, how should I know!"

"You *all* want to know, I gather, why we believe Miss Hewson was murdered. Our opinion rests to a considerable extent on post-mortem appearances. Dr. Natouche?"

It was a long time since they had heard that voice. He had been there, sitting apart in his splendid gown and scarlet slippers. They had shot uneasy, resentful or curious glances at him but nobody had spoken to him and he had not uttered.

He said: "You have sent for your police consultant. It would be improper for me to give an opinion."

"Even in the interest of justice?"

"It is not clear to me how justice would be served by my intervention."

"If you consider for a moment, it may become clear."

"I think not, Superintendent."

"Will you at least tell us if you would expect to find a difference between post-mortem appearances in these two cases?"

A long silence before Dr. Natouche said: "Possibly."

"In the case of an attack on the carotids you would expect to find external post-mortem marks on the areas attacked?"

"Superintendent, I have told you I prefer not to give an opinion. The external appearances from suffocation vary enormously. I have—" He waited for some seconds and then spoke very strongly. "I have never seen a case of death from a murderous assault on the carotids. My opinion would be valueless," said Dr. Natouche.

Pollock cried out shrilly: "You'd know how to *do* it, though wouldn't you? *Wouldn't you?*"

Hewson lowered his hands and stared at Natouche.

"Any medical man," Natouche said, "would know, technically, what death by such means involved. I must decline to discuss it."

"I don't like this," Lazenby said, turning his dark glasses on the doctor. "I don't like this, at all. It's not honest. It's not a fair go. You've been asked a straight question, Doctor, and you refuse to give a straight answer."

"On the contrary."

"Well," Alleyn said, "let's take another look at the situation. Before she left the *Zodiac*, Miss Hewson was in distress. She was heard by the constable on duty at the lock to scream, to break into a hysterical demonstration and to cry out repeatedly: 'Let me go. Let me go!' Is that agreed?"

Hewson said: "Sure! Sure, she was hysterical. Sure, she wanted to escape. What sort of deal had she had for Chrissake! Police standing her up like she was involved in this phoney art racket. A corpse fished outa the River and everyone talking about homicide. Sure, she was scared. She was real scared. She was desperate. I didn't want to leave her up here but she acted like crazy and said why couldn't I let her alone. So I did. I left her right here in the saloon and I went to bed."

"You were the last then, to go down?"

"Well—the Padre and Stan and I—we went together."

"And Doctor Natouche? Did he go down?"

"No, sir. He went up on deck. He went up soon as Sis began to act nervous. Pretty queer it seemed to me: go out into that doggone fog but that's what he did and that's where he went."

"I would like to get a clear picture, if 'clear' is the word, of where you all were and what happened after she was left here in the saloon."

They all began to speak at once and incontinently stopped. Alleyn looked at Caley Bard.

"Let's have your version," he said.

"I wish you luck of it," Caley rejoined. "For what it's worth I'll—well, I'll have a stab. I'd gone to bed; at least I'd gone to my cabin and undressed and was having a look at some butterflies I caught on the cruise. I heard—" he looked at Lazenby, Hewson and Pollock "—these three come down and go to the loo and their cabins and so on. They all have to go past my door, I being in Cabin 1. They were talking in the passage, I remember. I didn't notice what they said: I was spreading a specimen I picked up at Crossdyke. Subconsciously though, I suppose I must have recognized their voices."

"Yes?"

"All of a sudden a hell of a rumpus broke loose, up topside. Sorry, Hewson, I might have put that better. I heard, in fact, Miss Hewson scream 'Let me go.' Two or three times, I think. I heard a kind of thudding in the saloon here, above my head. And then, naturally, a general reaction."

"What sort of general reaction?"

"Doors opening and slamming. Hewson calling out for his sister, Lazenby and Pollock shouting to each other and a stampede upstairs. I'm afraid," Caley said with what could only be described as an arch glance out of his curious eyes, "I did *not* hurtle into the lists. Not then and there. You see, Alleyn, we had, to quote an extremist, supped rather full of horrors and, to be quite honest, my immediate reaction was to think: 'Oh *no!* Not *again!*' Meaning it in a general sense, you understand."

"So—what did you do?"

"In effect, listened to what seemed to be an increasing hubbub, had a bit of an argument with what passes for my conscience and finally, I'm afraid more than reluctantly, went up topside myself."

"Where you found?"

"Damn' all that could be distinguished. Everybody milling about in the fog and asking everybody else what the hell they thought they were doing and where was Miss Hewson."

"Can you say how many persons you could distinguish?"

He thought for a moment. "Well—yes. I suppose—I got a general idea. But it couldn't be less reliable. I heard—these three men again—calling out to each other and I heard the Skipper warn people not to go overboard. I remember Lazenby called out that he thought we ought to leave Miss Hewson alone and that she would get over it best by herself. And Hewson said he couldn't leave her. And Pollock, you were milling round asking what the police thought they were doing. So I yelled for the police—it seemed a reasonable thing to do—and a great bumbling copper landed on the deck like a whale."

Nobody looked, now, at the motionless figure behind the corner table.

"Do I gather," Alleyn said, "that at no stage did you hear Dr. Natouche's voice? Or hear him come down to his cabin?"

Caley was silent.

"I did, then," Pollock said. "I heard him just before she began to call out 'Let me go.' He was with her. He *said* something to her. I'll swear to that. Gawd knows what he *did.*"

"Did anyone hear Dr. Natouche after they heard Miss Hewson for the last time?"

As if they were giving responses in some disreputable

litany, Pollock, Hewson and Lazenby loudly said "No."

"Skipper?"

The Skipper laid his workaday hands out on his knees and frowned at them. "I can't say I did. I was forrard in my cabin and in bed when it started up. I shifted into this rig and came along. They were on deck and someone was bawling for the police. Not her. A man. Mr. Bard, if he says so. She'd gone. I never heard the Doctor at any stage and I didn't bump into him like I did the others."

"Yeah, and do you know why, mate?" Pollock said. "Because he wasn't there. Because he'd followed her and done bloody murder on her up the hill. Because he's not a bloody doctor but a bloody murderer. Now!"

Alleyn moved to face Dr. Natouche. Tillottson, who had been taking notes walked to the foot of the companionway. At the head of it the constable could be seen beyond the half-door.

Dr. Natouche had risen.

"Do you want to make a statement?" Alleyn asked and knew that they all waited for the well-worn sequel. But already the enormous voice had begun.

"I am alone," it said, "and must defend myself. When these men who accuse me had gone to their cabins I was, as Mr. Hewson has said, on deck. The mist or fog was dense and I could see nothing but a few feet of deck and the glow of the lockhouse windows and that only very faintly. The night was oppressive and damp. I was about to go back when Miss Hewson came very quickly up the stairway, crying out and weeping and in a condition of advanced hysteria. She ran into me and would have fallen. I took her by the arms and tried to calm her. She became violent and screamed 'Let me go' several times. Since I frightened her—she was I believe allergic to people of my colour—I did let her go and she stumbled across the deck and was hidden by the fog. I thought she might injure herself. I drew nearer but she heard me and screamed again: 'Let me go.' By that time these gentlemen were approaching. They came up on deck calling to her and plunging about in the fog. I waited, unseen, until I heard the Captain's voice and then, since obviously there was nothing I could do, I went below and to bed. I remained in my cabin until the arrival of your colleagues."

He waited for a moment. "That is all," he said and sat down.

Alleyn had the impression, an obscene and grotesque one, of Lazenby, Pollock and Hewson running together and coagulating into a corporate blob of enormity. They did actually move towards each other. They stood close and watched Natouche.

Caley Bard said: "I'm sorry. I'm terribly sorry but I can't accept that. It's just not true. It can't be true."

The group of three moved very slightly. Pollock gave a little hiss of satisfaction. Lazenby said: "Ah!" and Hewson: "Even *he* sees that," as if Caley were an implacable enemy.

"Why can't it be true?" Alleyn said.

Caley walked up to Natouche and looked steadily at him.

"Because," he said, "I never left the top of the companionway. I stood there, listening to the hullabaloo and not knowing what to do. I stayed there until after the Skipper arrived and after the constable came on board. He—" He moved his head at Natouche—"Well, look at him. The size of him. He never passed me or went down the companionway. Never. He wasn't there."

Natouche's arms rose naked from the sleeves of his gown, his hands curled above his head and his teeth were bared. He looked like an effigy carved from ebony. Before the curled hands could do their work, Alleyn and Tillottson grabbed him. They lurched against the bar. Troy's signs of the zodiac fell from their firmament and Hewson screamed: "Get him! Get him! Get him!"

Above the uproar, voices shouted on deck. A rival commotion had broken out and even as Alleyn and Tillottson screwed the great arms behind the heavy back, somebody came tumbling down the companionway, followed by Inspector Fox and two deeply perturbed constables.

He was a Dickensian little man: bald, bespectacled and irritated. He contemplated the outlandish scene with distaste and cried in a shrillish voice:

"Once and for all, I demand to know the meaning of this masquerade."

Fox arrived at his side and seeing his principal engaged in strenuous activity, lent his aid. Natouche no longer struggled. He looked at the men who had subdued him as if he himself was in the ascendant.

Alleyn moved away from him and confronted the little man. "May I have your name, sir," he said.

"My name!" the little man ejaculated. "*My name!*" Certainly you may have my name, sir. My name, sir, is Caley Bard."

X

CLOSED FILE

"And that," Alleyn said, laying down his file, "was virtually the end of the Jampot. He is now, together with his chums, serving a life sentence and good behaviour is not likely to release him in the foreseeable future. I understand he finds it particularly irksome not to be able to lepidopterize on Dartmoor where, as we know from Sir Arthur Conan Doyle, there are butterflies. Or perhaps, none of you has read *The Hound of the Baskervilles*. All right, Carmichael, I daresay you have.

"A little time before Foljambe arrived in England the real Caley Bard, who is a gifted amateur of the net and killing-bottle, had advertised in *The Times* for a fellow-lepidopterist who would share expenses on a butterfly hunt in South America. Foljambe's agents in England—Messrs. Dinky Dickson, alias the Reverend Mr. Lazenby, and Stanley Pollock—noted this circumstance. Further discreet inquiries satisfied them that Mr. Bard had left for a protracted visit to South America, that he was something of a recluse, and had private means fortified by occasional coaching in mathematics for tutorial organizations. So it was decided that the mantle of Lepidoptery should descend upon the Jampot's shoulders. Lepidoptery was his hobby as a schoolboy and he knew enough to pass muster with a casual enthusiast. If, by an outlandish chance, he had encountered an expert or an acquaintance of his original he would have exclaimed: 'Me? oh, no, not *that* Caley Bard. I wish I were!' or words to that effect. The only thing they hadn't anticipated was that the real Caley Bard should return, two months before his time, having picked up an unpleasant bug in the country beyond La Paz.

"So that when, at my suggestion, one of our chaps called at the address, they found the house occupied by an extremely irate little man whom they promptly flew by helicopter to Tollardwark for what I am obliged to call a confrontation.

"There was, of course, no doubt about the Jampot's identity and guilt, once we had established alibis for the others in the Andropoulos business. However, he did make a mistake. He talked about Miss Rickerby-Carrick's bit of Fabergé before he should have known it was anything of the sort. A rare thing, though, for him to slip up. He's a brilliant villain.

"He presented himself to my wife in exactly the light best calculated to produce a tolerant and amused acceptance. She was not likely, as he realized, to succumb to his well-tested but, to a man, inexplicable charms, but she found him companionable and entertaining. I am told that a swivel-eye is, to many people, sexually alluring. The Jampot's swivel-eye was the result of a punch-up or a jab-up with a rival gang in Santa Cruz. He subsequently underwent a bit of very efficient plastic surgery. Lazenby—Dickson to you—had lost *his* eye, by the way, in the Second World War where he was an Australian army chaplain until they found him out. He was born in the West Indies, went to a European mission school and had in fact been ordained and defrocked. He had no difficulty at all in passing himself off to the Bishop of Norminster who was very cross about it.

"That, more or less, is it. I'll be glad to answer questions."

Carmichael's instant boots had already scraped the floor when Alleyn caught the eye of a quiet-looking type in the back row.

"Yes?" he said. "Something?"

"Sir. I would like to ask, sir, if the missing pages from the diary ever came to hand?"

"No. We searched, of course, but it was a hopeless job. Lazenby probably reduced them to pulp and put them down the lavatory."

"Sir. Having read them when he sat on the bank, sir, and torn them out as a consequence?"

"That's it. Before the trial he ratted in the hope of reducing his sentence and will live in terror of the Jampot for the rest of his days. He told us the missing pages contained an account of the conversation Miss Rickerby-Carrick overheard in Tollardwark. Between—"

Carmichael's boots became agitated.

"—between," Alleyn loudly went on, "Foljambe, Lazenby and Pollock. About—. All right, Carmichael, all right. You tell us."

"About your leddy-wife maybe," Carmichael said, "sir. And maybe they touched on the matter of the planted picture, sir. And their liaison with the cyclists, and so on and so forth."

"Perhaps. But according to the wretched Lazenby it was mostly about Andropoulos. When Miss Rickerby-Carrick tried to confide in my wife, she was very agitated. She kept saying 'And—and' and 'Oh God. Wait.' I think—we shall never know, of course—she was trying to remember his name. Lazenby intervened as the Jampot did when Pollock became altogether too interested in my wife's drawing and altogether too ready to assist. The Jampot let it appear that he resented Pollock's overfamiliarity. So he did, but not for reasons of gallantry."

Carmichael resumed his seat.

"Any more? Yes?" It was the same man in the back row.

"I was wondering, sir, exactly what did happen on the night in question. At Crossdyke, sir?"

"The autopsy showed Miss Rickerby-Carrick had taken a pretty massive barbiturate. One of Miss Hewson's pills, no doubt. She slept on deck at the after-end behind a heap of chairs covered by a tarpaulin. Foljambe's cabin, No. 1, was next to the companionway. When all was quiet he went up through the saloon to the deck and, because she knew too much, killed her, took the Fabergé jewel and handed it and the body over to the cyclist—his name by the way *is* Smith—who had been ordered to wait ashore for it and was given his instructions. My wife remembered that, at sometime in the night, she had heard the motor-bike engine. Yes?"

A man in the third row said, "Sir: did they all know, sir? About the murder, sir. Except the Doctor?"

"According to Lazenby (I'll still call him that) not

beforehand. When Lazenby told Foljambe about the diary Foljambe merely said he would deal with the situation and ordered Lazenby to keep his mouth shut, which he did. No doubt in the sequel they all knew or guessed. But he was not a confiding type, even with his closest associates."

"And—the way they carried on, sir. Bickering and all that among themselves. Was that a put-up show, then, sir?"

"Ah!" Alleyn said. "That's what my wife asked me the next night in Norminster."

"It was all a put-up job, then?" Troy asked. "The way Caley—he—I still think of him as that—the way he blazed away at Pollock and the way those three seemed to dislike and fight shy of him and abuse him—well, the whole interrelationship as it was displayed to us? All an act?"

"My love, yes."

"But, Hewson's distress over his sister—" she turned to Dr. Natouche. "You said he was distressed, didn't you?"

"I thought so, certainly."

"He was distressed all right and he was deadly frightened into the bargain," Alleyn grunted, and after a moment he said: "You were among counterfeiters, darling, and very expert hands at that. Do fill up your glass, Natouche."

"Thank you. I suppose," Dr. Natouche said, "they looked upon me as a sort of windfall. They could all combine to throw suspicion upon me. Bard was particularly adroit. I must apologize, by the way, for losing my temper. It was when he lied about my going below during the uproar. He knew perfectly well that I went below. We ran into each other at the stairhead. When he lied I behaved like the savage they all thought me." He turned to Troy. "I am glad you did not see it," he said.

Alleyn remembered the uplifted ebony arms, the curved hands and the naked fury of the face and he thought Troy might have seen an element in Dr. Natouche's rage that he would never suspect her of finding.

In some sort echoing, as she often did, Alleyn's thoughts about her, she said to Dr. Natouche: "You must say at once— you will, please, won't you?—if it's an unwelcome suggestion, but some day, when you can spare the time, will you let me paint you?"

"If you look closely," he said with an air of astonishment, "you may be able to see that I am blushing."

They finished their dinner and talked for a time and then Troy and Alleyn walked with Dr. Natouche to the garage where he had left his car. The inquest was over and he was driving back to Liverpool that night. By a sort of tacit consent they did not discuss the sequel.

It was a sultry night and very still with a hint of thunder in the air. But there was no mist. They came to the top of Wharf Lane and looked down at the River. There was the *Zodiac,* quietly riding at her moorings with her cherry-coloured curtains glowing companionably. And there, on the right, were the offices of the Pleasure Craft and Riverage Company. Troy fancied she could make out a card stuck to the window and crossed the lane to see.

"They've forgotten to take it down," she said and the men read it.

> *M.V. Zodiac. Last-minute cancellation.*
> *A single-berth cabin is available for*
> *this day's sailing. Apply within.*

NGAIO MARSH

BESTSELLING PAPERBACKS BY A "GRAND MASTER" OF THE MYSTERY WRITERS OF AMERICA.

____	06341-X ARTISTS IN CRIME	$2.50
____	06818-7 BLACK AS HE'S PAINTED	$2.50
____	07105-6 CLUTCH OF CONSTABLES	$2.50
____	06715-6 DEATH AND THE DANCING FOOTMAN	$2.50
____	06224-3 DEATH IN A WHITE TIE	$2.50
____	06166-2 DEATH IN ECSTASY	$2.50
____	06177-8 DEATH OF A FOOL	$2.50
____	06716-4 DEATH OF A PEER	$2.50
____	06019-4 DIED IN THE WOOL	$2.50
____	05943-9 ENTER A MURDERER	$2.50
____	07074-2 FINAL CURTAIN	$2.50
____	06178-6 GRAVE MISTAKE	$2.50
____	06309-6 HAND IN GLOVE	$2.50
____	06820-9 KILLER DOLPHIN	$2.50
____	05966-8 LAST DITCH	$2.25
____	06496-3 A MAN LAY DEAD	$2.50